Tenderly Beats the Lonely Heart

K. J. Janssen

For information, or to order additional copies, please contact:

Beacon Publishing Group
P.O. Box 41573 Charleston, S.C. 29423
800.817.8480| beaconpublishinggroup.com

Publisher's catalog available by request.

ISBN-13: 978-1-949472-85-1

ISBN-10: 1-949472-85-1

First Edition. New York, NY 10001.

Printed in the USA.

CHAPTER 1

The woman fidgeted with the napkin, completely ignoring the cup of coffee in front of her.

The man sitting across the table had no such problem. He was busily scarfing down an apple turnover; his coffee cup nearly empty.

"How can you be so sure that it's him?"

He continued to chew until the large mouthful was fully masticated and swallowed.

"I just got this information yesterday. I can't be one hundred percent certain, but he is the only Thomas E. Mortinson that I've been able to locate. All the specifics are there. He is twenty-three years old, born on October 6th, 1993. He attended Owensburg High and he was raised by foster parents, Emily and Walter Peyton. Incidentally, the father is now the Police Chief of the town. Thomas graduated from Ohio State last year with a BS in Finance. He's working for a steel company in Akron, in their finance department. This is a picture of him from the Ohio State University Yearbook. It's the only picture I've found so far." He handed her the picture which was a slightly left side profile of Thomas Mortinson wearing a blue knit sweater. Miriam took the picture with a trembling hand. She tilted her head back in an attempt to keep the tears in; a gesture that was too late, as her eyes welled up and tears began their journey down her cheek, causing a line to appear in her makeup. "This is definitely my Thomas." With pride she added, "My little boy grew into such a beautiful young man. He looks just like his father, God rest his soul." As she ran her index finger over the picture a shiver ran up her arm.

"I must caution you to hold back on any conclusions. I realize that everything points to this young man as the Thomas E. Mortinson you gave up twenty-three years ago, but until I can do a little more digging, we can't be absolutely certain. Any premature contact could be very damaging psychologically to both the young man and yourself. You do understand that?"

"Yes, but I know it's him. The nose, forehead and chin are identical to his fathers."

"That may well be, but I know of cases where a man got two women pregnant with boys at the same time. He was a bigamist and to protect against a possible slip-up with either family, he named both boys exactly the same. There was even a similarity in their appearances due to the common sperm donor, so you can see where mistaken identity would be possible." He reached over and took her hands. "Sometimes identifications of long lost children or parents are not as clear cut as they seem. I read recently of a case where the paperwork trail on a young man led right up to age twenty-one and then hit a brick wall. It turned out that he had a sex-change operation and Patrick became Patricia.

"Compared to that we've been really fortunate. The state of Ohio deciding to open up their adoption files has been a real boon for these searches. Without that, it would have been close to impossible to trace Thomas down. So please don't do anything for few more days. Let me do my job. Give me time to make one final check."

"I can't promise you that. Tomorrow is the Owensburg's 200th Anniversary. There will be a parade, picnics and all kinds of activities during the day and a dance in the park at night.

Thomas grew up here. If what you've found is accurate he lives and works only a few towns over. He's bound to attend. We're both Alumni of Owensburg High. I received an invitation for the Anniversary celebration and I'm sure he did too and besides, his foster parents will be there, for sure. I just have to go, to see him if he shows up. I want to see what he looks like in person. Seeing this picture isn't the same. You can understand that can't you?"

"Sure I can, but I just don't think that it's a good idea to get too close to him right now." He looked into her tear-filled eyes. "I've got a feeling that you're going go there anyway. Will you at least promise me not to make any personal contact with him, accidently or otherwise?"

"I guess I can do that, but it'll take every ounce of my self-control, not to run up to him and hold him in my arms. My husband is on a business trip in Europe for the next two weeks. That should be more than enough time for me to do this. He doesn't know about Thomas and I didn't want to cross that bridge until I knew for sure that this is really my son. I'm just not certain how he will react when he finds out."

The tears started again and Mike Tolliver, who always considered himself to be a hard-boiled lawyer, felt his own eyes filling up as he handed her a clean handkerchief. "Hang in there, Mrs. Walton, were almost at the end of the journey."

* * *

Miriam Walton reflected on how she got to this position. Two months ago, she hadn't even heard of the attorney that she was meeting with for the third time. One day she was leisurely reading the local paper *The Spartanville Times* and noticed a small box ad on the personal page advertising investigative services for lost persons. It mentioned dead-beat dads, teen-age runaways and lastly searches for children or parents involved in adoptions. His office hours were by appointment only at his office in town. She cut the ad out and placed it between the pages of a book she was reading. There it remained for two weeks until she came across it when she reached the page where it was secreted. She held it in her hand, rereading it for several minutes. She knew that the only way to end the reverie was to find out what happened to the son she gave up when she was too young to know what effect it might have in her life as time passed.

She went to the kitchen and made a cup of tea, with fleeting glances of the scrap of paper she placed on the table. Finally, she picked it up and called the number listed in the ad.

"Good morning, you have reached the office of Michael Tolliver, Attorney at Law."

"Yes, Good Morning. My name is Miriam Walton and I would like to make an appointment to meet with Mr. Tolliver."

"May I ask the nature of your case?'

"Certainly, it has to do with an adoption case twenty years ago."

"I can fit you in at three this afternoon or eleven fifteen tomorrow morning. Are either of these slots good for you?'

"Yes, I can make it this afternoon."

"We'll look forward to seeing you then. Good bye."

Miriam didn't share the facts of her younger days with her husband on the premise that it would only muddy the waters. They both understood that there was baggage that would be best left unopened. That's the way it has been for the eleven years of their marriage.

Now doesn't this have all the makings of an emotional rollercoaster? Hold on!

CHAPTER 2

Thomas Edward Mortinson continued to live with his foster parents, Emily and Walter-Peyton until he finished college. They took Thomas in when he was three months old and provided a strict but nurturing environment for him for twenty-one years. They wanted to adopt him when he was old enough to understand what the procedure was all about, but he was dead set against it. Knowing how psychologically impacting the whole process could be, Emily and Walter acceded to Thomas's decision and the matter was never brought up again.

For reasons that Thomas would have difficulty explaining he always held out the hope that someday he would get to know his real mother. This deep desire had nothing to do with his appreciation for everything that the Peyton's did for him. He was happy living with them. It had more to do with the longing for a true identity that goes with being a foster child.

The Peyton's paid Thomas's way through four years at Ohio State where he graduated with a BS in Finance in 2015; Two Hundred and fiftieth out of a class of 11,000. He began his business career in the Finance Department of Matson Steel in

Akron. Although his employment site was within a short commute from Owensburg, he set up an apartment in Akron, adding independence to the long list of traits that slowly became the hallmark of the man Thomas Edward Mortinson was becoming.

Most notable of his good traits is a fierce loyalty towards his friends and acquired family; never finding fault or trying to compete with them. His only battles were with himself; to constantly better his past performance.

Best of all, is his high regard of women. His foster mother, Emily Peyton, is a staunch advocate of Women's Rights and an active campaigner against spousal abuse of any nature. Growing up in such an environment he developed a deep respect for women, an attribute that made him especially attractive to the many girls he dated in high school and college. Of course, the 2010 Ford Mustang convertible that the Peyton's gave him as a graduation present may have added to his attractiveness. He nicknamed the car "Cassy" after his first dog that was hit by a Mustang when Thomas was only ten years old.

Not that Thomas needed any help with women. At 6' 2", weighing 180lbs he was lean and lanky; any musculature on his frame coming from hard work helping out at home or from a variety of jobs he held as a youth and not from bodybuilding, an activity that he found particularly loathsome.

Thomas excelled at softball, playing on the Owensburg High Spartans team for three years as a star pitcher with a record of 30-2.

His cheeks were usually accented by three or four days of stubble that constituted his "bad-boy" look. His friends frequented sports salons to get their hair styled, but his ash-blond hair, neatly parted on the right side was trimmed once a month at an old-fashioned barber shop frequented by his foster father.

It was these attributes that helped Thomas capture the heart of Louise O'Neill, a fellow finance major at Ohio State. They met near the end of their last year at school and instantly fell for each other. Hailing from a small town in Pennsylvania, Louise started working in the Finance Department of a small company in her home town, immediately upon graduating, allowing her to avoid having to find her own place to live.

Being able to see each other only on weekends took a toll on the relationship, prompting Thomas to invite Louise to attend the Anniversary celebration with him with the intent of using the romantic setting of the evening dance to "pop the question".

He would also use the celebration to show off "Cassy", his prized Mustang, which he kept in pristine condition.

This is where things stand as Thomas prepares to participate in Owensburg's 200th Anniversary celebration, but there is much more in store for him, than being with his fiancé, family and friends at a town celebration, but that will have to wait until later.

CHAPTER 3
PREPARATIONS FOR THE CELEBRATION

Tiecher Park, named after one of the town's founders Joshua Tiecher, was bequeathed to the town of Owensburg by Jed Tiecher who died childless in 1998. Transference of the deed for the 169 acres, that once held his lavish mansion and stables, was delayed by a legal case brought by the corporation that Jed owned and operated. It took two years for a judge to rule that the estate was personal property with no ties to the corporation. It took another two years for the town zoning board to approve the plans to turn the property into a park.

Finally, in 2002 the buildings on the property were razed to make way for a concrete dance floor with a seventy-five hundred square foot bandstand as the centerpiece. The second phase was for a softball park with bleachers. Two lots, one at each end of the park, provided parking for a total of five-hundred cars along with bike racks. The architects took care to preserve the natural setting of nature walks with dozens of century old trees and pristine flower gardens, which they turned into a small Arboretum. The last phase of construction was for a man-made three-acre lake dubbed the "Pond" by town residents.

* * *

Five months ago, the 200th Anniversary Celebration, Dance Sub-committee voted unanimously to contract with Bobby V and the Rhythm Riders, a popular local band to supply the music for the dance and a special allotment was made to rent "The Beast" soundstage, a spectacular laser and fireworks structure, to be the centerpiece for the anniversary dance. The Beast was uniquely designed to fit over a towns existing bandstand, requiring little if any modification. The budget for the dance was easily exceeded by the cost of leasing the monster, but one of the sub-committee members, Payne Eaton, a town Elder wrote a check to bridge the gap. "After all," he said, "We want this celebration to be one that the town will remember for the next hundred years."

No one could have known then, how prophetic those words would become.

CHAPTER 4

Erecting "The Beast" required extensive planning and preparation. This marvel of sound and science boasted a stge with a revolving deck at the top that spouted pyrotechnics hundreds of feet into the air with multi-colored laser beams, synchronized to the music of the band, splaying an effusion of color over the stage and the audience. The sound system for the dance necessitated installing thirty Sytex Hi-Fi wireless speakers mounted on 20-foot poles, orchestrated to surround the dance floor with the "savage groans" emanating from the stage.

It took two trucks to haul the thirty tons of gear that made up "The Beast." A crew of ten workers and technicians required two days to assemble and test the equipment. The framework of the soundstage needed to be nested on top of the original bandstand, a task that required four cranes working in tandem. The Owensburg soundstage caused problems for the installation crew. When it was originally built, the construction crew ran into unexpected bedrock and the Steel I beams driven into the ground to support the metal foundation frame were eleven inches shorter than the design called for. As a result, the Owensburg soundstage was higher than it would normally be for the design code. On its own this was not a problem, but with a behemoth like 'The Beast" setting on top of it, a concern was raised.

Instead of settling to the ground, when "The Beast" was mounted over the soundstage an 11" gap resulted, but since "The Beast" came with 8" sliding panels around the periphery, even with them engaged, the super-stage was still sitting three inches from the ground. The panels gave the installation a finished appearance; although they did not provide any additional support for the 60,000 lb structure. To be safe, the engineers connected metal- rope guy lines to concrete blocks buried in the ground behind the stage with the other end hooked to fin plates at the top of the truss structure of "The Beast".

The construction of the bandstand wasn't without incident. In spite of the specialized training of the crew, several of the workers were injured; one with a shoulder dislocated by a fall from scaffolding and another with a twisted ankle from a slip off the edge of the stage.

"The Beast" needed to be tested so the band showed up on the third day to be indoctrinated on the high-tech features of "The Beast". Bobby and his guys were fascinated by the "big time" software and hardware associated with the massive soundstage that would provide the opportunity to showcase their new material that seemed to fit right in with "The Beast's" pyrotechnics and laser show's "warp and woof". This gig was the chance of a lifetime for Bobby and his crew.

Immediately after the rehearsal, a bus with the name Bobby V and the Rhythm Riders in psychedelic letters and colors emblazoned on both sides and on the back, headed south for a gig that night in Bluefield, West Virginia.

* * *

On Anniversary "eve" the soundstage program manager met with the Dance Sub-committee to sign-off on the preparations. With everything given the okay, they just had to wait until the next evening. The program was set to begin at 8pm sharp.

CHAPTER 5

Miriam Walton was nervous as she began dressing for the parade. Miriam lived in Spartanville, Pennsylvania with her husband, Nathan Walton, CEO of Walton Enterprises. Nathan was away on a trip, so she made the trip to Owensburg alone. This was her first trip back to the town where she grew up, since she gave up her newborn son two weeks after she graduated high school and now, thanks to the diligence of Attorney Mike Tolliver, she would finally have the chance to be reunited with her son and explain to him why she had made that fateful decision.

The boy's father, Thomas Wendell Mortinson left for a tour of duty in Iraq several months before her son's birth. They planned to be married upon his return, but two days after he arrived overseas, he succumbed to injuries received when an IED blew up two feet from where he was bunkered. Miriam knew that as an unwed mother she would be the subject of gossip and denigration and in a state of despair she decided to give the child up. She moved in with her aunt in Owensburg, Ohio and upon the birth, gave up her son who she named Thomas Edward Mortinson, after his father. She felt that that was the least she could do in the father's honor. Her son's middle name, Edward, was her father's first name.

Miriam left her aunt's home and attended Miami University in Oxford, Ohio, graduating with a B.S. in Kinesiology and Health. She obtained a job as a Sports Program Consultant for a high school in Spartanville, Pennsylvania. Several months later, while attending a retirement party for the assistant principal, she met Nathan Peter Walton, a very successful entrepreneur, who she married seven months later.

The nostalgia she was feeling at the moment had little to do with her own lifelong memories and more to do with locating the son that she had given up twenty-three years ago. She promised her Attorney, Mike Tolliver, that she would let him finalize his investigation before making any personal contact with her son. She knew, deep in her heart, that if she should see her son, the promise would be the hardest one she would ever have to honor. *I hope he shows up at the festivities today. I just want to see him; to feel his presence.*

CHAPTER 6

At first glance the town of Owensburg looked like a typical mid-west town on a typical mid-summer day. The sun as shining brightly, the high temperature for the day was forecast to reach 92 degrees and the only relief expected would be in the form of a gentle ten mph wind visiting from the northwest. On a day like today, most of the townspeople would normally stay indoors, but that wouldn't do for today, not by any measure, because today Owensburg, a quaint Ohio town with a population of 28,328 as of the last census, was celebrating the 200th anniversary of its founding and the natives were abuzz with excitement.

This was a town that took its celebrations seriously. Young and old alike lined Main Street for the opening ceremonies highlighted by the appearance of the Owensburg High School High Steppers; OHSHS for short. Led by Pop Weatherby, the venerable 83-year-old curmudgeon who put the town and the band on the map with multiple invitations to the Macys Thanksgiving Day Parade, the High Steppers awed the crowd with their flawless performances of town favorites.

Following the Steppers on the parade route were floats sponsored by local businesses. While attempting to keep with the centennial theme, they shamelessly advertised their companies, which was not unexpected, being that the parade was televised by NCTV, the prime TV station for Newcastle county, presenting an opportunity for free advertising. The Anniversary's organizers turned a blind eye to the overt commercialization of the event, ever cognizant of the economic contribution that the companies made to the town as both employers and as tax payers. They were more than happy to look the other way and allow a reasonable balance between business floats and an assortment of floats sponsored by Town of Owensburg departments and several charitable agencies. All told there were eighteen floats; a new record for a parade held by the town.

Bringing up the rear of the parade was anyone else who wanted to participate in the pageant. Civic organizations, book clubs, quilting bees, antique car owners and any group or individuals wanting to be a part of the celebration, made their way slowly down main street, stopping and starting as the procession of floats ahead of them dictated.

The parade slowed, then stopped, as the High Steppers reached the reviewing stand; first marching in place, then bringing their set to a finish and coming to rest.

It was time for the opening ceremony. The grandstand was filled with Aldermen and city department heads. John Martin, Owensburg's Mayor was already standing at the dais. Suddenly the quiet was shattered by his voice booming from the multiple of loudspeakers placed along the parade route. "What a wonderful day this is. I speak with certainty when I say that two hundred years ago, our founding fathers could never have imagined what a beautiful and prosperous town Owensburg would become, two hundred years hence."

He hesitated for a moment and then glanced at a sheet of paper an aide handed him. He returned to the microphone to announce, "Governor Fleming planned to be here today, but his plane is grounded in Seattle due to a sudden change in the weather. He sent an e-mail this morning. He regrets not being able to be here to share in all the merriment. The Governor congratulated us on our anniversary and wished us a festive day. Let's look at the bright side, folks, that's one less speech to listen to." He smiled as a few cheers came from the crowd. He turned his attention back to his prepared speech. "Now, I promise to be brief, so you good folks can enjoy the rest of this celebration, but I do want to give credit to Wendell Phillips his committee and all of the volunteers and vendors who spent so many hours putting this celebration together. Let's give them a rousing hand of applause."

After the clapping died down, the Mayor continued his speech, "There's a lot planned for your enjoyment, today, so instead of a roster of town officials and guests taking turns up here making speeches, they decided that it would be more in keeping with the spirit of the occasion for them to spend the balance of the day visiting the various activities and mixing with you townsfolk. They invite you to step right up to meet them and to discuss whatever may be on your minds or just to say hello.

"In case any of you missed the Anniversary section of today's paper, the planning committee has a scavenger hunt, three legged races, an egg tossing contest, car show, sharpshooting contest, pick-up softball game, pie eating contests and a host of other activities for the whole family. And, of course, the festivities will end tonight with the Anniversary Dance with our own Bobby V and the Rhythm Riders. You'll find the complete schedule and all the details at the Chamber of Commerce booth at the park entrance.

"I believe that I speak for everyone here when I say that on this, our 200th Anniversary, we're all proud to live in the beautiful town of Owensburg, in the bustling Buckeye State and in the greatest country in the world. You're not going to get another chance like this for another hundred years, so have a great time."

As the Mayor turned and exited the grandstand, he turned to an aide, "I certainly hope they appreciated me keeping that short."

"I'm sure they did, sir," the aide said with a big grin, "I sure did."

The crowd turned its attention back to the parade. As the Steppers resumed their play, they moved down the remainder of Main Street to the terminus of the parade route, where a large banner hung over the street. **HAPPY 200TH BIRTHDAY OWENSBURG - YOUR TOWN, MY TOWN, OUR TOWN**. Eventually all the marchers followed that course to the end and then headed off to their favorite activity.

* * *

Police Chief Walter Peyton scanned the crowd with a practiced eye. Peyton was reelected three weeks earlier on a platform of "Safety and Security".

One of his Officers, George Weisberg, on the force just 6 months, remarked, "Everything looks okay so far."

"It usually does this time of day, George. Wait until the sun goes down. That's when we'll have to be especially vigilant."

"Are you expecting trouble?"

"I'm always on the alert for potential trouble; it goes with the job. I don't want a reoccurrence of what happened last year at the Homecoming Dance."

"What happened?"

"What didn't happen is more like it? We had a full-fledged riot on our hands. Ten people were jailed, nine hospitalized, one with multiple stab wounds, charges of police brutality and thousands of dollars in property damage. Let's grab a cup of coffee over at the diner, George and I'll tell you all about it."

* * *

Wedged between a 1940 Cadillac Bohman & Schwartz convertible and a 1960 Pontiac Bonneville convertible, "Cassy", with Thomas at the wheel and Louise at his side, followed the parade route. They smiled as they waved to the crowd. Even tired arms couldn't spoil the excitement of the day. Being in a parade was not the sort of thing the average person does very often in their lives; except, of course, for members of marching bands.

Not only was Thomas home with his foster parents and friends, but he planned to finish the day by proposing to Louise. *What a great day this is going to be. I can't wait for the dance tonight.*

* * *

A woman was slowly walking up and down the street behind the onlookers. She paid little attention to the parade itself; with the hundreds of waving and smiling people, floats and cars. Miriam was scanning the crowds on the sidelines, for anyone who could be her Thomas. She searched both sides of the parade route several times.

For over an hour Miriam's pilgrimage continued up and down the street, until finally the last of the parade passed by and the throng of revelers began to dissipate. Miriam didn't notice "Cassy" with her son at the wheel when he passed within ten feet of where she was standing. Of course, she may not have recognized him anyway, with his face shaded by the baseball cap with the large red OH blazoned on it.

Disappointed at not finding Thomas among the onlookers she stopped at a food vendor and bought a hot dog and soda. She sat at a small table set up on a side street, ate her lunch and planned her next move. *I'm sure that I'll have better luck at the park. Mike's report said Thomas excelled in softball in high school. How could he resist the chance to play in the game today? Even if he isn't planning on playing, he's sure to be in the bleachers cheering on one of the teams...Please be there, Thomas.*

Thinking about his reported athletic prowess in high school stirred up a parcel of guilt. Not only did Miriam miss those four years, but the fourteen before them and the five after them. *How will I be able to explain to Thomas why it took all these years to search for him. My Therapist calls it Traumatic Amnesia resulting in "suppressed memories" of the events leading up to and following the death of Thomas's father. That's all fine, but why did I wait so long to get help for the depression that came over me several years ago? Why did I wait until eight months ago to finally start working with Dr. Wells to uncover my buried memories of Thomas's birth and subsequently abandoning him? What if he doesn't understand what I was going through at the time? What if he hates me for it?*

Life's often presents questions that only time can answer.

CHAPTER 7

Chief Peyton and his deputy ordered coffee and assorted pastries. When the food arrived, the Chief began his story:

"It started late that afternoon when several busloads of students from Towson High arrived for the Friday night football game between their unbeaten team, the Warriors, and our unbeaten Owensburg Panthers. Many of the visitors drove to the game, filling the parking lots around the stadium to overflowing. The game with Towson is part of a school rivalry dating back to the early sixties and the excitement was heightened by it being Homecoming night at Owensburg High. Even though both teams were undefeated going into the game, the Warriors were favored to win. Their quarterback, Nate Swanson, was County All-Pro. College scouts were often seen at their games.

"It's long been known that whenever two rival schools meet in a sports venue, 'all bets are off'. Current season records or past games don't mean a thing. Whenever town rivalries come into play the outcome of a game is up for grabs.

"The game started at seven sharp, with Owensburg kicking off to their opponents, who were determined to spoil the Panthers undefeated season and even up the number of victories in the rivalry.

"Towson High fans would be disappointed, however, as the Panthers rewarded the enthusiasm of the home crowd with a lopsided 48-0 score. Much to my surprise the Towson fans, with the exception of a few smart-ass teenagers, were civil during and after the game. Their buses left on time, sans a small number of fans who joined with other students that had driven to the game. I was glad to see the busses pull out of the parking lot.

"I assigned fifteen officers to be visible at strategic areas around town where any crestfallen teenagers might be inclined to congregate and stir up trouble. Only a few incidents actually happened and by ten o'clock I felt comfortable enough to return to the station, get a late dinner and watch a little television.

"Unfortunately, my rest would be short lived. Shortly after midnight we received a call from the 911 line that a brawl was taking place at the Homecoming Dance which was being held at the Newcastle County Convention Center on the northeast corner of the town.

"The Newcastle County Convention Center is the only indoor facility in town that could accommodate a dance of that size. Students from all four grades and their dates plus the Alumni were invited to the Homecoming Dance. Only a fraction of eligible students actually registered; slightly more than four hundred were expected to attend.

"The dance committee spent several days decorating the meeting hall with streamers, banners and balloons. A team of engineers from the county worked on the lighting and stage effects requested by Bobby V and the Rhythm Riders. I assigned ten of our officers to back up the twenty-man security force at the center.

"The fights broke out during the bands last set. It started when a young woman got past a security guard, jumped up on the stage, removed her blouse and bra and started dancing topless to the music. It was obvious to everyone that she had consumed too much alcohol.

Of course, alcoholic drinks were banned due to the ages of most students, but we both know that even the most stringent of measures by security will never prevent the smuggling of alcohol by underage students or even those old enough to drink. Hell, I did my share when I was young.

"When the crowd first saw the naked woman, they went crazy; guys left their partners and rushed to the front of the dance floor to gawk at the gyrating hips and bouncing boobs. Bobby V was nonplussed by the whole thing and kept the band playing since the set had only ten more minutes to run. He continued to sing and play, but he had a big grin on his face. To his credit, though, he finally stepped away from the mike for a minute and told the dancer that she had to put her clothes back on, but she just laughed at him and continued her dance across the stage.

"Guys started to push their way toward the stage as the security forces tried to keep them behind the yellow line on the floor that marked a no-pass zone between the dance floor and the stage. There was a lot of pushing and shoving and inevitably fights broke out among the students and with the security guys and a few of my Deputies. It didn't take long for several hundred students to get involved in the fracas. Finally, the head of the Center's security cops yelled, 'Okay, that's it. Pull the plug! Stop the music. This dance is over'. A few minutes passed, and finally the amps were silenced. There was still a remnant of music as the piano, sax and drums continued to play. It sounded disjointed, though, without the amplified instruments to accompany them and after several minutes, they all stopped playing.

"That's when things really got crazy. Everyone was pissed. They were chanting, 'Security sucks!' and 'Let the band play' and that set off a whole series of events. One of my deputies jumped up on stage and tried to put a table cloth over the dancer, but she just ripped it off and continued to dance; apparently to her own drummer.

"Two students were taken into custody when they refused to stop fighting each other. Their arrest set off a multiple of other fights. A security guard jumped up on the stage with a megaphone, 'Look, that's it for tonight folks. This dance is officially over. Please leave the Center at once.' The Center's staff opened the doors to let people out, and that was to be the end of it or, so they thought. When the students realized the dance was officially over and that the band would not be coming back, they started breaking tables and chairs. Students were milling around, refusing to exit the building. They were yelling at the band and yelling at the police. A Deputy attempted to take 'Chip' Miller, the captain of the football team, into custody for breaking furniture. Miller resisted and assaulted the officer, causing a minor cut to the forehead and a broken finger on his left hand. As additional police came to assist the injured officer they were attacked by four women and then by three men who came to the women's aid. It was really crazy.

"Finally, Principal John Clark stepped up on the stage and took the megaphone, 'Okay everyone, that's it. It's time to go home.' That's all he needed to say; disobeying the police or the Center employees was one thing, not listening to the school Principal, who had your future in his hand, was another. Reluctantly, the crowd started leaving, but once they got outside, a few of the students started breaking headlights and mirrors on the cars parked in the Valet Parking area immediately outside the doors. That's around the time that I arrived with backup cruisers and officers in riot gear. Once they saw the show of force the crowd dispersed immediately.

"So, we had ten overnight guests at the jail. The two students arrested for brawling were charged with disorderly conduct. The four women and three men that attacked the officers attempting to arrest 'Chip' Miller were charged with interfering with an official police action and resisting arrest. They were booked and held for court or bail. 'Chip' Miller was charged with destruction of public property, two counts of assault in the fourth degree and of resisting arrest. The young lady that started the trouble was never found. A warrant for her arrest is still outstanding for inciting a riot. The damage to cars and to furniture in the Center was extensive and we had several law suits brought against the Force for police brutality. Those were entirely unfounded; hell, we didn't even use our batons, pepper spray or tasers. Those cases were eventually thrown out."

Walter sat back in his seat and looked George straight in the eye, "Now you know why I am not looking forward to another dance that has

Bobby V and the Rhythm Riders on the bandstand. I'm not saying that they are responsible, but that bunch seems to draw trouble. I was very upset when the committee selected them for the dance tonight."

To himself he thought, *I've got a really bad feeling about it.*

CHAPTER 8

Thomas turned off the parade route and headed out to the Peyton house. Emily and Walter insisted that he and Louise stay with them while they were in town. Emily spent several days converting her sewing room back to Thomas's childhood bedroom; complete with model airplanes retrieved from their dusty attic storage.

"That was a lot of fun," Louise said as they drove. "I've never been in a parade before. It was really exciting, all those people cheering for us."

"Well they couldn't help cheering for the best car with the most beautiful woman sitting in the passenger seat."

"Oh, you," she said as she gave him a friendly poke in the ribs. "I bet you say that about every female passenger you have in this car."

"Au contraire, mon Cheri. First of all, there have been very few women allowed to grace the passenger seat of this car. Cassy can be very jealous. Second, none of those few could hold a candle to you when it comes to beauty."

"You're trying to tell me that you've been only dating homely women."

"I didn't say that. As it turns out I once dated a runner-up in the Miss Indiana Pageant. Most of the women that have ridden shotgun with me have been attractive. I'm just saying that, of them all, you are the most beautiful."

"Oh, that's so sweet."

"I just tell it the way I see it."

"Well, you can tell me romantic stuff like that anytime you want."

"No sweat. I intend to do just that."

"Not meaning to change the subject, but what's next on the agenda?"

"I've been meaning to discuss that with you. My buddy Carl asked me to officiate at the softball game. First, he asked me to pitch, but I'm too rusty for that and I know that I would wear myself out pitching even a few innings. Pitching a softball isn't as easy as it looks, you know. It takes a lot of ball control and timing and that's very exerting. So, I agreed to be the third base coach for the A team, instead."

"That's great. Then I'll be the head cheerleader for the A team. How would that be?"

"Super. Between the two of us, the B team doesn't stand a chance. Then, after the game, we can walk around and see what else is going on."

"That sounds great."

"I didn't play in the game because I don't want to be too tired to show off my moves out on the dance floor."

"You've got *moves*?" she asked, trying to hold back a laugh. "I've never thought of you as having *moves*."

"What's so funny? I can be quite the hoofer out on the dance floor."

"Don't get me wrong, Thomas, but from what little I've seen of your dancing so far, hoofer doesn't quite fit the mold."

"That's because I've been holding back. I don't like to brag, but when I attended that High School over there," he said, pointing at Owensburg High, "My partner and I won second prize at a Dance-a-thon during my senior year."

"Well, I can imagine that you and *he* must have been very excited."

"Very funny."

"Well, okay. I'll give you the benefit of the doubt and I'll be looking forward with breathless anticipation to seeing your *moves.*"

"You do just that. Well, that's the plan for today. There is just one thing; we have to be back by 6 o'clock. My folks are planning a light dinner for us."

"That's so nice of them. They're such nice people. In the short time that I've been here, they've made me feel like one of the family."

"Yes, they really are special people. I'm a lucky man to have been raised by them. I couldn't have picked better parents."

"Have you ever wondered about your biological parents?"

"Well, sure. That's only natural. I just know that my father died in the war before he and my mother got married. She gave me his last name, but being unable to raise me as a single mom, she thought it best to give me up so I could be raised in a good home. That's all I know about my birth mother."

"Well it looks like the Family Services people did a good job in finding the Peytons."

"Yes, they sure did. Emily and Walter can't have children of their own and looked to Foster Care as an alternative. I was just a few months old when they took me in. Emily is a Licensed Practical Nurse which made their transition to parenthood much easier."

"I have great admiration for people that open their homes to children in need, especially those who adopt. You lived with the Peytons from infancy. If you don't mind me asking, how come they never tried to adopt you?"

"Actually, they did try. When I was about eight years old, they sat me down and told me that they wanted to adopt me. We went over the pros and cons and when it came to me making the final decision, I decided that I didn't want to be adopted. It had nothing to do with the way I was being treated. Hell, I couldn't have had it better than I had living with Emily and Walter. What seemed to bother me most at that young age was that I would be giving up my true identity; who I really was and as I saw it then, any chance of ever knowing about my birth mother."

Thomas got thoughtful for a few moments. "Emily and Walter were devastated by my decision. I could see the tears welling up in their eyes as I told them how I felt, but, you know something strange, they never changed the way they acted towards me. In fact, if anything, they were more loving after that; if that was even possible."

"Wow, that's quite a story. Have you ever heard of anyone looking for you?"

"No, I haven't."

"How about searching on your own?'

"I've thought about it a few times, but I wouldn't know where to start. I guess the truth of the matter is that I'm a little scared."

"There are a lot of web-sites that you can use. I did a few preliminary searches a couple of years ago; nothing serious. It wasn't too hard to do.

They've got this locating people thing down to a science now and many States have begun loosening their rules regarding searching through records. A lot of laws have changed making it easier for someone to find parents and relatives so it's not rocket science any longer."

"Well, if you ever decide to do a serious search, I could help you with it. Would you work on it with me?"

"I'd love to."

"Well, we're here," he announced as he turned into the driveway of the Peyton's house.

"Why don't you get out here so I can park the car over there close to the hedges? That way I won't be blocking their driveway."

"Okay, I'll see you inside," she said, as she got out of the car and headed for the side door of the house.

CHAPTER 9

Miriam returned to her room at the Owensburg Inn. It wasn't that, having been brought up in the town, she was without kinfolk to stay with, in fact she still had a cousin and an elderly aunt residing in and around Owensburg, but the nature of her trip made it ill-advised to stay with them. As it was, she hadn't seen either of them for over twenty years and she didn't expect to have any free time to socialize with family, especially when the conversation stood a good chance of turning to the events of twenty-three years ago.

Her room was tastefully decorated. It was a room with double twin beds; not one she would have chosen, being used to a king–sized bed for the past eleven years, but unfortunately, because of the demand for rooms, she had not been given a choice. As it was, she was fortunate to have reserved the room considering the number of guests visiting the town for the Anniversary celebration; a point that was driven home by both the check-in clerk and the bellboy. *This place is as stuffy as I remember it. I better be on my best behavior or they may toss me out.*

The shower had an abundance of hot water and she indulged herself with five minutes on the pulsating massage setting. She dried off and donned the long white robe that came with the room. Planning to relax for only a few minutes, she settled on the bed with three pillows propped up behind her head. She poured a glass from the complimentary bottle of Chardonnay, took a big sip and settled back on the pillows. A warm peaceful feeling settled in and after a few minutes she was sound asleep. Two hours later, awakening with a start, she looked at her watch. It was one o'clock and she wasn't dressed for her afternoon at the park.

As she attended to getting ready, she glanced at the mirror several times; each time giving herself a nod of approval.

Miriam was forty-three years old. She kept her weight at one hundred and twenty-five pounds, which for her five feet-eight-inch height, gave her attractive proportions. She worked out twice a week at the "Club" to keep toned up.

She was a pretty woman with smooth features accented by light blue eyes with brown specks. It was her eyes that her husband Nathan liked most about her, but she kept the rest in shape because she had to look at herself in the mirror every day and she wanted to be sure that she could always maintain a high level of self-approval. She could still turn heads when she took a mind to. She put on a pair of denim shorts, a red three-quarter sleeve, V neck top and a pair of name brand canvas running shoes.

Miriam was one of those women that looked good without a lot of makeup, so she only needed to pencil a few strokes on her eyebrows and she was done. With one last approving glance, she headed off to the park.

CHAPTER 10

Tiecher Park was busy with fun and games everywhere one looked. The multiple committees had done themselves proud with well organized activities that made it impossible to walk more than fifty feet without coming across a booth, a contest, an exhibit or other festive activity.

When Miriam entered the park, the pie eating contest had just begun. A long table held an assortment of homemade pies, baked by the town's Ladies Auxiliary; fourteen in all, five different flavors. To the left of the table, twelve men and two women were lined up to participate in the contest. She walked on past several booths where jewelry, pottery and oil paintings were on sale.

She regularly attended fairs and festivals when she was back home, but today she would not be distracted by any of the exhibits. Her destination was at the far end of the park where the Mitchell softball field was located. The field was named after Archibald Mitchell, manager of the multi-trophy winning Owensburg High soccer team during the seventies and eighties, who succumbed to a lengthy bout with cancer several years ago. Behind her she could hear the oohs and aahs from the crowd watching the pie eating contest as fourteen people plunges their faces into their pies. *Never could get into that form of competition, but whatever floats your boat.*

Ahead, she could hear the noise of the crowd attending the ballgame, about hundreds of feet down the trail. As she walked past the last stand of trees, her heart skipped a beat. She could see bleachers, half-full with supporters, players on the field, a pitcher on the mound and a batter knocking mud from his cleats. Off to the side a small group of women were shouting encouragement to the batter. She made her way quickly to a seat in the bleachers where she would have an unobstructed view of the game. In her hand she held her I-Phone, camera ready, in case she spotted her son.

One by one, she eyed each player on the field; the task made difficult by the ball caps that each wore. The scoreboard showed that the B team was at bat. They were behind by two runs but had a runner at second with no one out. She hoped that they would stay on base long enough for her to methodically check each one out. The B team had a runner on, the batter and one man in the on-deck circle, which she quickly eliminated along with the first and third base coaches. The B team's dugout was on the opposite side of the field, too far for her to make a positive match with the picture she held tightly in her hand.

This is going to be a lot harder than I thought it would be. I wish I had thought to bring binoculars.

Team A was on the field except for six players in their dugout; each with their backs to her. One of the players on the field was a possible match, but she would have to wait until he came in from the left-field before making a positive identification. Miriam figured that she had enough time since they were only in the second inning of a scheduled six inning game.

Twelve minutes later, the game was tied up and the B team had three outs. The one possibility came off the field, removed his cap and she was able to eliminate him.

As the B team left their dugout and took up positions on the field, she eliminated them one-by-one. The A team players came up to bat she eyed each one. Two of the six that had been in the dugout were now in the game; one as the first base coach and the other was coaching at third base. The first base coach was short and plump, so Miriam turned to the young man waving his arms and shouting encouragement to the batter. *That could be him, but it's so hard to tell with that ball cap shadowing most of his face.*

The B team pitcher was having control problems and walked the first two batters. With the go-ahead runner on second, Thomas crouched down and prepared for action at third base. He removed his cap to signal the batter and as he did, he turned and flashed a broad smile to Louise who was jumping up and down on the sidelines with the rest of the cheerleaders.

Miriam let out a gasp. *Oh, my god, it's him. I'm sure of it.* She raised the camera and snapped several pictures before Thomas returned his cap to his head and pulled down on the visor. Her fingers immediately went to the review feature. She enlarged the best of the pictures and held the image next to the picture of Thomas. *It's him. I'm sure. It's my Thomas.*

Miriam moved over to the bleachers behind third base. She found a seat on the end of the third row that gave her an unobstructed view of Thomas. The woman seated two seats away turned to greet the newcomer. "Hi, I'm Shirley."

"Miriam."

"Pleased to meet you, Miriam. You A team or B team?"

"Definitely A."

"Well then, you're welcome to join our crowd."

"The third base coach looks familiar. Do you know him?"

"Of course, everybody in town knows Tom Mortinson. He pitched for the Spartans a few years back. He was a real superstar. I sure wish he was pitching today. Why do you ask?"

"I was just wondering. He seems so enthusiastic." Her heart was beating overtime. *It's him; it's my son.* Miriam wanted so much to tell Shirley that Thomas was her son; wanted to shout it out to the world, but of course that wouldn't be wise at this juncture.

"I think part of that enthusiasm is him showing off for the girl he came to the park with. I see him sneaking looks at her every once and a while."

"Which one is she?'

"Right down below there," she said, pointing towards a cheerleader with the blue top and white shorts.

"She's very pretty. Is she his steady?"

"I have no idea. I saw her for the first time today. I'm almost certain that she's not from around here. I've lived in Owensburg for ten years and I think I've seen just about everybody in town by now. I know that Tom moved away after he graduated OH and went off to college somewhere. I have no idea where he's living now. He's the son of our Chief of Police, Walter Peyton; well, actually he was raised by Walter as a foster child. They did a real good job too, as far as I can see."

Foster child? I wonder why they didn't adopt him. It seems odd that you would raise a child all those years and not make him one of your family. Well I guess, in a sense, that's fortuitous. If they had changed his name, maybe Mike Tolliver wouldn't have located him.

"So, I guess they're both here for the celebration."

"Looks that way. How about you?"

"That's why I'm here too. I'm an alumnus of OH. I left Owensburg over twenty years ago. It's my first time back. I just came for the festivities and to see how the town was prospering. It isn't every day that your home town celebrates its 200th Anniversary."

"Well what do you think of the place after all these years?"

"From what I've seen so far, things are a lot better. They've always had responsible town government. I'm looking forward to the rest of the day and the big dance tonight. I understand that they have a really spectacular show planned."

"That's what I hear, but unfortunately I have two elderly aunts visiting for the weekend and they don't want anything to do with pyrotechnics."

Shirley sighed as she added, "I'll just have to read about it in the papers tomorrow."

"What a shame."

"Well the night won't be a total loss. They go to bed early, so I'll be able to see the fireworks from my backyard and hear a little of the music. That's better than nothing."

The inning was over before Miriam could turn her attention back to Thomas. He was now sitting in the dugout again, with his back to her. The game moved along until, at the end of the fourth inning, it halted as everyone took time out to take the traditional stretch. The score was 5-3 in favor of the A team.

Thomas headed for the cheerleading squad and embraced Louise.

Miriam watched as they hugged, snapping pictures in such a way that Shirley wouldn't realize that Thomas was the true focus of her interest. She could tell by the expressions on their faces that this was a special relationship. A slight feeling of jealousy crept in and it took her totally by surprise. *What's on earth is the matter with me. I want Thomas to have someone to love and share his life with. She seems like a lovely girl and they seem to be really be into each other. Maybe I can even be a part of their lives. Listen to me, I sound like a typical mother.* Miriam smiled and popped out of her reverie after a few minutes.

The game resumed and by the end of the sixth inning the A team had held onto the two run lead and that was the way the game ended. Both teams headed for the sidelines where a tub of ice cold bottles of beer had been patiently waiting for over an hour and a half. The cheer leaders and game organizers joined them as they collectively toasted the town of Owensburg's 200th Anniversary.

The crowd in the bleachers disbanded rather rapidly, anxious to check out the many other activities the celebration had to offer. Shirley said goodbye and she and a few friends wended their way down to the exit passageway, leaving Miriam alone in the section. Not wanting to be obvious in her surveillance of the couple, Miriam eyed Thomas and Louise out of the corner of her eye, while she snapped picture after picture with her I-Phone, while pretending to be texting someone. After a half-hour of socializing Thomas and Louise took leave of the group and headed out of the park; with Miriam trailing close behind.

The urge to cause a chance meeting was prevalent as she reduced the distance between them. *How easy it would be, especially now that I know for sure that he is my Thomas, but I'd never forgive myself if I messed it up. I could do irreparable harm and maybe lose him forever. I promised Mike that I wouldn't make any contact, so that's what I've got to do, but it sure is hard.*

Miriam maintained a respectable distance as Thomas and Louise visited kiosks and stands, tried their hand at a few games. She saw Thomas checking his watch every few minutes and eventually started down the path to the parking lot. She was disappointed that she was losing contact with her son. *They look so comfortable with each other. I'm sure they'll go to the dance tonight; I'll see him there. Right now, I'll go back to my room, call Mike and tell him what I've found out.*

CHAPTER 11

The phone rang five times before he picked up. "Yeah, Jimmy Nordstrom, here."

"Mister Nordstrom, are you associted with the band Bobby V and the Rhythm Riders?"

"Associated? Hell, I'm their manager. Who wants to know?"

"Mister Nordstrom, this is Captain Davis of the West Virginia Highway Patrol. I'm afraid I've got some bad news for you."

Jimmy cut in, "What happened, has there been an accident? Is anyone hurt?"

"I'll get to that in a minute, sir. The band's bus was heading north on I-77 at ten o'clock this morning, apparently headed back to Owensburg, from Bluefield, where they played last night. Just south of Charleston they were hit by a tractor trailer operated by a driver who was distracted by a flapping tarpaulin on his cargo. According to the report, he veered off the rain slicked highway, over the median and collided head-on with the bus."

The Captain hesitated a minute to let that sink in, then continued, "I regret to inform you that the driver of the bus, one Thomas Meltzer, was killed on impact. Another member of the band, Pete Zahn, died on the way to the hospital. The band leader, Bobby Vincienti, is in intensive care at Charleston General with a broken hip, several broken ribs and a multiple break of his right arm. Several other members were shaken up and are under observation. Except for the driver, Mister Zahn, and Mr. Vincienti, the others were fortunate to come out of the crash with just minor scrapes and bruises. I'll give you the number of the hospital, if you want to speak with someone about their conditions."

Jimmy was at a rare loss for words, but it only took a few minutes for him to switch to the business side of his brain, "What happened to the driver of the rig? Was he cited?"

"There was no sign that the driver, Denver Manes, was impaired by drugs or alcohol, if that's what you're implying. He is, however, being held while the Accident Reconstruction Task Force attempts to determine, with some certainty, exactly how the accident occurred."

"Well, I hope that rig jockey gets the book thrown at him. The roads aren't safe with all that texting, CB'ing and pep-pill popping."

"Sir, we don't know that anything like that is involved here. That's why we hold these investigations. We need to get to the bottom of accidents in our State so that we can make the roads safer for every driver."

"Well that doesn't help Mrs. Zahn or her three children, now does it? It doesn't help Tom Meltzer's mother that he was providing care for. That ain't gonna help Bobby V who most likely faces a long recovery and may never be able to play again. Tell that to your 'task force'. Maybe that will help them with their investigation."

"I understand why your upset, sir. Rest assured the State of West Virginia will do whatever it takes to get to the bottom of this accident. We take safety on our roads very seriously, down here."

Jimmy calmed down. "I'm sure that you do, Captain Davis. I apologize for that outburst. I was just blowin' off steam. I'll get in touch with Bobby and the band members at Charleston General and make arrangements with an associate down there to transport the bodies of Thomas Meltzer and Peter Zahn back to Owensburg where they lived. I appreciate your calling, Captain."

"Please contact me or my assistant, Sergeant Harding if you have any questions." He gave Jimmy phone numbers for Charleston General, his own and that of his assistant and concluded the call.

Jimmy put the phone back in the cradle. *What the hell am I supposed to do now? I got that gig at Tiecher Park in eight hours*. Jimmy knew that the 'gig' was no ordinary performance. This one was part of the town's 200th Anniversary celebration. They were expecting the hometown favorite, Bobby V and the Rhythm Riders, to perform. They even contracted for "The Beast".

It was times such as these that Jimmy was glad that Bobby V didn't have an agent to complicate matters; that Bobby trusted him to look out for the band's interests. The two have partnered for a little over seven years and never had an argument that couldn't be resolved over a couple of beers.

Where the hell am I going to get a replacement band in such a short time; a band anywhere near as good as Bobby? Damn, sometimes I hate this business; all these headaches for a minuscule twenty percent management fee.

I've got to find somebody decent before I call the Anniversary Committee; they're going to be pissed-off big time, as it is. It's a good thing I included an emergency substitute clause in the contract, or I'd really be screwed.

Keeping his fingers crossed, that no one would find out about the accident before he had secured a replacement, Jimmy started to dial the numbers of bands within a radius of one hundred miles. An hour later, having had no success, in desperation, he called Bobby V.

It took several transfers, but finally he was connected to the private room where Bobby was laying in a hospital bed staring blankly at the TV screen hanging from the ceiling. He had monitors and IV drips hooked up to his arms and chest. It took him several minutes to manipulate the phone with his left hand; years of texting seeming to fail him. Finally, he got the hang of it and pressed the "TALK" button.

"Hello!"

"Bobby, is that you?"

"Jimmy?"

"Who else? How are you doing, Bud?"

"Not so good, Jimmy. I got busted up pretty good. One minute I was takin' a nap on the bus and next thing I know I'm flat on my back in a hospital bed."

"I heard. What did the docs tell you?"

"Just that I'm gonna live and that I'm going to be laid up for a long time; maybe as much as six months."

"Shit." Social graces weren't one of Jimmy's long suits; nothing in the way of empathy could be anticipated. Instead he got right to the real reason he called. "You know that we have a gig at Tiecher Park tonight. I've called everyone I know, and I can't find a band to stand in for you. You gotta help me out, here?"

Bobby wanted to say, *Christ, Jimmy, Pete and Tom are dead I'm busted up bad and all you care about is who you can get to replace me. You spend hours on the phone before you have the decency to call to see how I am.* But, he didn't. This was just Jimmy being Jimmy. Seven years had shown him many sides of Jimmy Nordstrom. He knew nothing would be gained by berating him now. So instead, he asked, "How about Vinny and the Cruisers?"

"Those pot heads? Why the hell would you recommend them?"

"They're clean now, Jimmy, and they're just looking for a chance to prove themselves. I sat in with his band during rehearsals a couple of months ago and they have a real cool program. Take my word for it; they'd be perfect for this."

Bobby felt a sharp pain in his arm and pressed the button for more pain medicine. "Look, I don't think they have any gigs right now. You give Vinny a call and tell him that I put in a good word for them." He responded to the silence at the other end with, "I gotta go."

Bobby pressed the "OFF" button. *I've got a real asshole for a manager.* He slumped back on the bed. Who played at Tiecher Park tonight was the least of his worries.

CHAPTER 12

Wendell Phillips had already banged the gavel to bring the emergency meeting to order. Wendell could be spotted easily in a crowd by his overall appearance. Whereby he was short in height, *5'5"*, he made up for it in girth, weighing in at slightly over three hundred pounds. A few townspeople referred to him as "Fatty" as in Roscoe "Fatty" Arbuckle, the silent picture star, with whom he bore an uncanny resemblance.

Marge Nelson, (The Committee Secretary.) took attendance for the minutes of the meeting:

"Wendell Phillips?" (Owner of four gas stations in town, and Chairman of the 200th Anniversary Celebration-Dance Sub-Committee.)

"Here!"

"John Clark?" (Principal of Owensburg High.)

"Here! "

"John Martin?" (Town Mayor and owner of three sandwich shops in town.)

"Here!"

"Payne Eaton?" (Town Elder and Family Law Attorney.)

"Here!

"Ralph Mason?" (Retired NBA Referee.)

"Here!"

"Peter Westlake?" (Owner/Operator of the local FM all-music radio station WOWM FM.)

"Here!"

Wendell, cleared his throat. "I move that we set aside the procedural stuff tonight and get right to the issue at hand."

"I second the motion," Payne said.

"All in favor say Aye."

"Ayes," around the table.

"Good, then let's get to this crisis with the band. We've got only four hours before the concert starts." He turned to Jimmy Nordstrom who was anxious to have his time. "What do you have for us, Jimmy?"

In his customary terse demeanor, Jimmy wasted no time. "You all know about the accident, so I'll cut to the chase. I'm obligated to provide the music for the dance tonight. I've already contacted a group that can do this gig for us. Vinny and the Cruisers are available, and they have experience with the pyrotechnics that will be used. Hell, the fireworks and lasers are what it's really about tonight. I just need to get your okay before I sign the papers."

"Whoa, hold on there." The speaker was Payne Eaton. "I'm not even sure that we should proceed with the concert, given the circumstances."

The other committee members shot quick glances at Payne. It was obvious that none of them had even considered calling off the show.

Wendell turned to Jimmy. "Wasn't that band in some trouble a few years back because of drugs; even did some time?"

"Wen, that was several years ago. They've cleared up their act since then. Bobby V vouches for them and in my book that's as good a recommendation as you can get."

Jimmy looked around the room. "Look, you guys, you have my word that Vinny can handle the job, but I need to get moving on this. We only have a few hours and they need time to work with the technicians from 'The Beast". Now, do I have your go ahead to sign them or not?"

Wendell looked around the room, making eye contact with each committee member. "It looks like a go, but we'll have to take a vote for the record."

Ralph made the motion, Peter did the seconding and it was approved unanimously.

"Okay, you have your approval, but I'm warning you Jimmie, you better be right about this."

"Don't worry, Wen, everything will be perfect."

Well now, that wasn't too difficult to predict. After all, the dance/show was the culmination of the 200ᵗʰ Anniversary Celebration. It just had to go on.

CHAPTER 13

The Peyton's had their special dinner set up by the time Thomas and Louise returned to the house. The screened-n porch was large enough to hold an assortment of wicker furniture and a large round table with a large heated plate in the center already stocked with assorted meats, shrimp and veggies. There were place settings for four with gold handled utensils and a long-stemmed wine glass rested next to each setting.

Thomas and Louise washed up as soon as they returned from the park and joined Walter and Emily on the porch, taking their seats just as Walter began pouring from a bottle of Cabernet Sauvignon. As he did, he explained, "Jim Rogers, the owner of the wine shop, said this is a good all-purpose wine for a light meal such as this."

Emily added, "I knew that you were planning to go to the dance tonight, so I didn't think you would want anything too heavy for dinner. I found this assortment in an article in one of those food and wine magazines last week and I thought it would be nice for tonight."

Louise looked over the food on the table. "This looks perfect, Mrs. Peyton."

"Oh, please, dear, call me Emily. Mrs. Peyton, sounds so formal. It makes me feel old."

"Thank you, Emily, I appreciate that."

Walter stood up. "I would like to propose a toast. Here's to love and peace; two passions that the world is much in need of, right now." He hesitated a moment before raising his glass. "Cheers."

They clinked their glasses with a round of "Cheers".

"Wow, that's a great wine, Dad. Your friend didn't steer you wrong."

Walter nodded his head, "Yes, it is good. I'll have to write down the name and get some more in."

"Dig in you guys, let's see if that magazine was right too."

Dinner ended about an hour later with a crème brulee cheesecake and coffee.

"That was really great, Mom. I really loved that cheesecake."

"Well, have another piece, then."

"Not now. I've had enough, but if you have any left, I might just raid the refrigerator when we get home."

"I'll make sure that there is some." She turned to Walter. "Did you hear that?"

"What are you picking on me for? I would never eat the last piece."

"Well, see that you don't," she said with a grin.

"How about you, Louise, can I save a piece for you too?"

"Sure, if it won't be any trouble."

"None at all. I'll stop off at Bensons and pick up another cake. That way we can enjoy it again tomorrow and if we have any left over, then you can take it with you when you leave."

"That sounds great, but please don't put yourself out." He rose from the table, "I think we're going to have to excuse ourselves. We've got a dance to dress for."

"Louise piped in with a mischievous look on her face, "Thomas promised to show me his moves."

Emily looked puzzled as she asked Thomas, "You have moves?"

Thomas snapped back, "Don't you start in on that too. You know I look good on the dance floor."

His mother shrugged her shoulders, and burst out laughing, "Whatever you say, dear."

As she rose from the table, Louise offered, "May I help you clean up?'

"Don't be silly, Louise. You go ahead and get ready. Walter and I will take care of this."

Back in their room, Louise and Tom busied themselves with getting ready for the dance.

"That was so nice of your parents to make that dinner for us. They are such a sweet couple."

"They are that. I could kick myself when I think of the time that I got into trouble as a teenager. I can still remember the painful look on their faces."

"You don't seem like the type that would get into anything really serious."

"Oh, you'd be surprised, if you knew."

"What? Tell me. Come on, you can't start that kind of a conversation and then not finish it."

Thomas looked at her with a frown. "Alright, but you have to remember that I was only fifteen at the time."

She sat down next to him on the bed. "I'm all ears. What did you do, Mister Capone?"

"Well, as you can imagine, being the son of a policeman makes you different from the other kids at school. Not that it makes life easier; far from it. In that environment, belonging requires proving yourself. In this case I needed to prove to four members of an elite clique that I wasn't what they kept calling a 'goody-goody'. I don't know why it was so important to me to get their approval. I've never been the kind of person that goes along with the crowd.

"Anyway, the test meant committing a crime. We broke into the high school and vandalized the library, chemistry lab and gym to the tune of over forty thousand dollars worth of damage. It took the police only two days to pin the break-in to the five of us and then, only because one of the guys told his girlfriend, who told her parents. Fortunately, the judge that heard the case was a personal friend of the parents. That happens in a small town. He only gave us two months of community service and fined each family eighty-two hundred dollars to pay for repairs and court costs.

"The parents of the other four boys were well off, financially, but the fine took a heavy toll on Walter and Emily. They had to take a personal loan to pay for it. Of course, having to pay the fine wasn't the worst of the situation. Their pride as parents took the biggest hit. Especially with him being the town Sheriff. Up until that time they never experienced even the slightest of difficulties in raising me. They were more concerned with why I had to get involved with the other boys, than my being involved in a crime that was high on the list with shoplifting and vandalizing cars parked on the street. I understood their concern and was willing to do anything to earn back their respect."

Thomas took a swig of water and continued, "Of course, while there was a happy ending, that didn't mean that I sailed through this incident unscathed. You don't know what anguish is until you hurt someone close to you. Emily and Walter, these two-wonderful people who had given me everything, were suffering because of my reckless actions. It tore at me like a knife gutting my insides. I couldn't look at them without feeling pangs of guilt.

"Once again, they came to my rescue. Both saw how repentant I was, and they were determined not to allow any negative energy into their household. To their credit, they let me tell them my side of the story and were sympathetic with my need for peer recognition.

"We talked for several hours and decided that I should get involved with after hour activities at the school, in particular, trying out for the school's softball program.

"Much too every one's surprise, I was a natural. My teammates readily accepted me. Many of them are still friends to this day and I'm happy to say that I never brought any shame to my parents since that time."

Louise reached out for Thomas and gave him a big hug. "That's a heartwarming story. No wonder you love Walter and Emily as if you were their flesh and blood."

"You're right about that. Sometimes I daydream that they really are my birth parents and that somehow my life has just been some kind of a social experiment to see how I'd turn out under foster care upbringing. I know that that's silly, but that's how I feel."

"It's not so silly, given what you just told me. It looks as if you have a void in your heart that won't be filled until you know the whole story of who your real parents are. We talked earlier about doing a search. If you are still interested, we could start when we get back home. There's a lot going on with the foster care/adoption process. I read something in the paper the other day that the State of Ohio has extended the Foster Care eligibility to the age of twenty-one. I know it's none of my business, but I want you to be at peace with your heritage."

"You may be right, as long as Walter and Emily don't know about it. Sometimes children searching for their real parents is upsetting to adoptive or foster parents. I think they would be happy for me, but I don't want to take any chances. Let's talk about it on the way home. Right now, we have a dance to go to."

"You're right. I get first dibs on the bathroom."

After Louise left the bedroom, Thomas opened his suitcase and removed a package. He quickly opened it and removed a ring box. He opened the box and looked at the one and a quarter carat, princess cut, diamond engagement ring. He placed it in the left inner pocket of his jacket. *I sure hope the answer will be yes.*

CHAPTER 14

"Tolliver."

Miriam was momentarily taken aback by his brusqueness; usually his soft speaking secretary answered the phone when she called. "Mike, its Miriam"

"Oh hi, Miriam. Are you staying out of trouble as you agreed you would?'"

"Yes, I am, but I've got the greatest news. I found Thomas. He is the one you located. He was at a softball game. I met someone from town who knew who he was, and it definitely is him. He's got a girlfriend and he's very popular here in Owensburg."

"Whoa, slow down. I'm not surprised that you found him. Everything pointed to him being your son, but I still have to check out a few more details. Your making a positive identification is an important step. Now remember, you and I need to sit down and go over everything before any one-on-one contact is made. You have to trust my experience with these matters. There are as many wrong ways as right ways to proceed when it comes to reuniting lost persons. You've come too far to make any last-minute mistakes."

"What could possibly go wrong, Mike?"

"Miriam you have to remember that you are looking at things only from your own perspective. You don't have any idea how Thomas will react to knowing that you're his birth mother. If you approach him the wrong way, you could lose him forever. We've been over this many times. Keep your distance until we've had a chance to consider everything."

"I hear what you're saying Mike, but you can't possibly know how hard it is. After all this time, to finally meet my Thomas. I get goose bumps just thinking about it."

"I think that I have a pretty good idea what you're going through. Now, tell me, what happened today."

"First, I went to the parade hoping that I would spot him in the crowd, but there were so many people and so much going on with the parade and all, that I must have missed him. You know that he played softball at OH, so I thought that there was a good chance that he would show for a softball game that was scheduled for the afternoon. I watched him coach one of the teams and I saw him hugging one of the cheerleaders. I took lots of pictures and then I followed them for awhile until they drove away together. Don't worry, I kept a respectable distance away so that he wouldn't see me. "I'll send you the pictures I took."

"That's really great, Miriam. I'm glad my investigation found the right man. What are your plans now?"

"Well, there's a big dance and show tonight. It's a big part of the Anniversary festivities so I'd be very surprised if they didn't attend. They're young and in love, take my word for it, they'll be there. That'll give me another opportunity to see them together. There's some kind of a light show planned, so taking a lot of pictures won't look out of the ordinary. I can't tell you how excited I am right now. I'll never be able to thank you enough for the work you've done in locating him for me."

"I'm just glad that we are this far along. You go to your dance, but promise me again, that you will not make any personal contact with him. Since he's with someone, who he may be important in his life, any personal contact could create a serious problem; he might react differently on her behalf. When you eventually do make contact with Thomas it's best that it be done privately and under controlled conditions."

"I promise you, Mike. I trust your judgment. We've come so far, I surely don't want to do anything to mess it up."

"Great. Then we're on the same wavelength. We're so very close now, Miriam. Thanks for doing things my way. Keep one thing in mind, Thomas is not a lost child, he's a grown man and that makes a big difference in how we eventually make contact with him. Now go and have a good time tonight and we'll talk in the morning. By then I should have my i's dotted and my t's crossed. I'll have enough background information know for us to be able sit down and make plans for you and Thomas to meet. Oh, and thanks for sending the pictures."

"Your welcome, Mike, have a good night."

"You too, Miriam."

She took a few minutes to send Mike the promised pictures. As she did, a strange feeling came over her. She had met with Mike several times and had talked to him at least a dozen times, but for some reason, today his voice caused a peculiar sensation that she could not make any sense of. Suddenly a number of random thoughts made their way through her thoughts. *Am I making more of this relationship than I should be? Hell, he does this for dozens of other women. Sure, I owe him a lot for finding Thomas, but that was his job. Is this some kind of transference thing? Shit, I've got to clear my head. Right now, I've got to keep my mind on one thing and one thing only and that is to see Thomas again.*

She called room service to order a club sandwich and coffee and set about getting her dress and shoes ready. The weather report for the night was for clear skies and temperatures in the 70's. The long sleeve night dress she brought for the dance was the perfect garment. It was warm enough when it was cool and cool enough when it was warm. The dress's heather gray color suited her complexion, as did the lipstick and nail polish she brought with her.

Miriam was very practical when it came to acquiring her wardrobe, refusing to be a slave to designer labels. Nothing disturbed her more than to see a group of people, each brandishing a designer's outfit that demonstrated their need to belong, rather than clothes that showed the wearer to be an independent thinker.

There would be some chairs and tables at the dance, but she expected that they would be reserved for the town's VIPs, so she based her choice of shoes solely on the expectation of being on her feet for several hours. She considered herself to be in good shape, jogging five miles at least three times a week so standing on her feet for several hours shouldn't be a problem. Miriam had packed several pairs of shoes, not knowing what to expect during her trip. She decided on a dark gray dressy platform pump, that experience told her, would serve her well for the night.

She inserted new batteries into the camera and put it into the shoulder bag she would be taking. When her dinner arrived, she ate slowly and watched the five o'clock news on a local channel. When she was finished eating, she put in a call to her husband.

"Hi, sweetie, I'm so glad I caught you in. I wasn't sure about the time difference."

"I'm so happy to hear your voice. For the last four hours, I've been negotiating through an interpreter. You can't imagine how difficult it is to carry on a conversation that long, under conditions like that. I'm totally drained."

"My poor baby. Are you through for the day?"

"It looks like it. I've going to use the rest of the day to get ready for a meeting in Brussels. tomorrow. I'll say one thing for the European Union, it's really easy now to travel between counties. I used to have to spend hours dealing with visas and money exchanges. Now, enough about me. Tell me how you're enjoying your trip down memory lane."

"It's really great. Owensburg is still the quaint town it has always been. They had a really great parade this morning and then I spent some time at the park with the games and stuff. Tonight I'll be attending the big dance and fireworks show. They brought in something called "The Beast". It's some kind of a pyrotechnical behemoth. I can hardly wait to see it."

"That sounds like fun. It's a shame I can't be there to share it with you. Well, you have a good time and don't let any gigolos try to pick you up. You're a beautiful woman and some guys frequent dances just to prey on women. I hate to admit it, but in my younger days, I did a little bit of preying myself, but never mind that, just be careful."

"Don't worry about me, sweetie. I know how to take care of myself."

"I know you do, but be on-guard anyway."

"Well, I'll let you go. You must have things to do."

"I'm sure you do, too. It was so good hearing your voice. Have a good time tonight and I'll talk to you tomorrow. Good night, my precious one."

"Good night, sweetie."

As she returned the receiver to its cradle, Miriam felt guilty. She hated to have to hide the real reason for her trip back to her home town; hated to keep such intimate details about her life from the man she married and shared vows with. He had every right to know, especially now that she intended to make contact with Thomas. *I'll tell him when the time is right, but I'm just not ready. I'm sure that he'll understand. And then there's those thoughts about Mike. God what a mess.*

She had at least two more hours before she needed to leave. She turned the TV back on.

CHAPTER 15

Nathan Peter Walton, CEO of Walton Enterprises was ten years older than his wife, Miriam. They met at a party for a mutual friend and they hit it off right away. They had a whirlwind courtship and married six months later.

Nathan built Walton Enterprises, a distribution consulting company, from scratch. Within five years the firm was on a list of the fastest growing consulting companies in the country. The last two years, however, several of his largest clients switched to full spectrum consulting companies. Walton Enterprises specialized in only one area of business and that was distribution. His trip to Europe was aimed at changing that by expanding his company's disciplines. Establishing a network of foreign consultancies would allow him to offer world-wide distribution expertise to his client base. He would provide a wide spectrum of services through partnerships and thus avoid the headaches and risks of building these networks himself. The survival of his company was riding on the success of this trip. Germany was all but assured, thanks to today's meeting. Belgium was next on the list.

Nathan was divorced and childless when he met Miriam. Early on in the marriage, they had a conversation about having children and they both decided that his business travel their life style didn't leave any room for raising a family.

He never told anyone about the child he fathered in his late teens. The girl he impregnated was a sister of his best friend and the daughter of his father's business partner. The birth was hushed up and the child, a boy, through legal maneuvers and sealed documentation, became part of the girl's family as a child of her aunt.

Nathan and the girl went their own way as if the pregnancy and birth never happened. He swore an oath to himself that he would never tell anyone about the child. Two years later the girl died from a drug overdose and the secret of his son's heritage died with her.

So, it seems that both Nathan and Miriam are harboring a secret about an abandoned child. What bearing will that have on this story?

CHAPTER 16

Aldo Vincent DeLuca the flamboyant leader of Vinny and the Cruisers walked the periphery of the sound stage to bsorb the energy of "The Beast". He frequently used lasers and fireworks with his shows and was familiar with the percussive interference that they could have on the flow of music. Positioning the band on the stage, then, became of paramount importance. He would not allow the Beast's engineers to put their show's reputation ahead of the professional performance of his band members.

"Hello, I'm Pete Honeycutt. I'm the Operations Engineer for Mystic Times, the developers of "The Beast". Honeycutt was six-five and heavily muscled; the type you would expect to be in charge of a project this large.

Vinny at five-eight looked up at the man. "I'm Vinny DeLuca. My band the Cruisers will be playing here tonight."

"Yeah, I heard. That was a terrible thing that happened to the other band. We worked with them for a while yesterday. They seemed like good folks."

"They're personal friends. I really feel for Bobby and his crew."

"I was watching you walk around. You seem to be concerned about something."

"Nothing in particular, I was just trying to get my bearings. I've had some experience with pyrotechnics. I was trying to figure out where the best spot would be to set up our instruments."

"Well, maybe I can help. We spent several hours this morning testing acoustics from various locations on the stage. You'd be surprised how every stage is different. It doesn't take much to throw the sound off. We marked a large oval area on the floor that should be large enough to accommodate your band. Anywhere within that area will have the lowest decibel reading from the pyrotechnics at the height of our display. I wish we could tie in better with your performance, but that just isn't the way we work. Our commitment is to provide a show for the townspeople and that's our priority. We went over everything with Bobby in a rehearsal, yesterday; he was set up right around the oval. We just don't have the time to do it again with your band. I'll make sure you get a schedule of when we will do our shoots. That's the best I can do for you."

"That's good enough, Pete. Under the circumstances I guess we'll both have to improvise.

I appreciate your candor. We'll be here at around seven-fifteen to set up."

"There's one more thing I need to caution you about. We had to use four guy wires behind the superstructure because 'The Beast' didn't fit well over the existing stage. Make sure that you and your band steer clear of them."

"No problem, we'll be entering through the VIP gate that's being set up over there," he said, pointing to a gate manned by a security guard.

"Super. See you at seven-fifteen, then."

Vinny stayed behind on the stage, looking out at the workers checking the flooring and stands. A memory came into his mind of a time several years ago when he and his band were at the top of the band circuit. He commanded top dollar then and the respect of fans and fellow bandleaders alike. That was before the band got involved in drugs; grass, horse and any party drugs they could get their hands on. With the drugs came the young girls anxious to party and some damaging headlines; one including a photo of him smashing his Fender on the stage at the end of a particularly wild set. Soon gigs began being cancelled, multiple lawsuits were filed and eventually they landed up in rehab for four months; it was either that or six months in jail.

Sober and wiser, the band, with two new members, worked hard to get back in the good graces of the soft-rock crowd. Tonight was the crown jewel. If all went well, he knew that the past would be forgiven. *There is a God after all.*

CHAPTER 17

The inspectors were just finishing their check of the dance floor, VIP area and concession stands. The town ownd portable dance floor decks which they stored on the left side of the soundstage. The Dance Committee rented additional panels to finish off a 100'X100' dance floor. Everything snapped together including matching edging. It took the crew of four just under three hours to complete the job. As soon as the floor crew completed the "stage left" flooring, workers set up chairs and tables for the VIP section.

Beverage concessionaires had set up their stalls as each section of the dance floor was laid. Beer and wine were approved for sale and consumption at the event. Signs listed beer and wine at six dollars each and soda at two dollars and reminded patrons that a yellow wrist band was required to purchase alcoholic drinks.

Still more crewmembers had cordoned off the main dance enclosure, establishing entrances at several "gates" at the far-right end of the area. Tables were placed there with boxes of white and yellow ID bracelets; white for General Admission, non-drinkers, and yellow for drinker's General Admissions. On the "stage right" side, adjacent to the stage, they erected a VIP/ Technician/ Performer/ Security gate where entry was by "VIP pass" only. Two propane powered, four passenger courtesy carts were parked by the VIP gate to provide transport across the Gap to the VIP tables at "stage left". The Gap, created by the construction crews, was made up of a strip of the town's original concrete dance floor between the stage and the beginning of the portable wooden dance floor.

Once the show started, the Gap would be quickly filled by the VIP quests wanting to get an up-front look at the performers on the stage.

It appears that everything's in order for the show to go on. With all that preparation, what could possibly go wrong? What, indeed?

CHAPTER 18
Tiecher Park 7:15pm

The General Admission gate opened fifteen minutes early. It was slow going at first as theearly-comers tended to be the youngest of the expected crowd, requiring a careful check of ID's for most, as they requested the yellow wrist band. A casual check of loose clothing, handbags and backpacks was conducted as well, to assure that no contraband, especially in the form of alcoholic beverages was being smuggled onto the premises.

The concession stands became busy immediately and within fifteen minutes a crowd of expectant devotees of the rock genre, cups in hand, was building along the temporary barrier set up along the width of the Gap. The Gap was reserved for VIP's and their guests.

Courtesy carts emitted a low beeping sound as they made their way slowly across the Gap transporting their passengers to the VIP tables. By seven-thirty the VIP area was almost filled except for the front tables which were reserved for the Mayor and The Dance Committee Chairman, their families and guests. As the guests of honor, they planned their arrival for several minutes before the show started.

* * *

Miriam went through the General Admissions gate at around seven-thirty, purchased a cup of red wine and started mixing with the crowd hoping to spot Thomas. After a few minutes she decided that he hadn't arrived as yet and positioned herself where she would have an unobstructed view of the main gate.

* * *

Around the same time, Vinny and the Cruisers arrived at the VIP gate and were escorted backstage. Vinny waved to Pete Honeycutt as they made their way to the chalked area on stage. Minutes later he and the four other musicians that made up the band, were setting up their instruments and engaging in instrument tune-ups.

* * *

When Thomas and Louise arrived at the VIP gate they were immediately passed in. He waved-off the offer of a cart ride, preferring to walk across the Gap and rub elbows with friends and town officials.

"Boy, you really are important," she said, as they walked over to a wine bar. "I'm extremely impressed."

"It's no big deal. They sent me two VIP passes with the invitation. I guess having once been

Owensburg High's star softball pitcher still carries some weight."

"Does that mean that we can be right here, this close to the stage, when the band plays and the fireworks show starts?"

"It sure does. I think the band and the lasers will start around eight, but the fireworks won't go off until its dark enough."

They both ordered a glass of red wine. When he offered to pay, he was told that refreshments in the VIP section were complimentary.

"This really is first-class. Any more surprises?"

Thomas thought about the ring in his pocket, as he answered, "The night is still young, my dear." He smiled, as he added, "Let's wait and see what develops."

They found their table and Thomas was pleased to see that several members of his school softball team and two of his favorite teachers and their wives or dates were at the same table. After several minutes of introductions, the couple picked up their cups to return to the Gap for the start of the program.

As they walked, an announcement came over the loudspeakers that Vinny and the Cruisers would be filling in for Bobby V and the Rhythm Riders. No explanation was given for the substitution and the announcement was immediately followed by piped in soft-rock music.

There was a soft murmur from the crowd as many Bobby V fans expressed their disappointment, followed by tumultuous applause from Vinny's fans.

Clearly, this was going to be a night of surprises or everyone.

CHAPTER 19

Aldo "Vinny" DeLuca finished tuning his Gibson guitar and set it down on its stand. He looked out at the crowd that was nearing capacity. He was momentarily upset by the crowd's initial reaction to the announcement that his band would be playing instead of Bobby V, but his angst didn't last long when a much larger part of the audience applauded the change. He thought to himself, *Looks like a lot of "Cruiser" fans out there. I'm betting that we'll convert the rest of the crowd before the night is over.*

Playing at Owensburg's 200th Anniversary celebration was the best gig he and the band have had on the comeback road from their drug experimentation. During the past six months they scratched their way back into the soft-rock band circuit, and now with this show under their belt, they could command bigger paydays and be choosier about gigs.

* * *

As they made their way back to the Gap, Louise said, "This is so exciting, I've never been to a laser show, let alone one with fireworks. Have you seen it before?"

"No, I haven't, but I'm really looking forward to it. 'The Beast' has been around for years now. It was quite a plum for the Town to snag them for their Anniversary." He looked up at the revolving platform at the top. "It has to be at least forty feet high. What a magnificent edifice. I read about some of their other shows and they got nothing but rave reviews. This is history in the making for Owensburg. We're very lucky to be a part of it."

As they passed through the entrance to the Gap, Thomas looked around for the nearest concession stand. "Wait here a minute while I get us refills. Once the show is underway it'll be damned near impossible to get anywhere near the stands."

* * *

Miriam was just about to give up looking for her son when she saw him cutting through the crowd up near the stage. Her heart was pounding as she started wending her way in that direction. After a series of accidental bumps, accompanied by some muttered expressions, some not too nice, she reached a point where she could get a clear shot of Thomas as he passed no more than twenty feet from where she was standing. She had the camera set for "video" so she could capture his every move. *Oh, this is so exciting. I knew he'd be here.*

Well, it looks as if the Owensburg 200th Anniversary Show is about to start.

Hold on to your hats folks. It's going to be a thrilling ride.

CHAPTER 20
Tiecher Park 7:55 pm

Mayor John Martin, Anniversary Committee Chairman Wendell Phillips, their wives and friends arrived at the VIP gate; six in all.

One of the organizers said, "Mr. Mayor, you're due stage-left in a couple of minutes for the opening remarks. It's too late to ride across the Gap because of the crowd. Anyway, the carts are on the other side.

Gus, one of the maintenance men, spoke up. "My convertible's parked right over there. I can scoot two of you gents over there if you don't mind a tight squeeze."

The Mayor turned to the others and said, "Fine. Wendell and I'll ride in his car." The others nodded as John and Wendell got in to Gus's 1995 Corvette.

Gus turned to the Mayor, "Ain't she sweet. That's the original leather. I drove her in the parade this morning. You guys are in for a real treat."

"It's a beauty, Gus, but can we get going? I've got a speech to make."

"You bet, hold on gents." That said he floored the pedal and headed the car around the back of the stage. Gus had driven behind the original Owensburg stage many times but had never driven behind "The Beast".

* * *

Gus had only one thought on his mind. *I've got to get these folks to the other side, pronto.* In his haste, he didn't see the guy wires until it was too late. The car caught a rear bumper on the first wire, spun around and while he frantically attempted to regain control of the 3,337lb vehicle, it hit the second wire head on. The car came to an abrupt stop, throwing John and Wendell head first, past Gus and over the front of the vehicle. Both hit the ground, rolled over for several turns and came to a dead stop; neither showing any signs of life.

The force of the car against the first two guy wires proved too stressful for the fin plates attached to the top of "The Beast". As the plates separated from the frame they created an eerie grating sound emulating the scratching of fingernails across a blackboard; only many times louder. The vibration created by the impact also short-circuited the laser panel and the lights started to strobe wildly across the stage and the audience.

At the front of the structure, the loud noise immediately got the attention of the crowd, but since it sounded like the ear-piercing noise of a mike/speaker feedback it caused no immediate concern. The sudden panoramic advent of the lasers acted as a confirmation that the show was about to begin. All eyes were riveted on the stage.

CHAPTER 21
Tiecher Park 7:59pm

Within seconds of the fin plate failure of the first two guy wires, "The Beast" pulled agaist the remaining plates for support and found them inadequate. Both plates also gave way within seconds causing the structure to pitch forward. The gap at the base, so artfully and only partially filled by the eight inch sliding panels, was soon filled by "The Beast" seeking purchase. The movement was slow to start, almost deliberate, as if structure was performing in slow-mo, but "The Beast" wasn't going to stop its forward journey until it was resting firmly on the ground; it's journey complete.

The collapse began with a slight wobble followed by the top rigging starting to tilt forward. The leaning continued and anyone watching the collapse unfolding knew that there was nothing anyone could do to stop it. 'The Beast" was going to devour the stage and part of the audience.

Thomas, his hands filled with two cups of red wine, was returning to Louise when the collapse began. He heard some screams from the back of the crowd; saw a few people pointing at the stage and when he looked back at the stage he saw the band, their instruments and several large pieces of scenery sliding across the stage in his direction. He turned his head and attempted to move away, but the crowd and time prevented his escape. Within seconds he was struck in the neck, head and upper back by several flying objects. He was knocked to the ground with several fans falling on top of him. Parts of the structure rained down on them as "The Beast" gave up pieces of its framework, followed by the complete collapse of the structure as it surrendered to gravitational forces. 60,000 lbs, that was once "The Beast", settled down into a massive pile of debris.

The audience was stunned beyond belief as the collapse enfolded before their eyes. As they attempted to run away from the stage; only a few were fortunate enough to elude its grasp. The screams of those beneath the falling stage were quickly snuffed out when it finally came to a stop. As a fog of dust settled, only a scattering of screams was heard, quickly replaced by a cacophony of shouts, cries of despair and prayers.

* * *

As she filmed her son, Miriam saw "The Beast" begin its collapse. She screamed, "Thomas, lookout," as she realized what was happening. She watched as he was knocked down by debris sliding off the stage. She continued to watch as the superstructure's collapse reached out into the audience, engulfing the spot where Thomas had been and stopping within three feet of where she was standing. The last moan of "The Beast" was deafening as it found its final resting place.

Several fans were suddenly thrust at her. She lost her balance and was carried backward by the force of the crowd, only to make contact with another wall of fans frozen in place by the shock of what was transpiring. Her movement came to a halt as she collided with several men. Either they fell on her, or she on them. It really didn't matter because as they fell, Miriam struck her head on the ground and was knocked unconscious.

* * *

Louise was watching Thomas as he was hit. She screamed, "Thomas, watch out," as she saw him engulfed by debris from the stage. As the superstructure completed its collapse she was thrown backwards by several fans rushing towards the sidelines. When she recovered her balance, Louise looked back at where Thomas had been standing and saw nothing but dust rising from a pile of debris. She felt faint but recovered enough to move out of the way of guards and maintenance men rushing toward scene.

* * *

Walter was enjoying an evening off with Emily, away from the hustle and bustle of the celebration activities that had kept him on duty for the greater part of the morning and afternoon. He answered the phone on the second ring, "Peyton, here."

He listened for a few minutes in utter disbelief as his deputy reported what happened.

"I'm sorry for the delay in calling you, Walt, but hell just broke loose, all at once."

"What have you done so far?"

"John and Wes are setting up an ECC and the rest of the guys are trying their best to maintain order. I called for the reserves and for all the emergency gear, including tents and chairs. I activated any trainees I could contact. Walt, there were several hundred-people standing up front when that thing came down. We found John Martin and Wendell Phillips behind the stage. They're both dead with broken necks and I fear we're going to have a lot more victims before the night is up. You've got to get over here right away."

"My son Thomas and his girlfriend are there. Have you seen them?"

"No, Sir, I haven't, but you have to understand that it's chaotic out here."

Emily perked up at the mention of Thomas's name. She nudged Walter to get his attention, "Has something happen to Thomas?"

Walter asked the deputy to hold on as he turned to Emily, "There's been an accident out at

Tiecher Park. It looks like that fancy soundstage collapsed."

Emily gasped. "Are Thomas and Louise all right?"

"George hasn't seen them, but that doesn't mean anything. I'm sure they're safe."

"We've got to go over there."

"Yes, of course we do." He returned to the deputy, "Do the best you can George. I'm on my way. If you run into Thomas, have him call either of us, right away."

"Will do."

* * *

Within minutes of the collapse, hundreds of fans, police and park employees swarmed over the wreckage trying to help those trapped in the ruble. Police quickly cleared an area by the admissions gate and set up an Emergency Command Center and temporary receiving area for the injured as they were freed from the wreckage. The emergency dispatch summoned EMT's, the town's emergency crews and private practice doctors and within minutes dozens of helpers converged on the park to assist with the injured. Hospitals within a thirty-mile radius of the park were at the ready to provide transportation and hospital rooms as would be needed. Fire Departments from surrounding towns dispatched their emergency vehicles and crews to help in the rescue efforts. The town's morgue made preparations as well as early word got to them about the size of the crowd and the possible extent of the casualties.

* * *

When she recovered consciousness, Miriam was lying on a cot in a make-shift tent set up in the parking lot; one of the many that made up the Emergency Command Center. She attempted to sit up but was immediately restrained by a woman wearing a yellow safety helmet. "You're going to need to stay quiet, dear. A medic looked you over and said that you probably suffered a concussion from a blow to the right side of your head. We're not going to know how bad it is until we can check you out at the hospital. You're on that IV to keep up your fluids; sometimes dehydration can be worse than actual injuries. You'll be transferred to the hospital as soon we get you identified and we can get some transportation."

"No. I can't go anywhere until I find my son. He was out there on the floor when that thing fell. I've got to help him, he needs me."

"There's nothing you can do for him right now, dear. The debris is just too heavy. They've ordered in some cranes to lift off the heavy wreckage and until that happens, there's little anybody can do."

Miriam's voice took on an air of urgency, "But, I can help. I know where he was standing when it came down. I can show them the spot." She started to rise only to be restrained again.

"From what I can tell it will be a while before they can remove enough of the wreckage to help those that are trapped. I know it's hard to just sit back and do nothing, but it's all any of us can do right now. Give me his name and I'll post it with the list of missing people that they're compiling. That way as soon as they find him we'll know it right away."

"It's Thomas Mortinson. He was up close to the stage when it happened. I've got pictures on my cell phone. Give it to me and I'll show you."

"I'm sorry ma'am; you were brought in here without any effects. Whatever you may have had with you was probably lost in the confusion that followed the collapse. We don't even have your name. Can you give that to me now, along with your address so that I can add it to the list? By the way, I'm Patricia."

"Hello, Patricia. I'm Miriam… Miriam Walton. I remarried". She gave Patricia her home address and phone number and added, "You need to find my purse, too. I have my identification in there. It must have been right there where they found me."

"Miriam, I'm so sorry about your things, but I guess getting you to safety was a priority. Work with me here and before you know it you and Thomas will be back together again. I've volunteered for a number of these emergency situations and I know for sure that it's best to stand aside and let the professionals do their work. Eventually everything will get sorted out. You'll see. The more we stay out of the way, the better."

"I guess you're right, but it's hard just doing nothing."

"I understand how you feel. Now that you're in stable condition and we've identified you, we're going to move you along to Owensburg General. They're been designated as the First Responder Care Center. They'll be coordinating the names of persons being treated at outlying facilities and they'll be cross-referencing that with the list of those that are reported as missing."

"No. I won't leave here until I know Thomas is safe."

"Miriam, you'll be better off at the FRCC. When they do find Thomas, he'll be moved immediately to one of the area hospitals. If you're lucky he may even be sent to OG. Either way, they will know everything about him, where he is and the care he's receiving."

"I don't care about any of that, I'm staying here."

"You'll be best off at OG, I promise." Patricia released a mild sedative into Miriam's IV and the issue was settled.

A procession of EMT vans and ambulances began transporting their cargos of the injured to local hospitals and the dead to hastily set up, makeshift morgues. In one of the ambulances, Miriam Walton and another survivor lay strapped to gurneys as the vehicle wailed its way through traffic headed for Owensburg General Hospital.

CHAPTER 22
Tiecher Park 8:12pm

The most listened to all-music radio station in town WOWM-FM interrupted Rod Stewart's *Maggie May* for a "Breaking News" announcement. A solemn voice reported:

"This is Warren Sutter of Station WOWM-FM. We interrupt our regularly scheduled broadcast for a special news bulletin. I'm speaking from Tiecher Park in Owensburg where moments ago, the soundstage known as 'The Beast' collapsed onto an audience of at least six hundred fans, that were here attending Owensburg's 200th Anniversary celebration show."

He spoke louder as he continued, *"Scores of townsfolk are milling around me, frantically pressing keys on their mobile phones in a desperate attempt to contact their loved ones known to be attending the festivities. I saw a few people throw their phones on the ground in frustration; one even stomping on his. I've never seen anything like this. It's reminiscent of the chaotic scenes following the collapse of the Sugarland stage in August of 2011.*

Warrens voice started to crack, *"I . . .".* The broadcast ended abruptly.

CHAPTER 23
Tiecher Park 8:25pm

Walter and Emily arrived within minutes thanks to the siren and flashing lights clearing thir way to the park. George met them in the parking lot.

"Any sign of Thomas, yet?"

George tipped his hat to Emily. "Evening Emily" Turning to Walter, "I'm afraid not, Walt. Why don't you and Emily come on over to the EEC. That'll be the best location for receiving any information. Gordon Dalton has a crew compiling a list of missing people and they're in touch with the FRCC to coordinate both sides of this. Things are going real slow. They're moving cranes in from Merryville where they had to store them. They have to raise the stage platform high enough to begin rescue operations. It's going to be a really slow, painstaking job. Until they get that done, we won't know the extent of injuries to the crowd."

They made their way to a table set up in the corner of a large tent. Gordon greeted them as they approached. "I'm glad to see you Sheriff Peyton. I just got a message from one of the first-aid stations to add the name Thomas Mortinson to our missing persons list. Isn't that your boy?"

"Yes, that's him. Where did you say it came from?"

"One of the first-aid stations. I can't tell you which one. They just write names on a sheet of paper and send someone over here with it. The courier is already gone."

Emily interrupted. "I'll check the other stations and find out who reported his name. Maybe it was Louise. Is the name Louise O'Neill on your list?"

Gordon scanned the lists. "No one by that name has been reported, but I'll add it now."

Emily turned to Walter, "You must have a lot to do, let me follow up on this. I'll call you when I find out anything.

"Okay, I'll do the same. Be careful. People do crazy things at times like this."

"Don't worry about me, I'll be fine."

* * *

Emily visited three stations before she located the one where Patricia was working.

"Sure, I remember that. She said her name was Miriam Walton and that Thomas Mortinson was her son. She has a concussion, possibly severe, but she didn't want to go to the hospital. She got so adamant about it that I had to sedate her. She was transferred to Owensburg General about twenty minutes ago."

"Thank you, Patricia, you've been a big help."

Miriam called Walter to update him and to tell him she was headed over to Owensburg General to check up on Thomas, the mysterious Miriam Walton and to look for Louise.

"You go ahead and do that. I've got a couple of situations I have to handle. Would you believe that there are some people taking pieces of the debris as souvenirs? What's wrong with people? Look, I'll send a car over there to take you to the hospital. Call me when you know something. Love you."

"I love you too."

CHAPTER 24
Tiecher Park 8:30pm

Channel NCTV, "The pride of Delaware County", had several cameras assigned to Tiecher Park to cover the opening of the Anniversary show. The police allowed them to set up their equipment just inside the General Admissions gate. One camera was fixed the stage and a second panned the crowd; editors planned to merge them for the Eleven-O'clock News.

Minutes after "The Beast" fell into the crowd, John Taggart, the field reporter in charge of the filming, called his manager and requested that a NCTV interrupted their regularly scheduled broadcasting and go "live" to Tiecher Park starting at 8:30pm.

Dreams of an award-winning documentary danced in John's head as his crew concentrated on filming the rescue effort. Live footage started with EMT's carrying a woman on a stretcher and transferring her to one of the waiting ambulances; then switched to the makeshift crews continuing their rescue efforts, frustrated by the weight of the massive rubble.

"This is John Taggart, coming to you live from Tiecher Park where minutes ago the superstructure known as 'The Beast' collapsed onto an audience of rock lovers estimated to be as many as seven-hundred. It is impossible to know at this time just how many people are buried under the rubble or what their condition is. The main problem hampering rescue efforts is that the pieces of the stage are too large and too heavy for the rescuers to lift" He stopped speaking as he read a piece of paper handed to him by one of the security guards. *"I've just been notified that the cranes used to build the soundstage several days ago are on their way back here to help move the wreckage, but I hear that it'll take time for them to get here because they'll have to take the side roads to avoid utility wires."*

Taggart moved over to the sidelines where anxious fans were crowding around, looking for the opportunity to have their "moments of fame". The first interview was with Bill Corborn, and his girlfriend Debbie Fraily, both residents of Owensburg. They explained that they had arrived late and were at the back of the audience when the catastrophe occurred. Debbie clung to Bill's arm, too shaken-up to say anything, but Bill blurted out, *"We're all right, but I feel for the people under that wreckage. It was just awful; people were running and acting crazy. We were looking at the stage when it happened. It was horrible, those people could see the stage starting to topple and they just couldn't get out of the way."*

The reporter inquired, *"Do you know anyone that might be in the wreckage?"*

"Hell, yes. Most of our friends were in the front of the crowd. We got here late, or we would have been there with them." His face tightened as he added, *"I wish they would let us help, but in the meantime, I guess the only thing we can do is pray."*

"Yes, that appears to be all we can do. Thanks for talking with us, Bill," John said as he turned to another couple, that appeared anxious to talk on air. *"Can I have your names please?"*

The couple were older than the average soft-rock devotee; probably in their sixties. *"Hi, I'm Marshall Gibbons and this is my wife Melody."* Melody was weeping softly.

"Where were you folks when the stage collapsed?"

Marshall answered, *"We were pretty far in back of the audience. We positioned ourselves to be in between the speakers. Neither of us can handle loud music anymore, so we tried to get the best position possible. We were watching the stage when we heard that awful screeching sound. The next thing we knew, the top of that contraption started to lean forward, and it didn't stop until it crashed down on those people. It was the most terrifying thing we've ever seen. I hope help gets here soon. There are a lot of people buried under that rubble."*

Melody reached out and touched John's arm. *"This is so terrible. I just pray that they can get here quickly and get those people out."*

A broadcast engineer motioned to John to join him. John shook Marshall's hand, *"Well, thank you both for speaking with us. Excuse me, but I've got to check with my engineer."*

John made his way over to the sidelines where the broadcast engineer was standing with a tall man. Pointing towards the man, he made the introduction. *"This here's Peter Honeycutt from the company that installed 'The Beast'."*

Taggart extended his hand. *"I appreciate you taking the time to tell our audience how this tragedy could have possibly happened."*

Honeycutt jumped right in, *"I just want to say up front that that soundstage was safe when I signed off on it the other day. We had some issues with the original bandstand. It wasn't built to A-27 Soundstage specifications. Apparently when it was erected they ran into bedrock problems and it was eleven inches higher than the specs called for. We run into that kind of thing a lot, so when we positioned The Beast on top of their soundstage we added guy wires for extra support. I don't know what happened here and I don't want to get into fixing fault.*

There'll be plenty time for that after we're sure everyone is safe. The four cranes we used to build the soundstage are on their way here. They should be in position in about one hour. We'll need them to raise the pyrotechnic platform that's hindering rescue operations right now. That platform is in one massive piece and it's about thirty feet both ways and weighs over ten thousand pounds. To avoid doing any additional harm to those trapped under it, we'll have to use all four cranes to slowly lift the platform straight up in the air so that rescue workers can get in underneath it."

"Can't you disconnect the sections that make up the platform There must be dozens of them and they wouldn't be as heavy to lift. You must have done it that way to build it."

"You would think so. Actually, there are over thirty sections bolted together, but if we attempt to disconnect any of them there's no telling what damage we could do to anyone underneath them. No, we're just going to have to wait until we can lift the entire platform at one time."

"You said an hour. Why will it take that long? How long do you think those people can survive under there?"

Honeycutt's voice piqued as he replied, *"Look, it's out of my hands. I just know that the cranes had to be stored in the parking lot of an abandoned warehouse in the next town over. They have to take back roads to get here because of overhead utility lines. Then when they get here, they'll have to be painstakingly positioned at the four corners of the platform in order to raise it straight up. We're not sure of conditions under the platform. If they don't do this right and the weight shifts to any one corner, who knows the damage it would do? I mean, just look at that platform, you can see that it's only inches off the ground. We can't be sure what's holding it up. It's probably rubble, we hope that what it is, but it could be people. Some of the rescue team played lights under it, but it's so low you can't be sure what you're looking at. I know it's a tough call, but we're just going to have to err on the side of caution. That's all I have to say right now. If you need more information, you're going to have to get from the Command Center."*

Sensing the irritation in Honeycutt's voice, Taggart said apologetically, *"Look, Peter, I wasn't trying to put you on the spot. I apologize if it sounded that way. I appreciate that you took the time to explain to our TV audience what is happening."*

"That's okay, John. I understand that you have a job to do, too. Right now, I've got to get back to the Command Center. Our role is to operate the cranes and to secure the platform so the rescue teams can do their jobs. You're going to have to talk with them if you need more."

Looking directly at the camera, *"There you have it. This is going to be a long night. I just pray that those trapped under the wreckage will muster the strength to hold on while these valiant crews of men and women continue their rescue operations. Our thoughts and prayers go out for those injured and their families."*

He looked once more at the scene before him, turned to the camera and said, solemnly, *"That's all for now from the tragic collapse of the soundstage here at the 200th Anniversary Dance in Tiecher Park. We're returning to our studios, but we'll be back later to follow up on the rescue efforts and to report on those rescued from the bowels of 'The Beast'."*

CHAPTER 25
Tiecher Park 9:50pm

Dozens of rescue workers flooded the area, each executing their particular specialty. Years of training and periodic exercises showed in the professionalism they demonstrated. If anyone was attempting to shout or otherwise communicate their existence from under the debris, it was lost amidst the hubbub of activity and the din of the ongoing rescue efforts. Part of the clamor was created by three men and two women circling the downed platform, bullhorns in hand, urging those trapped in the ruble to stay calm and wait for the rescue workers to get to them. They alternated their messages so as to give the appearance of being in control of the situation. They added assurances that help was on the way; that everything would be all right.

Two reception areas were cordoned off to process the rescued. Gurneys and stretchers awaited passengers, as it were and hospital ambulances and EMT vehicles waited for their human cargo.

A half-dozen strobe light columns were moved into the area accompanied by a mobile generator. They were set up in a circle to provide light across the surface of the platform. When the power was turned on they created a macabre mix of light and shadow that added to the grisliness of the scene.

A half hour later, John Taggart and Channel NCTV resumed live coverage of the scene just in time to broadcast the distant arrival of the four cranes. Two cameras focused on the narrow access road as word of their arrival quickly spread.

TV sets within the broadcast area, which were tuned to NCTV, showed the emergence of the cranes onto the access road about one-half mile away. At first it was difficult to make out what it was that was moving, ever so slowly, toward the cameras. Clouds of dust, raised by the massive OTR tires swirled around the behemoths as they made their way single-file towards the park. First one took form, then a second, until eventually the four could be clearly seen.

The two cameramen conferred with Taggart while keeping a close eye on their prey. They decided to split up coverage of the machines once they were in their final positions; Camera 1 to cover the northwest and southwest corners of the stage and Camera 2, the two remaining corners. Ahead of their entrance into the area, bands of workers scurried about removing any small objects or debris that lay in their paths.

The bullhorns made their final appeal for patience to those trapped under the platform. They urged the trapped fans not to try to move or do anything to escape until the platform raising operation was completed and for them to wait until a rescue worker could get to them and determine the best method for their extraction.

Close to two hours had elapsed since the fatal collapse.

The cranes moved onto the site amid the cheers and applause of onlookers. Members of Peter Honeycutt's team took over directing them to the proper staging area and supervised the rigging of the grappling hooks. Once the hooks were secure, the workers stood down. An eerie silence spread over the crowd as they realized that the "moment of truth" had finally arrived. Over the next several hours the cranes would lift the soundstage and reveal the full extent of the catastrophe.

Mostly unnoticed, due to the drama of the cranes arriving, was a truck delivering several hundred cinder blocks and metal shims that would be used to construct ersatz columns to support the platform once it reached a height sufficient to begin the rescue of the trapped victims. No rescue workers would be allowed under the platform until the four corners were secured. A crew of six construction workers, donning hardhats, exited the truck and began loading hand-trucks with the blocks and distributing them near the four corners of the platform.

On a signal from Honeycutt the crane operators started their engines and engaged the lift mode. He signaled a second time and the operators slowly tightened the wire cables until the slack was removed. Peter took a deep breath and signaled once more. On this final signal the operators began raising the platform. Each crane was locked into "click-one" position so that they lifted in unison, one anguishing fraction-of-an-inch at a time. The crowd was silent; anxiously watching for the enough space to be created to allow rescuers to crawl underneath. Some held their cell phones over their heads as they recorded the scene. Many stood silently praying for their friends or their family members, or perhaps just for anyone trapped under the ruble that needed solace and courage to hold on a little longer, or for the safety of the rescue workers.

As the cranes began their work, the TV cameras moved in for a close-up of the south side of the platform hoping to show a measurable difference in the raising of the platform, but it would be several minutes before any noticeable change would become visible to the stations viewers and even then, it would only be about six inches at best. At least thirty-six inches would be required to accommodate the rescue workers and their equipment.

John Taggart, a seasoned professional, was content on allowing the cameras to tell the story for a while, although, some of his silence was due to the fact that he too was somewhat mesmerized by the drama as it unfolded before his eyes.

Finally, he returned to narrate the operation. *"What you are viewing is the raising of a platform that weighs over five tons. The cranes that you see at the four corners of the platform are synchronized to lift it so that no additional pressure is applied to anything or anyone trapped beneath it. These are the same cranes that were used several days ago to construct the soundstage called "The Beast, that now lays in ruins. The cranes are operated by seasoned veterans experienced at lifting massive amounts of materials. They have to lift that platform carefully. This is going to take time, folks, so stick with us as the drama continues to unfold. All we can do now is wait and pray."*

What will they find when the veil is lifted? How many dead? How many crippled? How many too injured to identify? We will know soon enough.

CHAPTER 26
Tiecher Park into the night

An hour passed before the platform was raised sufficiently for the emergency workers to begin the grim task of rescuing those trapped under it. Honeycutt gave the signal to the crane operators to stop the lifting. Workers rushed to install the final concrete blocks at the four corners of the platform. One more wave from Honeycutt and the operators reversed direction and as the cables became slack, the platform settled onto the four columns with a soft thud.

A hush came over the crowd. Even over the hum of the neutralized engines, first rescuers, standing close to the scene, could hear screams, moans and calls for help from beneath the platform; the first sounds of life any of them had heard since the collapse. Honeycutt and four of his workers pushed against the platform on the three sides that afforded access, to check the stability of the workspace. Once assured of the rescuers safety, he turned the rescue operations back to the Emergency Command Center to conduct the actual rescue operations.

The space created was very narrow and the work of approaching the victims promised to be slow. No amount of training or simulations could have prepared the rescue workers for what they were about to encounter. Equipped with handheld concrete cutters and drills, small claw hammers, flashlights, bottles of water and emergency first-aid kits, they crawled cautiously into the space from three sides. The first victim they located had been decapitated, followed closely by six others whose bodies had been crushed beyond recognition. It wasn't until the death count totaled twenty-one that they finally came across a cluster of injured fans that were fortunate enough to be trapped in a pocket beneath the platform. Some of them suffered serious wounds, but they were just glad to have been found alive.

Slowly the unofficial death toll climbed close to fifty and the number of victims reported as injured to over two hundred, including six who required immediate amputations of arms or legs; one with multiple limbs removed.

The Command Center was disciplined and well organized, handling immediate care and dispatch to hospitals at a level of efficacy totally unexpected from a group of professionals totally devoid of any actual experience working on a disaster of this magnitude.

Six hours after the rescue of the first victim, the platform was raised to six feet from the ground and a secondary sweep of the area beneath it conducted. Eight additional fans were located; one dead, five with minor injuries and two suffering from shock. The last ambulance finally left as the Emergency Command Center became a "Crime Scene" complete with yellow tape and police security. The booths and stalls so hastily set up many hours previously, quickly became populated with officials from the State Health and Safety Bureau and multiple local, state and federal departments and agencies, all bent on determining the how's and why's behind the most memorable disaster in the State's history; close to sixty dead so far and hundreds more injured, many, seriously. Investigating a disaster of this magnitude would probably take months if not years.

As predicted, it turned out to be an Anniversary Celebration the town of Owensburg will never forget.

CHAPTER 27
Owensburg General Hospital 1:27am

Owensburg General Hospital, an award-winning facility with over 450 beds was prepared for the influx of patients. The Emergency Command Center at Tiecher Park named them as the First Responder Care Center to manage the processing and care of the victims recovered from the collapse of the soundstage. Being the FRCC meant that they would be responsible for coordinating the services provided by area hospitals and clinics and maintain a data base of people reported to have attended the show, including cross-referencing the names on that list with anyone reported as receiving care at any of the facilities in the network.

The fifty-year-old medical hospital was rated 6th in the State and housed several of the country's most renowned specialists in Acute Care, Pediatrics and Oncology among the roster of over 600 doctors who practiced there. In the previous year admissions totaled over 22,000 and a total of 48,789 visits were made to their Emergency Room. They housed a first-class Trauma Center and were rated among the highest in patient safety.

Owensburg General was a hospital at the ready. The switchboard was already being swamped with calls from people looking to locate their friends or loved ones. Most callers responded to the lack of information with anger, making the job that much tougher for the operators.

The first patient they treated had a laceration on her arm that required twenty stitches. She was moved to a waiting room and told she could leave after 30 minutes. She was followed by two men and four women that were treated for shock. They were not among the fans directly impacted by the collapse, just bystanders who were having difficulty processing the horror of the situation. The Hospital did its best to process these patients as quickly as possible to make room for the more seriously injured victims that were sure to follow.

Within the next twenty-four hours, OG would process two hundred and twenty-nine patients. Of these, they treated and released ninety with superficial injuries, transferred thirty-seven to neighboring Hospitals and released three patients who died on the operating table to one of the makeshift morgues.

Ninety-nine patients were permanently admitted to OG. Among these, the Hospital performed sixty-two operations ranging from broken bones to amputations. Another thirty-two were admitted for minor injuries, concussions and shock.

Another five patients arrived at the hospital in an unresponsive condition. All five were diagnosed with blunt force trauma to the head or neck and immediately moved to an ICU. Treatment of patients in a coma, varies greatly, depending on the cause. As a precaution, a doctor/nurse team was assigned to the care of each.

CHAPTER 28

Miriam opened her eyes and was greeted by a blurry image of Mike Tolliver, the Attorney she hired to locate her son. "Mike, what are you doing here?" She sat up and looked around. As the room came into focus, she added, "Where am I?"

Mike put his hand on her shoulder and eased her back to the pillow. "You think you can go missing and I'm not going to find you? You're in Owensburg General Hospital. You suffered a concussion out at the dance last night and they brought you here for treatment. The nurse said that you have been in and out of consciousness for several hours.

Suddenly she realized what happened, "Oh my God, Thomas was hurt. Is he here? I've got to see him." Miriam started to rise again and Mike gently restrained her.

"Calm down, you've got to rest. The nurse said you have a Grade 3 concussion and that there is a risk of serious brain damage is you don't remain quiet."

"But, I've got to find him."

"I understand that, but there is nothing that you can do right now. You've got to do as the nurses say and rest as much as possible. If you don't you'll hurt yourself more and then you won't be of use to anyone. Let me be your proxy. Does that make sense?"

"Of course, but we can't just sit here while he's off somewhere, hurt. We have to do something."

"You're right and we won't. If you give me your promise that you will remain here, do everything the nurses tell you to do and give your body a chance to heal properly, I'll go check out what's going on with Thomas. The number of injuries from the collapse is so high that they're being pretty lenient regarding access to patients. Usually, I wouldn't have been able to see you, but I convinced them that I was a relative from out-of-town who knew you were at the dance. They appreciated the fact that I was able to fill them in on your personal data, since you came in without any ID or personal effects.

"Okay, I promise. I remember talking with a nurse at the park. Her name was Patricia. She said that this hospital was acting as some sort of a communications center and they would know where Thomas was sent." Her tone changed to a plea, "Find him Mike. I can't lose him again."

"Don't you worry, if he's in the system I'll find out where and get back here as soon as I have all the facts. In the meantime, remember your promise. I don't want to be worrying about you too."

"You have my word. You're right; I am feeling a bit woozy. I think I'm going to close my eyes for awhile." With that said, Miriam dozed off.

* * *

"My name is Nathan Walton. I'm calling from Brussels, Belgium. I'm trying to contact my wife Miriam Walton. She's staying at your hotel for the weekend. I spoke with her yesterday, but today my calls aren't being answered."

"I'm sorry about that, sir. She's in Room 217. I'll try the room for you." After several minutes, he came back on the line. "I'm not getting an answer either. Let me check the door monitor." Again, several minutes passed. "Our records show that your wife exited the room early last evening, but there hasn't been any activity since then. The only other explanation I can offer is that she may have been involved in the situation out at the park last night."

"What do you mean? What situation?"

"There was an accident with the soundstage. According to the TV reports a lot of people were killed and scores more were injured."

"Why didn't you tell me that right away."

"I'm sorry, sir. Our switchboard has been inundated with calls. The management instructed us to avoid any discussion about the incident at the park and to concentrate on the welfare of our guests."

"Okay, okay. Look, do you know what hospital they might have taken her to?"

"I only know that Owensburg General Hospital is acting as a central communications center for anyone hospitalized because of the accident." He gave Nathan the number and added, "I hope that you find her and that she is well."

"Thanks. You make sure you hold her room. If there's any problem, I'll take care of it when I get there. When she shows up please tell her that I called and that I'm cutting short my trip and coming home. I should be in Owensburg tomorrow afternoon. Got that?"

"Yes sir, I'll put the message in the room slot."

"Thank you for your help."

"You're welcome, sir. I wish you and your wife the best.

CHAPTER 29

A large group of parents, friends and relatives were amassed at the information desk in the ground floor lobby of Owensburg General Hospital. Security guards were busy keeping the crowd inside the roped-off areas and behind the white line that separated them from the two beleaguered volunteers busily checking for names and locations of accident victims admitted to hospitals anywhere in the surrounding region.

It took Emily forty-five minutes for her turn to arrive. "Do you have any record for Thomas Mortinson?" She wrung her hands nervously as she watched the young lady key in the name and press a few keys. At first there was no sign that she had a match, but after what seemed like minutes, the reply came back positive.

"Yes, there is a Thomas Mortinson listed as missing, but we don't have any record of him being admitted anywhere."

"Are you certain?"

"Yes, Ma'am, but our records are only being updated every twenty minutes or so. I'm sure he'll show up soon."

"Thank you. Would you please look up two other names for me? The first is Louise O'Neill."

Once again, the young lady keyed in the name. "We have a Louise O'Neill listed, but she too, is still missing.

"I guess I should be relieved that they're not in a hospital somewhere. How about Miriam Walton?"

"We have a Miriam Walton in Observation Ward. Room 359."

"Well that's a start. Thank you for being so patient. I can't imagine what it must be like having to deal with so many anxious people."

"I'm just glad I can be of some help during this crisis."

"Well, God bless you," looking at the woman's ID tag, she added, "Brenda."

* * *

Mike Tolliver was also on the line at the information desk and when his turn came up he also encountered Brenda.

When he asked about Thomas, she volunteered, "I just had another person inquiring about Thomas Mortinson. I'll tell you what I told her, Thomas Mortinson is listed as missing on our data base. That's all I have, but check back later. They are constantly updating the databank."

"Can you give me the name of the other person who made the inquiry?"

"I'm sorry, I didn't take note of it. I don't know who she was, but she inquired about two other persons as well, Louise O'Neill and Miriam Walton."

"Are you certain that she asked for Miriam Walton?"

"Yes, sir. I directed her to Observation Ward, Room 359."

"Well, thank you for the information. You've been a big help."

Mike left the desk and headed back to Miriam's room.

CHAPTER 30

Twenty minutes after Mike Tolliver inquired about Thomas, the computer records were updated and the name Thomas Edward Mortinson was entered as admitted to the Intensive Care Unit with a Traumatic Brain Injury.

Five patients, admitted to Owensburg General Hospital's Emergency room that day, were diagnosed with TBI's. Four were quickly stabilized to prevent secondary neuronal injury and transferred to OG's in-house ICU. One of the five patients was classified at a GCS of 5 and was immediately transferred to the ICU at the George Bennett Baxter Trauma Center.

Traumatic Brain Injury (TBI) accounts for over 52,000 deaths every year. It is the leading cause of death for ages 1-45. Healthcare professionals use the Glasgow Coma Scale (GCS) to score the severity of head injuries. A score of 3 being most severe and 15 the least severe.

* * *

Dr. Frederick Jensen, Staff Director of the Trauma Center, scanned the patient's chart. When he was admitted, Thomas Mortinson was in a coma, totally unresponsive to any stimulus. The doctor nervously tapped his fingers on his desk as he studied the results of the CT scan and MRI.

"When will Dr. Freenold be arriving," he asked his assistant.

"We're expecting him in about two hours. He's driving over."

"It can't be quick enough."

* * *

Dr. Arnold R. Freenold, MD, is an Assistant Professor of Neurosurgery at Brewster Medical School and Staff Director of Medicine at St. Leonard's Trauma Center in Carrolton, Pennsylvania. He is known, worldwide, for leading teams that have been successful in the rehabilitation of celebrities and prominent athletes suffering severe TBI's with Glasgow scores of less than 7.

When he heard the news of the stage collapse, Dr. Freenold immediately volunteered his services to Owensburg General and was immediately appointed by OGH's Director, Dr. Philip Owens to lead a team of Neurologists, Anesthesiologists, Respiratory Therapists, Neurosurgeons, Facial and Head Reconstructionists, Critical Care Nurses and other specialists that would be providing immediate care for Thomas Mortinson, the newest patient at the Trauma Center. Thomas, a twenty-five-year-old male was admitted with a Level 10 concussion, (crushed skull with bruising of the Brain), broken left collarbone and severe facial abrasions and contusions and a GCS score of 5.

* * *

Owensburg General Hospital, thanks to a generous grant of several million dollars from George Bennett Baxter, whose son fully recovered from a severe skull fracture received while playing soccer, housed the country's newest and best equipped Trauma Center. Only once, since it opened, had the center treated a patient with a GCS of 5 or less. The patient was a four-year-old child who fell into an empty backyard swimming pool, suffering a crushed skull. The child's condition worsened each day until, on the third day of treatment, she died.

It was here that Dr. Freenold and his team would provide immediate care to stabilize their patient. They would eventually be joined by Rehabilitation Nurses, Occupational Therapists, Orthopedists, Physiatrists, Psychologists, Nutritionists, Physical Therapists and Speech Therapists.

Successes and failures over the two years since the center opened, highlight the fact that no two brain injuries are alike; each requires specific individualized care, with the hospital team, patients and families each playing a vital role in the process.

CHAPTER 31

Miriam looked with disdain at the tray in front of her. She had a throbbing headache and a high-pitched ringing in her ears. On a plastic plate there was a small piece of baked fish, a dollop of mashed potatoes and eight skinny string beans. A small salad with oil and vinegar dressing, a roll with a pat of butter, a cup of rice pudding and a glass of lemonade rounded off the meal. *This is supposed to be health giving nourishment?* She decided to eat everything but the roll and butter. She ate the food quickly hoping that it would help with the headache.

She pushed the tray aside. *I wish Mike would get back with news about Thomas.*

She glanced at the door as if that would summon his appearance, but instead she saw a woman peeking into the room; looking first at Miriam and then at the other two women in the room, while trying not to be too conspicuous about it.

"Are you looking for someone?"

Caught in the act, Emily responded, "I'm so sorry to disturb you, I'm looking for Miriam Walton. I was told she was in this room.

Surprised, Miriam replied, "I'm Miriam Walton. If you're here to introduce me to Jesus, somebody already beat you to it. I'll tell you what I told him, I'm okay in that department, but I do appreciate your concern."

Emily laughed, "Oh, it's nothing like that. Actually, I came to ask you a question. I'm Emily Peyton. I believe that my son Thomas Mortinson and his fiancée were at the dance when the stage collapsed, and we can't locate either of them. Patricia at the Emergency Command Center in the park told me that you asked about him and insisted that his name be added to the missing list. She also told me that you claim to be his mother."

Miriam froze. What little color she had quickly drained from her face.

Concerned about the woman's condition, Emily rushed to the bedside. "Are you okay?"

She grasped Miriam's hand and felt a strong response. "What's wrong? Do you know something about where Thomas is?" When she received no reply, she reached over to the side table and poured a glass of water. She handed it to Miriam, who sipped it very slowly to create as much time as possible before she would be compelled to reply.

Finally, Miriam put the glass down and turned to Emily. Their eyes met, and something passed between them; some sort of an empathetic bond. With a shaky voice she said, "I'm Thomas's birth mother. Thomas's father, Thomas Wendell Mortinson, died in combat in the war. Thomas was born two months later." She stopped to collect her thoughts. "I was so shattered by his death, so full of self pity that I gave up my son. I'm not proud that I did. At the time I had no money, no job and no permanent place to live. I wanted Thomas to have a better life than the one I was heading into; one with no future in sight. I saw him briefly the other day and in a way I'm glad that I made that decision. You and your husband have raised a fine young man."

Miriam saw the look of surprise on Emily's face. Emily grabbed a chair and sat down as the news caused her legs to feel weak. "I can see that this comes as a shock to you. I'm sure you never thought that after all these years, I'd come looking for my son."

Emily remained silent for a while as she mulled over what Miriam was telling her. She reached out for Miriam's hand and grasped it firmly. "You're right. Walter and I talked about it often as Thomas was growing up. I'll be absolutely honest with you; I hoped that you would never show up and ruin the perfect story-book family we became. Yes, he is a fine young man. My husband and I are so proud of what he has become, but most of the credit goes to Thomas himself."

Miriam hesitated for a moment and then asked, "Has he ever asked about me?"

"Well, there was a time when he was eight. We thought that he was old enough to understand what was at stake. We asked him if he would be agreeable to our adopting him. He thought about it for a few days and then told us that he didn't want to be adopted. He said something about keeping his *true identity*. While he didn't speak of you specifically, we were certain that somewhere in the back of his mind he harbored the thought of meeting you some day. He believed that if he was adopted that opportunity would be cut off. We honored his decision and never discussed it again."

"His *true identity*. That's a pretty mature concept for an eight-year-old."

"I agree. He's always had a serious nature. I'm glad you're here, Miriam. I think Thomas will be anxious to meet you. Walter and I will help in any way we can."

"I appreciate that."

"Have you seen him tonight?"

Tears welled up in Miriam's eyes. "Yes, I have. I was at the dance when the stage collapsed. I was filming him on my cell phone when the stage fell on top of him. I was pushed backwards as I tried to do something to help him. Then I was knocked down and suffered a concussion when the crowd of people tried to escape. It was awful. Thomas was hurt, and I couldn't help him." She saw the look on Emily's face and realized that she hadn't known about Thomas being injured. *The poor woman.*

"You saw Thomas get knocked down by the stage?" she asked, half knowing the answer and half hoping that she had misunderstood Miriam.

The answer came amidst the tears streaming down Miriam's face, "Yes. I thought you already knew. I screamed to him, but it happened so quickly. He couldn't hear me."

Emily leaned over and put her arms around Miriam. Tears flowed freely from both.

"A friend of mine, Mike Tolliver, is trying to locate him right now. He's the attorney I used to find Thomas. I'd show you the pictures, but I lost my phone in the confusion. I can't even call my husband because my phone records were in the phone. He must be worried sick."

Miriam sat back against the pillow. "You know, life is really funny at times. When I married Nathan, we agreed not to have children because his business required that he travel frequently. He felt, and I agreed at the time, that it wouldn't be fair to put the responsibility of raising a child squarely on my shoulders, but freedom from parenting comes at a price, as does all freedom. In this case the price was loneliness; loneliness so overpowering that I needed to seek help from a psychiatrist. I never told Nathan about my feelings or visiting a shrink because I was afraid that I wouldn't be able to explain my feelings without telling him about Thomas. I know that a marriage is supposed to be based on trust, with no secrets, but I guess I felt too much guilt about giving Thomas up for adoption. Even though I received professional help for several years, the loneliness never left me. A day doesn't go by that I don't think about what it would have been like to raise my son. I know that this must be difficult for you to understand."

"Not as much as you may think, Miriam. I'm no stranger to feelings of loneliness. The reason that Walter and I took in Thomas as a foster child was mostly because we were unable to have a child of our own. When we were first married I became pregnant and had a miscarriage. The second time, I was so careful, thinking that the miscarriage was my fault. When the baby was born, it was a boy and we named him Thomas. He only lived four days. We were both heartbroken. Walter took it especially hard; he wanted a son. The doctors ran some tests and hit us with a bombshell. There were some genetic defects on both our sides that greatly reduced the odds of a healthy child. They advised us not to attempt to get pregnant again."

Emily stopped for a minute to wipe away the tears that were cascading down her cheeks.

"Now you talk about feeling lonely. I was not only depressed, but I was impossible to live with. I was certain that my marriage was going to end at any time. All the joys of impending motherhood that I had experienced for nine months came crashing down into my miserable world."

Miriam leaned forward in the bed and hugged Miriam. "I'm so sorry."

"Don't be. It wasn't until I hit an emotional rock bottom that I finally hit on an answer.

Adoption would take too long but becoming a foster parent could provide the solace that was desperately needed in our lives. I was surprised when Walter enthusiastically supported me.

We received Thomas when he was three months old. The minute I held him in my arms all feelings of sadness left me. The similarity of the name wasn't lost to us. It strengthened our resolve to be the best parents we could possibly be. We believed that there was a force somewhere that wanted Thomas to be with us. The road wasn't without challenges, but Thomas turned out to be a fine young man who has made us very proud."

"Didn't anyone else ever try to adopt him?"

"That's the funny thing. The only time adoption came up was when Walter and I considered it. I guess that force was looking out for us, Other than that time, the agency seemed content with keeping Thomas in a stable environment."

Suddenly the room was silent. They looked at each other and suddenly burst out laughing. Miriam said, "Aren't we a pair?"

"Yes, but a pair of what?"

Laughter again.

"You know, Miriam, I think that if we had met sooner, we would have become good friends."

"I believe you're right. Let's make sure that nothing gets in the way of that happening now."

They hugged once more.

* * *

As Mike Tolliver approached Room 359 he saw that Miriam had a visitor. "Well, what do we have here?" As Emily turned around, Mike recognized her immediately from the pictures of her and her husband in his files.

Miriam turned towards the door, "Oh, Mike, this is Emily Peyton," she said excitedly.

"I'm pleased to meet you Mrs. Peyton. They told me downstairs that you were looking for Miriam. I'm glad you found her. I 'm afraid there is no news of Thomas yet."

"I told Emily about what I saw."

"They are still bringing patients into the hospital. It takes time to get enough information to identify everybody and enter the data into their computers."

Miriam spoke, "I was out at the park about an hour ago. It was really chaotic out there. Why don't I call my husband? He's in the best position to tell us what is going on."

Emily stepped out into the hall. She was about to call Walter when she received a call from him.

"Emily, thank God you answered."

She responded with, "I was just about to call you."

"Look, they found Thomas and he's on the way to Owensburg General right now. I don't know his condition. All they told me that he is not conscious. The ambulance left about five minutes ago."

"Thank God they found him. I've got news too. His birth mother, Miriam Walton, is here in the hospital. She was out at the park and was taking pictures of Thomas when the stage fell."

"Oh, my god, the poor woman. Did she see it happen?"

"Yes. She was taking pictures when she saw the stage fall on him. Then she was knocked unconscious. She seems very nice. I feel so bad for her."

"Well, it looks as if the rescue effort is well along now. Wes and George can take over from here. I'll be right over. I sure hope Thomas isn't hurt too badly. Is there any sign of Louise yet?"

"Not yet. I'll go back down to information desk. They have a record of her being at the park, but she still hasn't showed up anywhere. She should have been close to Thomas when the stage fell. Look, I'll meet you downstairs in the main lobby. I'll keep after the information desk until they have a record of what room Thomas is in. Please get here soon!"

"Don't worry, the siren will be on. Love you, Em."

"I love you too, Walt."

* * *

Emily returned to the room to share the news about Thomas. They were relieved, although all they knew was that he had been found and that he was on his way to them.

"I'm going to go down to the main lobby and hound that information desk until they tell me where they've taken him. Walt's on his way. I'm meeting him down there."

Mike thought for a moment and said, "Maybe I should go with you."

Miriam asked, "What about me?"

"I know that you want to be there, but that just isn't possible," Mike answered. "You've been confined to that bed with a serious concussion. We talked about this before, Miriam."

"I know we have. That was when we didn't know anything, but now we know that Thomas is going to be here in the same building, if he not here already, I've got to see him."

He gently took her hand in his. "Miriam, we've been on this journey for many months now. Another day or two isn't going to make a bit of difference in the great big scheme of things. If you don't follow the doctor's orders you will jeopardize your health and make a reunion with Thomas that much more difficult. Work with me on this."

"I know you're right Mike, but it's so damned hard. Okay, I'll be good." Looking first at Mike and then at Emily, she added, "But promise me you'll keep in touch, no matter what you find out. It's going to be unbearable just sitting here waiting."

Mike squeezed her hand. "I know it will be and I promise that I will keep you updated as soon as we find anything out. I have your phone number."

He and Emily smiled at Miriam and left the room.

* * *

Louise wandered around Tiecher Park for several hours, trying to find some news about Thomas. She asked at every tent that was set up; stopped every person who would take the time to speak to her and then backtracked in case they had more information. "Have you seen Thomas Mortinson?" Nothing! Most of the people she talked to knew who he was, but no one had seen him. Finally, exhausted, she sat down on a bench and dozed off.

She was awakened some time later by a policeman. "Are you all right, Miss?"

She explained her dilemma and asked if he knew where Chief Peyton was. The deputy called on his radio and was told that Walter had left the grounds to go to Owensburg General Hospital.

"Can you contact him for me? I was at the dance with his son, Thomas. I'm sure he'll want to talk with me."

"Louise, are you okay. We've been frantic looking for you. We thought you were hurt in the accident."

"I'm okay, but Thomas was under that thing when it fell. I've been trying to find out something about his whereabouts.

"We know where he is. He was rescued awhile ago and transferred to Owensburg General.

I'm headed there now. Put Officer Gordon back on. I'll arrange for him to transport you to the hospital. I'll meet you there."

Minutes later Louise was sitting in a police car, with the siren wailing, on her way to join Walter and Emily at the hospital.

CHAPTER 32

Emily and Mike stood together on the information line. "The wait is shorter this time. They opened up two more desks," Mike said.

"Well I guess they have more people to deal with now. It shouldn't be much longer. At least we know that Thomas is in the system."

Minutes later, they reached the front of the queue. This time they were processed by the other lady at the desk. Emily asked, "Can you tell me where they've taken my son, Thomas Mortinson?" She spelled the last name for the lady.

"He's been moved to the ICU."

"What floor is that on?"

"Oh, not the one in this building. You have to go around, past the west wing to the George Bennett Baxter Trauma Center. They will guide you from there."

Emily's legs went weak for a moment, but Mike stepped forward to support her. "What's wrong with him?"

"I don't have that information, Ma'am. They'll be in a better position to tell you about your son's condition over there. I don't have that kind of information."

Mike guided Emily to one of the few seats that were empty in the lobby. "Now, don't get all worked up just because they sent him to some other building. It may just be that they ran out of beds in this building and borrowed the space. In this kind of situation, I'm sure they do that all the time. Walter should be here any minute. He'll have his siren on and parking sure won't be a problem for him.'

Emily no sooner got the words out than his car pulled up in front of the building; he jumped out and spun through the revolving doors. He headed right for Emily. 'How're you holding up, Em?"

"I'm good Walt. They told us at the desk that Thomas was around the corner at the Trauma Center." Emily stopped for a minute and said, "Where are my manners. Walt this is Mike Tolliver. He helped locate Thomas for Thomas's mother. Mike, this is my husband Walter Peyton." The two men shook hands.

"I've located Louise. She called me while I was on the way here. I had a car pick her up, so she should be here any minute now.' As he was speaking, they heard the approaching siren. "That must be her now."

They met in front of OG and headed to Walt's car. Two minutes later the four passed through the ultra-modern entrance to the George Bennett Baxter Trauma Center.

They could never have imagined what lay behind those doors.

CHAPTER 33

Dr. Jensen greeted Dr. Freenold, when he arrived at George Bennett Baxter Trauma Center at 7:25am. "I'm so glad to see you Doctor. We have the patient set up in Room 333"

"I got here as quickly as I could. The traffic was unbearable. I'd like to take a look at the patient and his charts."

"Of course, this way Doctor. Your patient is Thomas Mortinson. He was in bad shape when he arrived. We cleaned him up as best we could. He wasn't conscious when he arrived. We saw some early signs of recovery and felt it best to induce a coma to prevent any further damage to his head."

As Freenold approached the bed, his face became drawn and he shook his head slightly. He hastily reviewed the results of an MRI and CT scans, then spent several minutes inspecting Thomas's head wound and ordered that Thomas be moved to the operating room and prepped for immediate surgery to repair his crushed skull and reverse the buildup of cranial fluids. The next three hours would be crucial.

Dr. Freenold wasted no time in removing the portion of scalp that had been pushed down into the brain; a procedure that was performed over the course of an hour to allow for a gradual restoration of the brains natural formation. The broken skull bone was in three pieces making it improbable that they could be fit back in the skull after the surgical procedure was complete. He ordered that a temporary plastic implant be molded to ultimately replace the skull pieces.

During the procedure Thomas's vital signs were being monitored to assure proper oxygenation, blood pressure and intracranial pressure. Several times corrective actions were needed to restore the patient to the support range required to continue the procedure.

The next hour and one-half was dedicated to stimulating the soft brain tissue; a course of action that called upon the expertise acquired from close to three dozen Craniectomies. Using his fingers and specially designed instruments Freenold massaged the tissue, attempting section by section, to restore it to its original shape and size, something that could only be attained over time. He could only do so much; nature would have to do the rest. Freenold was one of forty-six neurosurgeons in the world able to perform the reshaping procedure.

Once satisfied that the he could go no further with the reshaping, he placed a soft surgical cushion into the space left by the broken skull parts. The cushion would allow cranial fluids to return to the top of the brain. It would remain there until he was satisfied that his patient had stabilized or recovered sufficiently that the molded plastic implant he ordered could be inserted into Thomas's skull.

Lastly, he and a neurotrauma specialist placed a protective helmet on Thomas's head. The model he selected had a clear top section so that the surgical cushion could be observed without disturbing the patient with constant removal.

Freenold ordered that Thomas be transferred back to Room 333, where a team of nurses and technicians waited to connect him to machines that would measure his vital signs 24/7. Surgical supplies, catheters, anti-embolic stockings and special dressings were required to support the monitoring process and prevent further damage to the patient's body.

The doctor finished his notes then returned to the top of the page to enter the new diagnosis codes that had become effective several weeks earlier. These codes, known as ICD-10 (International Classification of Diseases) were designed to help health officials track the quality of care given to patients (and Health Care Policy holders). He shook his head, as he often did, at the amount of paperwork required. Usually paperwork would be handled by his office staff but being miles away and without this support it became his responsibility. After one-half hour he was finally ready to join Dr. Jensen in the section of the hospital known as the "Family Room". Here he would meet with the assembly of people that had waited for hours to find out anything they could about Thomas's condition. It was another part of the "job" that he loathed. He was a highly trained and skilled medical professional accustomed to concentrating on minute, sometimes unseen, parts of the human brain. Trying to explain to parents and love-ones, what he was going to do or had done, was not an activity he relished.

CHAPTER 34

Walter and Mike went up to the reception desk, while Emily and Louise sat down on the last two seats in the waiting area.

Louise turned to Emily and asked, "Who is that man?"

"Oh, I'm so sorry. I should have introduced you, but we were in such a hurry to get over here. His name is Mike Tolliver and he is an attorney. He's here because his client, a woman by the name of Miriam Walton hired him to locate the son she gave up at birth. They believe that Thomas is her son. Apparently, she was at the dance last night, wanting to get a closer look at him. She saw when the stage collapsed on Thomas. Then she was knocked to the ground herself and suffered a serious concussion. She's in a ward over at Owensburg General."

Louise was stunned. "Oh my God, you're not going to believe this, but Thomas and I were talking about his birth mother before we left for the dance. How certain are they that Thomas is the son that they are searching for?"

"Pretty certain from what Mike says. I haven't seen any of the paperwork, but he was able to see records that had been previously sealed. It must be heartbreaking for Miriam to come all this way to meet Thomas, only to see him injured like that."

Walt returned. "Thomas is definitely here. He has multiple injuries that they're attending to right now. Mike's getting whatever details they are able to give us. It looks as if it's going to be a while before we'll know anything for sure about his condition. From what they did tell us, Thomas was unconscious when he arrived at OG. Due to the seriousness of his injuries they moved him over here where he could get the specialized treatment he needs. Right now, they want us to move upstairs to a special room to wait for any additional information.

Mike joined them. He did a quick introduction to Louise. "They didn't have anything else to share with us. Why don't you folks go on upstairs while I go back to Miriam's room and update her on what we know so far. You can give me a call when they are ready to talk with us." He handed Walt a slip of paper, "This is the number of her room. Okay"

"Sure," Walt said.

* * *

Four "visitors" sat together in the center of the Family Room awaiting the arrival of the doctors; four Styrofoam coffee cups were on the table in front of them along with several wrappers from snack food.

The Family Room was tastefully decorated in an ultra-modern motif with comfortable reclining and lounging chairs, several cots with pillows and bed linens and a twenty-foot, three shelf, bookcase with books chosen to meet a variety of reading tastes. Complimentary coffee and other beverages, in addition to snacks and light meals were available along with a small laundry and shower facilities. These impressive amenities were the Trauma Centers attempt to make relatives of trauma patients comfortable while they endured the arduous wait for optimistic news about their loved one.

Twenty minutes earlier, after several hours of waiting, they had been informed that the doctors would meet with them soon to discuss Thomas's condition. This would be the first solid information they would receive since they arrived four hours earlier. As soon as the staffer left, Walt called Miriam's room to alert Mike and he rejoined the team minutes later, using the courtesy van that the hospitals provided to ferry visitors and staff between the buildings.

Walter and Emily Peyton, Louise O'Neill and Mike Tolliver sat looking at the French doors though which the doctors would probably enter.

Dr. Frederick Jensen was the first to arrive. He nodded to the occupants as he moved two chairs over in front of the table facing them. As he awaited Dr. Freenold's arrival, he began to prepare the group for what to expect. "Good afternoon, I'm Dr. Frederick Jensen. As you can imagine, we've been through this procedure many times since we opened the Center. As a result, we've developed a set of protocols that we believe are in the best interests of the patient, their loved-ones and the Center. I know that you are anxious to learn about Thomas's condition and I can tell you that I just left his room and he is resting, comfortably.

"That being said, the details of the care we have administered, our future plans and all other details concerning Thomas's condition will be covered by Dr. Freenold who is scheduled to join us shortly. He is the Neurosurgeon in charge of the team assigned to Thomas's care and rehabilitation. He is in the best position to answer your questions and address your concerns. So just relax for a few more minutes."

A feeling of relief was immediately apparent on the faces of the four, but it was slowly replaced by expressions that exhibited the need to ask questions. Jensen expected that and rather than get involved in a discussion on the rules, he asked them about their relationship to Thomas. Walt was the first to speak. Putting his arm on Emily's shoulder, he said, "I'm Walter Peyton. My wife Emily and I raised Thomas as his foster parents until he graduated from college and went off on his own. He's staying with us while he's visiting here for the Town's Anniversary celebration. He brought his girlfriend Louise O'Neill with him." Louise half raised her hand at the mention of her name.

Mike Tolliver introduced himself as a proxy for Miriam Walton, who he described as a friend of the family who was in the main hospital suffering from a concussion received in the accident out at the park.

Jensen continued, "The reason I asked that question of you, is that in order to protect the patient's privacy, you will need to determine who will be a spokesperson for the patient; someone who can receive medical information and share it with other family members or associates. That person will also have the authority to approve of any necessary surgery or medical procedures that require consent. I won't ask you to decide on the spokesperson right now, but I will need to know by the time were finished here."

Mike called Miriam's room and set up his cell phone as a speaker-phone. He took a few minutes to bring Miriam up-to-date on their progress. "We're going to be meeting with the doctor that will be in charge of Thomas's recovery."

"Thanks for including me, Mike. You can't imagine being cooped up here without knowing what's going on."

They didn't have to wait long. Dr. Freenold walked into the room, looked around at the furnishings and took the empty chair facing the group. "Good afternoon, I'm Dr. Arnold Freenold. I've been assigned by the Center to head up the team of specialists treating Thomas Mortinson, who sustained multiple injuries due to the collapse of a stage last night." He held up his hand to quell any questions. "I'm going to ask you to hold all questions until I'm finished. I promise you that before I leave, all your questions will be answered. Would each of you please tell me your name and your relationship to Thomas?"

Once again each explained their relationship to Thomas. As this was being done, he looked at each person, nodded his head and made notes about each on a yellow pad. When they finished, he hesitated for a few minutes before addressing them. "First of all, I want to tell you about the extent of Thomas's injuries. When he was rescued from the rubble out at the park, he was unconscious, and his breathing was much labored. His vital signs indicated that he had injuries that were not apparent to the naked eye. He was ventilated, given fluids at the site and immediately transported to the emergency room at Owensburg General. Once there, he was given a battery of tests that showed that he had suffered a severe head injury, a broken left collarbone, facial abrasions and contusions, bruising to several ribs and lacerations on both arms. The attending doctors wisely transferred Thomas to the Center here and a team of specialists were immediately assigned to his case."

Freenold took a moment to gather his thoughts. He looked out at the concerned faces before he continued. Louise had tears streaming down her face, Emily was wringing her hands and the men seemed to be hanging on every word hoping to hear something, anything, optimistic to latch onto. *I hate this part.*

"The diagnosis is that Thomas suffered a Traumatic Brain Injury as a result of the accident. When he arrived here, Thomas was placed in a medically-induced coma to prevent any additional harm, should he suddenly return to consciousness. In cases such as this, given the extent of his injuries, the calmer the patient, the better. As to the nature of his injuries, we measure the severity of brain injuries using the Glasgow Coma Scale. A level 3 being the most severe and 15 the least. Thomas was diagnosed at a level 5."

It didn't take long for them to do the math. Emily gasped, and the others paled a shade or two.

Freenold continued, "Don't let the number concern you. We are equipped here at the center to provide the very best care for every level of cranial damage.

"Now as for the care we are giving him, as soon as I got here, I examined Thomas and decided that a procedure was needed immediately to relieve the pressure on his brain. I performed an emergency Craniectomy earlier and my first assessment afterwards is that the operation stabilized Thomas's vital signs. He was transported back to the ICU where specialists are addressing his other injuries. He will remain in a coma until we are satisfied that he is strong enough to maintain a certain level of stability on his own. It could be days, perhaps weeks; there is no way to tell at this point, but when that occurs, his secondary injuries will be addressed. Suffice it to say we will be constantly monitoring his condition. As a precaution, a Respiratory Specialist and an Emergency Care RN will be with him for the next twenty-four hours or for as long as needed.

"You must understand that for his sake and for us all, we want him to return to consciousness as quickly as possible so we can proceed in earnest with his rehabilitation. I ask you to remember one thing and that is that no two brain injuries are alike, so please don't go running to your computers and trying to second-guess us. Trust me when I say that Thomas is receiving the best care possible."

Emily could no longer maintain silence, she blurted out, "I have to see my boy. When can I see him?" The others wanted to ask the same question but were too reticent to do so.

"I wish I could give you an answer to your question. As I said, Thomas is being treated for a number of injuries. Injuries as serious as his require that he be held in a very controlled, sterile environment. As for the injury to his left collarbone, it won't be addressed until we feel that he is strong enough to undergo an additional operation. I cannot allow anyone to see him until all emergency care has been completed and he is resting satisfactorily. That means that no one will be allowed into his room for at least two more days. I'll leave it to Dr. Jensen to make such arrangements. The initial visit and all subsequent visits must be strictly controlled for Thomas's welfare."

Louise asked, "Are you saying that we can't visit Thomas or even see him?"

"Until personal visits are allowed, you will only be permitted to *view* him and only from behind a glass wall. That will be arranged by Dr. Jensen as soon as he gets the okay from the ICU staff. I understand your anxiety. I don't think it will be that much longer, but you will have to be patient." He looked at the group. "Are there any other questions?"

Walt half raised his hand. "Can you explain a little about the operation you performed?"

"Yes of course. A Craniectomy was necessary because the upper back side of Thomas's skull was broken into three shards. They were pushed down onto his brain. I removed the pieces and manipulated his brain matter to as near normal as possible. You understand that I'm simplifying the complexity of the procedure but be assured that it is a standard protocol in cases such as these. The hole in his scull will eventually be sealed up with a synthetic skull piece because the damage to the pieces we removed was too extensive to re-use them. Right now there is a soft cushion sealing the skull to allow us to monitor brain activity. He's wearing a protective helmet as well to assure that no further damage can occur. Once everything heals to our satisfaction and the synthetic skull piece is sealed in place, Thomas's head should be as good as new."

Walt wasn't the only one taken aback by the grizzly details of the operation. Emily spoke up, "I mean no offense, Doctor, but shouldn't you have discussed the details and secured our permission from one of us before undergoing such a serious operation?"

"I understand your concern, Mrs. Peyton. Under normal circumstances we make every attempt to gain such approval, but as you can imagine, with conditions such as these, we must put the patient's survival ahead of any protocol. Thomas's vital signs were in the extreme range and any delay in performing the Craniectomy could have resulted in his death."

Emily gave a reserved nod, indicating that she understood and that under the circumstances she approved of the decision.

Louise asked, "I understand that you will keep Thomas in a coma until you are sure that he will be able to deal with his injuries, but I need to know is if he is feeling any pain from his injuries?"

"That's an excellent question and the answer is no. As long as he in a coma, induced or otherwise, he is not feeling any pain. That is one of the reasons for the decision to induce one. I'm sure that you can imagine how he would feel, given the extent of his injuries, if he were conscious. At this early stage, he would have great difficulty dealing with the extent of his injuries. We would need to administer heavy doses of pain medicine. By the time Thomas is conscious we will be able to control his pain to allow us to perform the secondary surgery and get him ready him rehabilitation."

Mike asked, "Just how long does an average rehabilitation from something like this take?"

"Once again, Mr. Tolliver, there is no average rehabilitation. I can't emphasize that enough. Much depends on the patient, family support and advances in medicine and technology. It could be as short as nine to twelve months or as long as three to four years. I refuse to speculate about Thomas's case. Is there anything else you want to know?"

Emily had a concerned expression on her face. "Doctor, will Thomas return to normal when he completes his rehabilitation?"

Looks from the others indicated that they wanted to know the answer to that question, as well.

"You're asking a question that is extremely difficult to answer, since every Traumatic Brain Injury affects motor functions, thinking, memory, reasoning, sight, hearing, touch, taste, smell, expression, behavior, mental health and personality. With such a broad range of factors to be considered, it's difficult to determine what is normal given the introduction of the trauma into a person's life. The road back to normal is often a slow, arduous one and it requires patience on the part of the patient, family and care givers. It can be very disconcerting and frustrating to watch a patient attempt to remember basic movements or information as simple as the current year or name of the country's president. That being said, whatever the extent of damage, our goal is to get Thomas back to his life and family and as much as possible back to way he was prior to the accident. Keep in mind that you may experience a new normal for Thomas.

"I can share with you that I have seen some miraculous recoveries over the years. Sometimes a patient musters up a high degree healing power that doctors are at wits end to understand or explain. Again, it depends on the patient and the quality of familial support."

"I'm sure that you will have many questions in the coming days and weeks. Feel free to ask Dr. Jensen or anyone that he designates to dispense the information about Thomas. Prayer is always helpful. Don't forget to ask for wisdom and guidance for us doctors and all the professionals looking after Thomas, as well."

That being said, he shook everyone's hand and hastily left the room.

Dr. Jensen picked up the pace where Dr. Freenold left off. He quickly finished his notes, stood up and announced, "I'm going to check with the ICU staff to determine when we'll be allowed to see Thomas. It shouldn't be long now. I also have someone bring in Thomas's personal belongings. While I'm gone I'll need you to assign the Family Spokesperson we discussed earlier." He handed Walter a form to fill out that contained all the contact information the Hospital required.

They wasted no time deciding. Miriam excluded herself because she was from out-of-town and was, at the moment, a patient, herself. The rest unanimously decided on Emily as the most practical choice based on her years as Thomas's foster mother and because she resided in Owensburg.

As Emily was completing the form, a nurse entered the room carrying a banker's box. She laid it down on the table. The name "Thomas Mortinson" was printed with a black marker on a white label on top of the box. Emily, in her new role as Family Spokesperson was asked to sign for the box.

Walt removed the cover and began to remove the contents. It was a very large box for the few contents inside. The first item was Thomas's wallet. He flipped it open and looked at the photo ID on the Drivers License. It was a picture of Thomas from a year back, when he was trying hard to grow a mustache. Tears welled up in Walt's eyes as he closed the wallet and handed it to Emily. The next item was a belt, followed by a baggie containing loose change, keys, a handkerchief and a comb. He laid them on the table. Lastly, he removed a cell phone.

He pressed a few buttons, but nothing happened; apparently the battery had gone dead. He chuckled as he recalled that Thomas had a bad habit of forgetting to recharge his phone and as a teen, very often used "my phone went dead" as an excuse for getting home late.

Walt pushed the box aside and as he did he heard a clunk from inside. Reaching back into the box he was surprised to find a small jewelry box. Curious eyes were on him as he opened it up. Inside was a diamond engagement ring. Walt looked at Louise, who by now had a flood of tears flowing down both cheeks. He reached out and handed the box to her, "I think Thomas would want you to hold on to this."

Louise accepted the box as Emily put an arm around her. "If it's any comfort to you, he didn't even tell me that he was going to pop the question. I guess he wanted it to be a complete surprise to everyone." As she gave squeezed Louise's shoulder, she thought for a minute and added, "He certainly got his wish, there, didn't he?"

Louise looked at the ring and snapped the box shut. "I'll hold this until Thomas is well enough to ask me in person. Of course, I'll say yes."

Suddenly a voice came from Mike's cell phone. It was Miriam asking, "What's going on over there?"

Mike picked up the phone, shut off the conference call feature and motioned to the others that he was taking the phone outside so he could bring Miriam up to date on everything.

Walter also excused himself to make a call to his Deputy.

Louise and Emily held hands as they discussed Louise's and Thomas's plans for when this ordeal was finally over.

Do you remember that thrilling ride I promised you earlier? Well, this is only the beginning; there is so much more to come. Just sit back and enjoy.

CHAPTER 35

The emergency meeting of the Owensburg Town Council was gaveled to order at 7pm with much consternation among the Council members attending. Behind the locked doors of the Council chambers, they could hear the murmur of the crowd in the halls that was usually allowed to attend Council meetings; Media included. The attendees did their best to ignore the chatter outside and the occasional knocks on the door.

Peter Westlake addressed the small group, "I'd sure like to know how those people knew about this meeting. Boy, I sure am grateful to the Sheriff for having the foresight to assign a few deputies to protect City Hall. So, let's get on with it before they break down that damn door."

Continuing, "According to the By-Laws of Owensburg's constitution, when the elected Chairman is unable to perform his duties and in the absence of the Mayor, the longest seated member of the Council is to assume the Chairmanship of the group. That being me, I want to begin this meeting with a moment of silent prayer in memory of

Wendell Phillips and John Martin and for all our friends and neighbors who died in that tragic accident out at Tiecher Park." He solemnly bowed his head along with the rest. That being done, he took a quick vote to legitimize the change in leadership and, in the light of what happened, Peter made the motion that they dispense with customary stilted Rules of Order of the Council and all the protocols that usually followed and move immediately to a discussion of what occurred at Tiecher Park and how they should proceed to run the town now that the Mayor was dead. John seconded the motion and they all voted to free the meeting from the Rules of Order.

The group, made up of John Clark, Payne Easton, Ralph Mason, Peter Westlake and the Council Secretary Marge Nelson, moved to a circular table in the chambers. Peter said, "If you want to get something to drink, you best do it now." Marge rolled a serving cart with a coffee service, soft drinks, water and assorted chilled pastries she found in the small refrigerator in the corner of the room. Each served themselves and settled down for the work at hand.

Peter started the meeting. "It's probably going to be months before we know anything for sure about the cause of the stage collapse. As the governing body in the town, until we have all the answers, we must be extremely careful about what we say and to whom we say it. I have no doubt that there will be a multitude of frivolous and some not so frivolous lawsuits filed against the town and perhaps even against one or all of us. I suggest that if you are served with any papers that you give them to Payne. If that alright with you?" he asked, turning to Payne Eaton.

"Sure, I was going to suggest that, myself. Just forward them to my office," Payne replied. "I'd like to suggest that we seek the counsel of a law firm that specializes in disasters of this magnitude. We not only have the deaths and injuries of our townspeople to deal with, but Jimmy Nordstrom and four members of the band Vinny and the Cruisers also perished. There's no telling who was in the audience or how they will respond."

Peter volunteered, "I'll handle the Media, so send me all requests for interviews. Most of these people are personal friends of mine. I don't expect any problems with unfair coverage of the incident from the locals, but I have no idea how out-of-town news people will behave. This is big. It's already gone national on TV and social media. I'll do my best to handle them as they come along. That's all we can do."

He turned to John Clark, the Principal of Owensburg High, "Have you made any decision yet as to when you will reopen the school?"

John was over six feet tall, but the sheer magnitude of the tragedy made him appear several inches shorter. "It's not really up to me, Pete. The Board of Education is looking at that now. You know that the State has mandatory school days, but nothing of this magnitude has ever happened before." Suddenly he choked up, "I lost twenty-three students and another seven have injuries that will lay them up for at least a month or two. We're planning to have trained counselors meet with all our kids to help them get over the loss of their friends and classmates. Suddenly I realize how towns involved in mass shootings at schools had to feel. It staggers the imagination that a tragedy of this kind could befall our student body."

Peter placed his hand on John's shoulder. "I know that this is a special burden for you, being that you personally knew all of the students that were lost. My heart goes out to you and to the surviving students and to all the families involved. If the State isn't responsive quickly enough for you, we can bring in specialists on our own to work with the students. Several corporations in town and the surrounding area have volunteered the help of their Personnel Department psychologists. These are some of the best therapists in the country and an asset we shouldn't overlook. Perhaps we should set up an advisory council composed of State and private specialists to weigh in on this issue. One way or the other we will get the job done."

"Thanks, Pete. I might very well be looking for that sort of help. The biggest problem I'm dealing with is that we have no precedent for handling the loss of so many students at once. We were lucky that more students weren't in the area of the collapse."

Ralph Mason raised his hand. "I'd like to volunteer to be sort of a liaison for the town. It seems to me that we're going to have people coming at us from all over, with the oddest issues. I spent my adult life refereeing some of the toughest coaches and players, so I'm used to handling people that are determined to have their way. What do you think?"

Peter looked at Ralph. "That's an excellent idea." Then he chuckled, "I feel sorry for anyone trying to take advantage of you over this situation. You make sure that you wear your whistle so that everyone knows that you mean business."

That brought a smile to everyone's face. The levity helped ease the tension that was building up as the full scope of their responsibilities to the town of Owensburg was becoming clearer.

Peter turned to Marge. "Marge, will you see to communicating information with all the town offices. Everyone needs to know as quickly as possible that we are on top of this and functioning as a team. We must avoid as much confusion as possible."

"I'll get on it as soon as we're finished here. By the way, has anyone heard anything about the condition of the Sheriff's son?"

John answered her, "The last I heard is that he's over at the George Bennett Baxter Trauma Center in a special intensive care unit. Apparently, he was right under that thing when it fell. He's in pretty serious condition from what I hear. I also heard that they brought in a trauma specialist from out-of-town to handle his case. Please say a special prayer for him and for Walter and Emily."

John added, "I remember Thomas from when he pitched softball for the school. He was an outstanding athlete and he was an excellent student; a really fine young man. What a tragedy."

The remainder of the emergency meeting consisted of splitting up the Mayor's routine duties until they were prepared to set up the machinery for a special interim election. They agreed to meet at the same time the next day or immediately if an emergency situation came up.

As they prepared to leave, Peter turned to the group, "I think it would be a good idea if we check with each other before we finalize anything major. Make sure you have everyone's cell phone numbers and that yours is with you and on 24/7."

CHAPTER 36

Dr. Jensen returned to the Family Room at 7:30pm. "Well folks, I have good news. We have a clearance to visit Thomas, but before we do, I have to go over the ground rules. As long as Thomas is in what we call a "restricted status', all visitations must be scheduled by the nursing station on the third floor. That's in case he is receiving special treatments or under special observation. At this time your visits will be restricted to viewing from behind an observation window. There is a red line on the floor in front of the window and all viewing must be done from behind that line. Under no circumstances is the window to be touched."

He stopped for a moment to judge the level of comprehension. "All this must seem to you as very picayune, but you would be very surprised at the lengths that some visitors have gone to communicate with their loved ones. Tapping on the glass in the hope of getting the patient's attention is the most egregious, followed closely by attempts to paste pictures or messages on the glass for the patient to see during or after their visit. Now, please don't get me wrong, I thoroughly understand their frustration with not being able to be in the room with their loved one and if I were in their shoes I might even resort to the same behavior.

"The last item involves a prohibition against taking pictures with any type of device. There are several reasons for this. The first is the possibility that a sudden flash in such a controlled environment may have a deleterious impact on the patient. The second reason is that some of the equipment and techniques we use here at George Bennett Baxter are proprietary; some may even be experimental. Violations may result in revocation of visitor privileges, so if you have a problem with any of these restrictions, now is the time to say so."

He looked at the group and was satisfied that the rules were both understood and agreed to. "That being said, I want to prepare you for what you will see. I mentioned earlier that after his operation, Thomas was returned to his room and attended to by a team of specialists. His room, number 333, is equipped with a bed that is customized for patients with head trauma. It is placed away from the wall to allow rapid access from all sides. Thomas is connected to multiple monitors via wires and tubes; many of these hanging from the ceiling. He will have anti-embolism stockings on his legs and, what will probably be the most startling to you, he will be wearing the protective helmet I spoke of earlier. I'm going to show you a photo of a patient that went through a similar experience at my home hospital. It will give you a very good idea of what to expect."

He handed the photo to Walter, who looked at it for a few seconds and then gave it to Emily to pass around. Looks of surprise and disbelief appeared on each face as they saw the equipment and wires; not much being seen of the patient.

"Now that you've seen that picture, I can't caution you enough, that the person you will see occupying the bed in Room 333 will not resemble the Thomas Mortinson that you all know and love. Returning *that* Thomas Mortinson to you, will be our 24/7 activity for as long as it takes. It will be a herculean undertaking, but I can assure that it is one that each and every member of the team is well trained to accomplish. That's all I have to say for now. Do you have any questions at all before we go there?"

Louise looked at the others before she spoke. "I guess we all want to know how long we will be able to visit."

"This first visit will pretty much be up to you to decide. Subsequent visits are limited to fifteen minutes as long as Thomas is in a coma. Once he is conscious and cognitive, visits will be scheduled based on his medical condition so that we can control his reactions to visitors. We find this to be an effective way to personalize rehabilitation. Specialists will be on stand-by during those visits, either behind the glass or in the room; in case an unexpected reaction shows up on one of the monitors that may require immediate attention. These extra precautions are mostly for the first stage of Thomas's rehabilitation. We will discuss what is expected from you as we approach each stage. Your Family Spokesperson will also have all this information in a packet we provide and will be notified as each stage is reached. I believe that Dr. Freenold explained that the rehabilitation of each patient is individual, so once again I urge you not to spend a lot of time on the web trying to analyze Thomas's progress. There won't be another case the same as Thomas's. Only time will tell. Okay, then, let's do it."

Dr. Jensen started for the door with the others close behind. Mike held back long enough to explain to Miriam that he needed to turn off his phone, "As soon as we're finished I'll come right to your room and fill you in on everything as soon as the visitation is over. I promise."

* * *

Miriam pressed the button to summon the nurse. When she arrived, she asked for help calling the Owensburg Inn.

"This is the Owensburg Inn, how may I help you?"

"This is Miriam Walton, I'm sorry that I didn't call sooner. I'm afraid I have a bit of a problem. I was at the park the other night when the accident occurred and now I'm at Owensburg General Hospital with a concussion. The doctor wants to keep me at least another day. I'll need you to hold my room for me."

"That won't be a problem at all, Mrs. Walton. What an awful thing happened out there. I'm sorry that you were injured. Incidentally, your husband called earlier looking for you. He asked me to tell you that he cut his trip short and is on his way home. I told him that you hadn't returned to your room and may have been at the show when the accident occurred. I certainly hope that it was okay to disclose that information."

At first the news took Miriam aback, but she quickly regained her composure. "Of course, you did nothing wrong. If he should call again, please tell him that I am at the hospital and give him the phone number. I'm in Room 359."

"I'll make sure he gets the message. Be well, Mrs. Walton."

"Thank you very much. I expect to be seeing you soon."

CHAPTER 37

Nathan Walton was fuming; nothing seemed to be going right. First, his cell phone charger went missing and then his connection at Logan was out of service with no replacement in sight. He was sitting in a bar at the airport nursing a Rusty Nail, his favorite drink. The Public phones had long lines. *I've got to calm down. All this stress is no good for my blood pressure.*

He turned, for what must have been the twentieth time, to check the lines at the payphones. They were still at least ten people deep. *What a time to be without a charger.* Then it hit him, *there must be a cyber shop in a big airport like this. I'll buy a charger or if need be, one of those throwaway phones.*

Thirty minutes later and seventy dollars poorer, he had a new battery pack and a charger. Relieved, he placed a call to the Owensburg Inn.

"This is Nathan Walton. I called earlier about my wife Miriam who is a guest there."

"Yes, of course, sir. I believe that you spoke with me then. I have news for you. Your wife called a short time ago. Apparently, she was injured at the show out at the park and is in the Owensburg General Hospital. She called to make sure we were holding her room and I informed her about your earlier call. She asked me to give you the telephone number at the hospital and her room number." He relayed the information to Nathan adding, "I hope we will see you both, soon."

* * *

Satisfied that Miriam was safe, he returned to the information booth near his previously scheduled departure gate. The "closed" sign continued to tell the story. He crossed the aisle to the bar, got a small table in the corner where he got maximum bars on his cell and had a clear view of the gate. He ordered another Rusty Nail and settled in to call Miriam.

It took a while for the call to go through.

"Hello, Precious. How are you?"

Miriam was half asleep when she answered the phone. Groggily she muttered, "Nathan is that really you?"

"It's me, but unfortunately I'm still a thousand miles away. What's going on with you? The man at the hotel said that you were injured. What happened?"

"Oh, it's the damnedest thing. There was a terrible accident at the show I attended. This monstrous stage collapsed onto the audience. Luckily, I was far enough away when it fell, but the crowd stampeded, and I got knocked down and hit my head. I lost my purse and everything I had in it. That's why I didn't have them call you. All my phone numbers are in that damn phone. There's something wrong with the way we depend entirely on something so expendable. Anyway, they say I have a Grade 3 concussion, whatever that is. Apparently, it's serious enough for them to keep me until tomorrow for observation. I feel okay; just have a slight headache."

"Thank, god. Did the doctor say when you will be able to travel? I know that you'll be glad to get back home after that ordeal."

There was silence on the other end of the phone. Miriam had to think quickly, but the effects of her injury made concentration difficult. Finally, she spoke, "Look, I'm going to be alright. You don't have to cut your visit short."

"Nonsense. I need to be there for you. The main objective of my trip was accomplished today. The rest was just going to be public relations. I can't help thinking that if it hadn't been for that trip, I would have been with you at the park and you wouldn't be in a hospital bed."

"Or you might be in the bed next to me or in another hospital, entirely. So, count your blessings. What's the story about your trip back?"

"It's an absolute disaster. Everything that could go wrong has gone wrong. I expected to be there by now and I would be, except the connecting plane developed mechanical problems and is out-of-service. So, I'm stuck here at Logan Airport in Boston. There is no information about a replacement plane, so it looks as if I'll have to wait until tomorrow morning before I can get out of here." He sighed, and continued, "I thought about renting a car, but it's a ten-hour drive at least and I am really beat. The last thing I need is to fall asleep at the wheel and land up in a ditch somewhere or kill somebody. Anyway, the next flight is at 6am tomorrow morning and I'm booked on it. It's coach, but any port in a storm, as they say. I should be out there between 8am and 9am, unless through some miracle, the rocket scientists solve the plane problem before then, but I'm really not holding out any hope of that happening. I just thank god it's a relatively short trip."

"Well, why don't you find a bar and have a few of your Rusty Nails and a nice, thick, juicy steak. That always helps you feel better and it will help you wile away the hours."

"You know, that sounds like a great idea," he said, as if he needed any prompting in that direction, "I'll have a good meal and try to catch a nap later. At least the chairs by the gate are well padded. It won't be the first time I've slept at an airport."

Knowing that Mike was on his way, Miriam needed to cut the call short. "I should go now, sweetie. I'm sharing the room with several others and they want us to get all the sleep we can get. Give me your cell number in case I need to call you." She wrote it down and added, "I love you my dear Nathan and I can't wait to hold you again."

"Same here. Sleep well, my Precious."

Miriam returned the phone to its cradle. A sudden feeling of dread flooded her body as she realized that in less than half a day her husband, who was totally unaware of the search for her son, would be there wanting to whisk her back to the safety of their home.

Where the hell is Mike? I got to know about Thomas.

CHAPTER 38

Dr. Jensen led the group to the elevator and pressed the button for the third floor. As they approached the window Room 333, Jensen reminded them about the rules. "Please remember everything I said downstairs. This is probably going to be the most difficult visit you will have to make. Over time, some of the wires and tubes will be disconnected and you will get to see more of the Thomas you are familiar with."

They stepped up to the line and looked in on the figure prostrate on the bed with dozens of tubes and wires connected to him. Two nurses were in attendance checking the monitors. Emily gasped, and Walter reached over to support her arm. Louise's knees gave out and Mike wrapped an arm around her waist, for support. He led her over to a nearby bench. She looked up at him, "Thanks Mike, I thought I was ready to see him. I know I saw the picture, but since it wasn't a picture of Thomas, I was expecting something less upsetting." Her eyes switched to Dr. Jensen. "Are you sure that that is Thomas in there?"

"Very certain, Ms. O'Neill. Please remember what I said before. Many of the tubes and wires you see are only there to monitor Thomas's condition during the first 72 to 96 hours. If everything goes as planned, the next time you see him some of them will be gone and the time after that still a few more. In cases such as these, we prefer to err on the side of too much monitoring rather than too little."

Emily joined Louise on the bench. She put her arm around her and held her close for several minutes.

Walter took Dr. Jensen's arm and they stepped aside. "Look, Doctor, I can see that visiting Thomas like this is very difficult for the ladies. Hell, it's taking all the self control I have to stop from breaking down in tears myself. You've been through this a lot of times. Do you have any advice for me on what to say and do? I sometimes put my foot in my mouth when it comes to talking with the fairer sex and I don't want to make matters any worse than they already are."

"I understand what you're going through. Don't be too hard on yourself. There is no right or wrong when it comes to circumstances like this. As far as I know, none of you have ever been in a situation like this, so just try your best to be supportive of whatever the others want to do. Things tend to be overly emotional in the beginning, but that improves over time. Just play it by ear. Remain the calm, reasoning one; the rock.

They will listen to you as long as you show you understand where they are coming from. Let them vent and be slow with any criticism. That's about all I can advise."

"Well, that's a lot, but it makes sense. Thank you, Doctor."

"You're welcome."

Emily got up and returned to the red line, followed by the others. Looking in at Thomas she asked, "My poor baby, why did this have to happen to you?"

Walter squeezed her shoulder and she looked at him with tear fill eyes, "Whatever it takes, we're going to help him get through this." Another squeeze followed.

Mike stepped away from the line. "I'm going to go back to Miriam's room to bring her up to date. She must be going nuts having to wait like this."

Emily touched his arm, "You shouldn't have to do that alone, Mike. Why don't we all go back together?" She looked at Walter and Louise and they both agreed.

Mike looked relieved, "I sure would appreciate that. I'm not too good at this sort of situation and I sure wouldn't want to mess it up. I've dealt with failed searches galore and many disappointed clients, but his is another thing entirely."

The men shook Dr. Jensen's hand and the women gave him a hug. Somewhat embarrassed by the gestures, Dr. Jensen's face changed several shades of red.

"We'll be in touch with you Emily as soon as we know anything more about Thomas's condition.

"Thank you Doctor, for everything."

Walter got out his keys. "Well, let's get going then. The sooner we can relieve Miriam's anxiety the better."

What the four of them just experienced may well turn out to be the easiest part of this ordeal. We'll just have to wait and see, won't we.

CHAPTER 39

The minute they entered the room, Miriam snapped out of the reverie she had slipped into.

"How is he?"

Mike fielded the question as the others gathered chairs from around the room. "We couldn't see much of Thomas because they've got all these wires and tubes hooked up. You heard what the doctor told us. It was exactly as it was in the picture he showed us."

She looked around her bed at each of them. "I guess it must have been hard seeing him like that. Did the doctor tell you when they will bring him out of the coma?"

Emily spoke up, "The doctor can't tell us that yet. Everything depends on how well his body responds to the operation they performed and their success at treating the secondary injuries he received."

"I don't like the fact that they operated on Thomas without any of us knowing anything about it; especially such a serious operation. It doesn't seem right."

Emily reached out and took Miriam's hand. "We all felt that way at first, but Dr. Freenold explained that it was a life or death situation. The good news is that he also said that it looked as if the operation was successful." Changing the subject, she asked, "Have you heard anything yet about when you will be released?"

"Not yet. If it wasn't for the fact that beds are in short supply, I'd think that they were keeping me here just to make a few bucks. Something else happened while you were gone. My husband called me. He called the hotel right soon after I called them to tell them I was here. When he hadn't heard from me he cancelled his trip and headed here. He's stuck in Boston right now because of a plane shortage and won't get here until tomorrow." She suddenly stopped talking and her eyes teared up.

Louise asked, "Why do you seem so unhappy about that? I would think you would be happy to see him."

Miriam answered, "Yes, one would think so, but the problem is that Nathan doesn't know about Thomas."

"Oh, I'm so sorry. I didn't know."

"That's okay, dear. You had no way of knowing. I thought that since Nathan was going to be abroad for at least two weeks, I'd have time to meet Thomas and figure out where we would go from there. Now I have to figure out how to deal with him when he gets here tomorrow. He was talking about me being released and the two of us returning home. I don't know what I'm going to do. I'm not going to leave Thomas." Her voice quivered as tears flowed down her face.

Emily grabbed a tissue and handed it to Miriam. "Maybe I can help you with that. I know it won't be easy, but I'm willing to spend some time with you now, if you want to fill me in on the details." She turned to her husband, "Why don't you take Louise home while Miriam and I have a long talk. It may take a while, so I'll call you when we're finished."

"That sounds like a good idea. I need to check in with the office, anyway, and I'm sure that Louise could use some private time."

Louise nodded affirmatively. "This has been a very trying day." She looked at the ring box and added, "I need time to let this all sink in and a long nap on a soft bed wouldn't hurt. That concrete bench I was on last night left me numb in a few places."

Mike gave a quick wave to Miriam. "I'll go check out the cafeteria. I can use a strong cup of coffee right now. Maybe I'll even try out some of that notorious hospital food to go with it."

"Don't expect much, if it's the same as they served me, you're going to be disappointed."

Mike turned to Emily. "When you two are through, call my cell. I'll give you a ride home, so Walter doesn't have to come all the way back here."

Walter looked at Emily, saw an okay, and thanked Mike. He gave his wife a quick kiss and he and Louise left for home. Mike left the room with them, leaving Emily and Miriam to work out a plan to explain Thomas to her husband.

Oh, what a tangled web we weave...

CHAPTER 40

Emily pulled her chair closer to the bed so that their conversation would not be overheard.

Miriam spoke first. "This is going to be the most difficult thing I have ever done. Nathan and I have never kept secrets from each other. Now here I am with a whopper like this."

"Are you certain that he will be upset? After all, you're in the hospital with a concussion, lucky to have escaped serious injury. Your son is in an ICU with a serious head injury. How could he be upset with you under those circumstances?"

"You've got a point there. He will be very thoughtful at first, but what I fear is what happens when the initial feelings wear off. That's the Nathan I don't want to face. We've had a very happy marriage for the most part, but there is a dark side to Nathan that comes from his childhood and especially from his relationship with his mother. Apparently, she never wanted children and made no effort to disguise it. Loyalty is very important to him. We've had some real donnybrooks over the years and they were mostly about relationships. He highly values our union and doesn't want to share it with anyone. Would you believe that he even felt that way about a cat I rescued? He made me take it back to the shelter because he said that the cat was cutting into our 'alone' time."

Emily looked shocked. "You poor woman." "Oh, I didn't mean to paint a totally bleak picture about our marriage. When we're alone Nathan is the gentlest man I know. He is thoughtful and considerate as long as no third party is involved. He can, at times, blur the lines of civility and get downright cruel, especially if he feels that he has been betrayed. He's done it with members of his family and with a previous business associate. So, you can see why I'm concerned. Having Thomas in my life threatens to destroy my marriage, but I can't see any way to avoid it."

"Do you think it would help if Walter or I, or perhaps both of us were here when you tell him about Thomas?"

"Oh, no, I think that would just muddy the waters. He'll have enough to handle with me being in the hospital and then with the news about Thomas. I can't get you involved in my web of deceit. I'll just have to deal with it as best I can and hope that his love for me and sense of decency are stronger than his hurt feeling. He's really a wonderful man."

"Well if you change your mind, the offer stands."

"That's very sweet of you Emily. No, I got myself into this mess and I'm going to have to live with the consequences, no matter what they are. It's helped a lot talking with you about it, though. I think I know how I'm going to approach the subject of Thomas with Nathan."

A smile replaced the frown on her face. "I feel much better now. You're a very kind person. I'm so glad that Thomas grew up with you and Walter. You did such a wonderful job with his upbringing."

Emily smiled, "Careful now, you'll give me a swelled head. Are you certain that you're going to be okay?"

"Yes, I'm certain. Go now, Walter and Louise are going to need you." She stopped for a second and added, "She's such a lovely young woman, isn't she? Thomas has such good taste when it comes to women; his future wife as well as his foster mother."

"That's so kind of you to say and I certainly agree with you about Louise. Okay then, I'll go home, but remember I'm just a phone call away."

"How could I forget my new BFF?"

Emily smiled as she gathered up her coat and bag. She waved as she left the room but waited until she was in the lobby before calling Mike for a ride home.

CHAPTER 41

"E-Coli, are you certain?" The question came from a dumbfounded Director of the Owensburg General Hospital, Dr. Philip Owens. "How could that happen, we've never had a problem in our commissary?"

"The only thing I can figure is that it might have come from the delivery of meat and produce that we've been getting from Owensburg Catering."

"When did we start ordering from a caterer?"

"That was the idea of our Chief Dietician. Apparently, there's a move underway among hospitals to 'humanize' hospital food. You know, make it like the food you get at home; hamburgers, hot dogs, Mac and cheese, stuff like that. So far, it's been well received by patients and is faster for the commissary to prepare. We've been on that regimen now for about a month, now. Much of what OC supplies are ground beef and fresh vegetables; the type of food that unfortunately can cause a problem if not handled properly. That's the only thing I know that we've done differently. Notwithstanding that they may be the source of the E-Coli, it was a good thing we have that resource available, since this influx of patients has put a real strain on the Commissary."

"That makes sense I suppose, as long as we watch the preparation; especially with the raw beef, however, under the circumstances I think we should suspend any further deliveries from Owensburg Catering until we locate the source of the contamination. They may not be the source, but we can't take any chances. You should notify them right away of our decision and enlist their help in the testing protocol. You're going to have to alert Legal too, about what's happening, and we need to start a dialogue with the CDC and the State Health Department right away. I don't want to be caught short on this."

"Of course, but I'm have an even greater concern."

Impatiently, Dr. Owens asked, "What else?"

"Our commissary chefs took a liking to the convenient packaging of the cuts of chicken and tubs of salads that Owensburg Catering provided, especially with the greater demand for meals due to the accident. They ordered extra of both and mixed it with some of their own meals. I guess what I'm saying is that it's possible our entire food supply is at risk including the food we send over to George Bennett."

"Damn it. That's all we need now. At least you can distinguish their food by the packaging. Have GB isolate that food in case we have to test it. Do we have any count on the number of patients that could be involved?"

"I can't give you an accurate count because we have discharged over ninety patients during the time frame that we were dispensing the contaminated meals. Of course, many of them were not fed during their stay here.

"We're dealing with a five to ten-day incubation period. To complicate matters many of the symptoms such as fever, diarrhea, headaches, fatigue and nausea are common to what we are treating them for."

"You need to get stool samples from any patient showing symptoms. Expedite processing with any lab that can do E-Coli testing. Get our lab busy on finding the source. Change the menus to meals from our emergency food supply and any food that is cleared from the lab until further notice.

"One other thing, I see no reason for this outbreak to be discussed outside of this room. Only discuss it with the Authorities and those that have a 'need to know'. Any testing or treatment should be presented as part of the standard protocol for the patient's care."

He shook his head. "We need to isolate the cause of this outbreak … STAT."

CHAPTER 42

As soon as she came in the door, Walter grabbed Emily and held her tight. "I'm so glad you're home. It's been quite a day hasn't it?"

"That's for sure. I caught a little bit of the news on the way home. It's really bad isn't it?"

"Yes, it is. So many unsuspecting people were killed. They don't have the final numbers yet, but I heard that this is the worst single disaster in the State of Ohio and possibly the country. I waited until you got home because I didn't want to leave Louise alone, but I really need to get back out there. This situation has left us shorthanded."

"Of course, you go right ahead. Where is she?"

"She went to her room as soon as we got home. She said she needed some alone time. I heard some sobbing going on for about five minutes, but then she probably went off to sleep. She was thoroughly exhausted when we got here, poor girl."

"I'll keep an ear out for her. She may need a shoulder to cry on when she wakes up. You go on now, the town needs you. Just give me a call occasionally so I know you're okay."

They kissed at the door. Walter left with the siren wailing.

CHAPTER 43

"Get out of my way. I've got to see my wife. She's in there. Her name is Miriam Walton."

It was Nathan Walton doing the shouting while attempting to push two orderlies aside. "My wife's in that room and I want to see her…now!"

"Sir, you can't go in there now. Please return to your seat until we call you."

"You don't understand. She's had a concussion. I've been travelling a day and a half to get here. I want to see her right away. Now get out of my way, before I have to get rough."

One of the orderlies motioned to a security guard who quickly joined the fracas. "You're going to have to come with me, sir." He grabbed Nathan by the arm with just enough pressure to broadcast that resisting might not be in Nathan's best interest.

Nathan immediately turned to the man and, under the assumption that he now could reason his way out of this predicament. He repeated his message.

The guard was unmoved by Nathan's argument. "When hospital employees give you directions, they are to be followed. We have a hospital emergency on our hands and we won't tolerate any unruly behavior on the floor. Is that clear?"

All the fire went out of Nathan and he meekly replied, "That's clear."

The guard pointed to the waiting area. "Now you go on over there, sit down and be quiet until they come for you. If I hear a peep out of you, I'll turn you over to the Sheriff's Department and charge you with disturbing the peace and resisting arrest. Got that?"

A docile Nathan answered, "Yes Sir. I understand."

* * *

Meanwhile in Room 359, nurses and candy stripers were busy handling a case of severe nausea being experienced by the patient in bed 1. Miriam was doubled over holding her stomach as a nurse and a candy striper did their best to steady her and aim the contents of her stomach into a large pan. As they assisted her, another nurse slipped a bed pan out from under Miriam, but instead of taking it over to empty it in the lavatory, she filled out a gummed label noting Miriam's name and the room number, affixed it to the pan and directed the orderly to take it to the lab down the hall.

It took several minutes for Miriam to empty her stomach of the previous night's dinner two cups of water she drank first thing after she arose and some oatmeal and coffee she ate for breakfast but empty it she did. Totally exhausted from the ordeal she fell back against the pillow. A nurse stood next to the bed taking Miriam's vital signs, made notes on the chart and advised Miriam to try to rest. When the room cleared of helpers, the head floor nurse entered to check on Miriam. The first thing she did is give Miriam an extra blanket. "How do you feel now? Are you up to having a visitor?"

Miriam's face brightened. "I'm okay now. Is Nathan here? Is my husband outside?"

"Oh, yes, he certainly is, and he caused quite a commotion; almost got himself arrested."

"I heard some disruption, but I was too busy barfing to pay any attention. You say that that was him making all that noise?"

"That was him all right, but they finally calmed him down. He's waiting down the hall."

"Oh, please let me see him. The poor man's been through so much to get here."

Unmoved, the nurse replied, "And you haven't?"

"Oh, you know what I mean, please let him in."

"Okay, but you make sure he behaves himself. The atmosphere at the hospital right now is very edgy. It won't take much to set off any of the people working here. Keep in mind that we're all doing our best in what has to be the worst situation any of us has ever experienced in our professional lives."

"He'll be fine, I promise."

* * *

Nathan headed straight for her bed and leaned down to kiss her. "My poor Precious, how are you?"

"I told you about the concussion. It seems that sometimes you get a bit of nauseousness along with the other symptoms. It held off until this morning and then everything I had in me came hurling up. That happened just a while ago. It felt as if my stomach and intestines were coming up as well. It was awful, but I'm okay now that you're here."

Nathan sat down on the bed and held her against his shoulder. "Well we're going to get you better and then back home where I can look after you. I should have never left you alone."

"That's nonsense and you know it. You had to go on the trip; nothing short of face to face meetings would have worked. The proof-of-the-pudding is that you were successful in setting up the network you wanted and now you're home safe with me."

"I guess you're right, but I still wish I had been here for you."

"Of course you do, that's natural, but all's well, that ends well. The important thing is that you're here now. Right?"

"I suppose."

"You know I'm right. Now, no more of that kind of talk from you. Tell me about your night and the trip here."

"You don't really want to hear about that stuff. Suffice it to say, that this was the worst return trip I have ever been on. Let's talk about what's going on with you."

"Well, you can see the condition I'm in. I'm so weak that I'd fall flat on my face if I tried to get up. That vomiting took back all the energy I had built up by resting for two days. It's like setting the clock back and starting over. Aside from that, I'm good. No broken bones or serious lacerations, just that conk on the head from when I was knocked down."

"What would you say about our getting an ambulance service to take you to Spartanville General? It would only take a few hours and that way you'd be close to home and be able to settle in as soon as whatever you have wrong with you passes. You'd have Doctor Welch there to treat you, too."

"I can't go back to Spartanville yet."

"Why on earth, not?"

"Nathan, you and I have to have a talk about something and you're not going to like it."

"What are you talking about? Is there something else wrong with you?"

"No, it's nothing like that. It's about the real reason I came to Owensburg."

CHAPTER 44

Emily prepared some tea to have ready in case Louise woke up.

She didn't have to wait long. Just about the time that the kettle started whistling, she heard the bathroom door close and the water running. She waited until the water stopped and called upstairs. "Louise, I have some tea brewing if you would like to come down to the kitchen."

She heard no response for about a minute and then Louise called down, "That sounds great, Emily. I'll be down in a few minutes."

Louise took about five minutes to show up at the kitchen door. She had on a silk robe and a pair of Yogi Bear slippers that Thomas had given her on Valentine's Day. Her hair had been combed and her face, though washed several times, still showed redness from the cascade of tears that had travelled down her cheeks.

"Hello, dear. Come on over here and sit down. I have tea and some mixed berry scones"

"That will be great, Emily. I finally got my appetite back."

"Cream or sugar with your tea?"

"Just some sugar, please."

Emily poured the tea, placed two plates, a sugar bowl and utensils on the table and got a bakery box with the scones from the refrigerator and brought it to the table.

"There we are, help yourself."

Emily waited for Louise to select a scone before she spoke. "I can't imagine what you must be going through. This weekend was to have been so special for you and Thomas…and look where we are."

Tears began to well up in her eyes as Louise reflected on the reality of those words. "You're right. Everything was going along so nicely, and it looks as if Thomas was going to propose sometime that night. And then this catastrophe happens, and Thomas is wrapped up like a mummy, unable to know where he is or probably even know what happened to him. I don't know how I will be able to endure the coming months not knowing if my Thomas will be coming back to me."

Emily moved her chair next to Louise and put her arm around her shoulders. "We have to be strong for Thomas's sake. I know it looks dire right now, but Dr. Freenold assured us that the condition that Thomas is in right now is temporary and that when they bring him out of the coma they induced, Thomas will start on the road to recovery. He's going to need every bit of our support to get through the ordeal of recovery. He's strong and he has you to fight for."

"You're right, of course, but it's so hard."

"I know it is dear, but if we all stick together and don't waver in our faith, we'll all get through this. Have you thought about what you are going to do?"

"Only a little, it's so hard to make any plans without having all the facts. For one thing, I will quit my job, so that I can be here."

"Well, of course, you'll stay with us. Consider the room your using as yours for as long as it takes. It goes without saying dear that you are part of our family now and Walter and I want to keep you close."

"That's very kind of you. I was hoping you would want me to stay here in Owensburg. I'll call my boss and ask for a leave of absence. I think that under these circumstances they'll understand, but if not, I'll just resign. I've got to be here for Thomas"

"Say no more. We'll do this together."

CHAPTER 45

Miriam began, "Nathan, when we first met, you and I agreed not to spend endless hours talking about our past lies. Unfortunately, there was one part of my past that I probably should have revealed to you. I think the reason I didn't was partly because I wanted to keep those memories suppressed, but also because it was a part of my life that I was ashamed to tell anyone about."

Nathan squirmed a bit in his chair. "What on earth are you talking about? What could be so shameful that you couldn't tell me? Our love for one another is certainly stronger than that."

"I believe that too, but what I have to tell you is not a trifling matter." Miriam decided to blurt it out and end the suspense, "I have a grown son. His name is Thomas Mortinson. I gave him up for adoption when he was born and recently I felt the need to find him and let him know that I was his birth mother." She stopped to see Nathan's reaction; it wasn't good. She knew that look from years of marriage and it meant that he was extremely disappointed in her. *I guess that shouldn't surprise me. He feels betrayed.*

Continuing on, she related the details of Thomas's birth, her decision to give him up, his eventual foster care by the Peyton's and then to his accident at the park. "I hope you can forgive me for keeping this from you. I need you understand."

Nathan let her speak without interruption, mulling over in his mind the significance of what she was telling him. When she stopped, he lowered his eyes and said, "Miriam, what I hearing from you is that you buried a secret about having a son for twenty-three years, a good bit of that time, married to me and then went about traipsing all over the Midwest to try to find him. You did all that behind my back. I'm very disappointed in your behavior. Do you really expect me to just ignore it, to pretend that it's okay that you deceived me? Am I supposed to pat you on the head and say, 'good work Miriam'?"

"There's no reason to be sarcastic. None of this was intentional. I suppressed my memory of Thomas for years and it was only because we decided not to have children of our own that my thoughts seemed to turn to him. I continued to do nothing for several years until finally, a few months ago, I went to a Family Law Attorney who was able to locate Thomas and authenticate his birth."

"Oh, I'll bet your attorney friend was more than happy to be of assistance. I can just see the two of you making plans to come to this desolate town and uncover your lost son. Is something going on between you two? Is that the next thing that you're planning to spring on me?" Nathan's face was beginning to take on a light pink shade.

"Don't be silly. I came here by myself, and besides, Mike is a real gentleman and obviously good at what he does."

"Mike is it. How cozy. I'd like to meet this joker."

"You won't be meeting anyone with that attitude. You are making no attempt whatsoever to understanding what I've been going through. All you care about is your damn ego."

"Maybe so, but I'm not the perfidious one here; you are. To think I spent the past 24 hours worried sick about you and all the time you're playing footsy with some shyster, using the excuse of looking for some long-lost mistake."

"Nathan, how can you be so cruel? I've told you the truth about everything. I was praying that you would understand and support me."

"Are you kidding? You expected me to be a part of this charade? Don't make me laugh. If I hadn't ruined your plans by cutting my trip short, you would have gone on with your deception; who knows for how long and doing who knows what. There's no telling what I would have come home to. Now that I think about it, what other antics have you been up to during my business trips? Got any other surprises for me; maybe another husband hidden away somewhere?"

"Now you're being ridiculous. Please calm down and let's discuss this rationally."

Nathan's face was now a deep pink, "Don't tell me to calm down. You're the one who's being irrational if you expect me to accept this mistake of yours as calmly as if you just changed your hairstyle. It's not that simple, Miriam. This is as bad as being unfaithful…it's a betrayal of our life together and any future we may have had together."

Miriam's eyes dropped, and she began to cry. "Oh, Nathan, I never wanted to hurt you. I love you and I wish this could have been avoided, but my heart was lonely for the child that I brought into this world. I knew that I would never have a child of my own again and I needed to know that he was all right and to be there if he wanted me to. Can't you at least give me the benefit of the doubt?"

He calmed down a little and took a sip from a bottle of water before he answered, "I want to, believe me I do, but I'm finding it hard to wrap my mind around all this. I just can't understand how you could keep such a secret like that from me. You apparently didn't trust me enough to share this with me."

"Believe me when I say I wanted to tell you everything. When I first had these feelings, they frightened me. I hadn't thought about Thomas for years. I was happy with the decision you and I made to not have children. I guess that my consciousness had to play out the drama of the suppressed memories of my giving up my own flesh and blood. I knew that I had to close that chapter in my life. I didn't tell you about it because I didn't want you to be disappointed in me. I thought you would be ashamed about my abandoning my son even though I was convinced at the time that it was the best thing I could do for Thomas. I didn't think it through. I never gave a thought to unintended consequences. Now here I am, and Thomas is lying in critical condition in another hospital. Things are a real mess."

Miriam reached out for Nathan's hand, which he gave reluctantly. "If you truly love me, you will understand what I'm going through and be there for me."

"How can you ask that of me? I came here to take you back to the comfort and security of our home, not to get involved in a missing persons case. Give up this chase of yours and return with me to Spartanville. From what you just told me, there's little you can do for that young man anyway and you'd just be in the way." He raised his voice and gave her an ultimatum. "So, what is it going to be? Are you coming home with me or not?"

Miriam stared at him in disbelief. "Please don't speak to me like that? I've never seen this side of you and if that's the best help you can offer me, then I suggest that you go on home to Spartanville, because I'm going to stay here until I can meet my son and he can meet his mother; no matter how long it takes and no matter what the consequences are. I lost him once and I'm not going to let that happen again. Thomas needs me now and I'm going to be here for him, whatever it takes."

Nathan was taken aback. His grip on her hand tightened.

Miriam grimaced, "Nathan, let go, you're hurting my hand."

He released her hand and retorted, "That's not all I'd like to hurt. Well then, it looks as if you've already made your choice. So be it. I'm going home, but don't expect any welcome from me when you come crawling back. You may have just taken the first step to ending this marriage. We'll see. Goodbye, Miriam."

With that said, Nathan left the room without as much as a goodbye kiss or any sign that he had feelings for the person he was leaving behind.

Miriam watched after Nathan as he hurried from the room. Eleven years married to the man, and she had never seen him so angry or so ambivalent. She saw hate and resentment in his eyes that she had never seen before. *Is he serious? Is he really thinking of ending our marriage over this? Why can't he understand that my wanting to be with my son, who is close to death, isn't choosing Thomas over him? My love for him hasn't changed, or has it?*

Exhausted physically and mentally from the afternoon, Miriam easily gave into sleep.

She had a brief dream, one in which she was chasing a man through the streets. No matter how fast she ran, the distance between them remained the same. Finally, he came to a barricade in the street and stopped. As he turned around, Miriam expected to see the face of her husband Nathan. To her surprise she found herself looking at Mike Tolliver. She was jolted back to consciousness by the intrusion of Mike into her dream. *Why do I keep thinking about him?*

* * *

She grabbed the phone before it could ring a second time.

"Nathan?"

"No Miriam, this is Emily. How did everything go?"

Miriam was quiet for a minute. "Not well, I'm afraid. He was very angry because I wouldn't go back to Spartanville with him. He didn't take the news about my son very well. He stormed out of here. He said that he's going home, and that this situation may very well jeopardize our marriage."

"Oh, I'm so sorry."

"Well, I shouldn't be surprised, but I was hoping that our love was strong enough that he would understand the situation. Now you can understand what I meant about having a lonely heart."

"What are your plans?"

"I really haven't had time to make any, except that I'm committed to the long run for Thomas, whatever that requires and however long that turns out to be. I won't desert him again."

"Look, I think it would be best if, when you get out of the hospital that you move in with Walter and me. That way all of Thomas's loved ones will be together to help with his rehabilitation. We have plenty of room and you will get a chance to know Louise. We really won't take no for an answer."

Tears were welling up in Miriam's eyes. "I don't know what to say."

"Just say yes. Look at it this way. You are going to need to rest up for a few days, you'll will need help getting around and we can all go together to visit Thomas. It makes the most sense. What do you say? Remember, we're BFF's."

"How can I possibly say no? Thank you, Emily. You don't know how much your friendship means to me. God bless you and Walter."

"Let me make all the arrangements at this end. Give me a call when you know about your release. I'll pick you up and bring you home."

"Oh, you don't have to bother. Mike said something about dropping me off wherever I need to go. I need to spend some time with him, anyway. It looks as if, now that he's finished his investigation, he'll be returning to Pennsylvania soon."

"You two have been working together for some time now. He seems to care a lot about you and Thomas."

"Mike is a very wonderful man. He really cares about the work he does; it's not just a business with him."

Emily noticed a softness in Miriam's voice when the subject turned to Mike. "Do I detect an interest beyond the professional?"

Miriam was slow to answer. "Don't be silly. Everything has always been strictly business between us."

Doubting this, Emily replied, "If you say so."

"I say so. No more talk like that. I will give you a call when I'm released. Thanks again."

"You're welcome. Have a good day, Miriam."

"You too, Emily."

* * *

The next day Miriam was released from the Hospital with a long list of do's and don'ts to follow for the following week. Mike Tolliver was there to pick her up, but instead of driving her directly to the Peyton house he stopped at a small café to have some coffee and private time with her.

Settled in a booth in the back of Jeffery's Café, they waited for their coffee and Danish orders. Once the order arrived, Mike was the first to speak. "I'm worried about you, Miriam; not so much physically, although you've been through a lot lately, but mostly, emotionally. Your problems with Nathan and the prospect for a long rehab process with Thomas have got to be taking a toll."

Miriam closed her eyes for a minute and thought about her answer. "I know that you are concerned, I can see it in your eyes. I don't have any readily available response for you. Things got out of hand so quickly. This business with Nathan is very troubling for me. He left no doubt that he will never forgive me and that he will probably move toward divorcing me. You know he hasn't even called me since he left."

"I'm sorry to hear that. I've been nervous since I heard he was on his way. I knew the encounter could go either way, but I was hoping for your sake that he would understand your situation. I want you to know that I'm not going to disappear from your life just because we've located Thomas. Unfortunately, I have to leave tonight to go back to Spartanville for another case, but I'll always be a phone call away. If you need me for any reason, promise me you'll call. After all, you and I have become close friends and I don't want to give that up."

"I promise, Mike. I don't know how I would have gotten this far if I didn't have you as my rock. It's going to be a long road for Thomas's recovery. I can't wait for the day he's strong enough physically and emotionally for me to tell him that I'm his mother."

Tears were rolling down her pale cheeks. Mike reached out for her hand.

"I know it will be tough, but you hang in there, Miriam. Actually, it's quite possible that since he had already expressed an interest in locating you, that when you do tell him, it may give a very positive boost to his rehab progress."

"You may be right. I hadn't thought of that."

They finished eating and looked at each other, neither wanting to end their time together. Finally, Mike said, "I guess I better get you over to the Peyton's house. Oh, by the way I located your rental in the parking lot out at the park. I got another set of keys from the rental company and arranged to have the car delivered to the Peyton's. Here are the keys. Also, I checked you out of the Owensburg Inn. They packed up your personal things and delivered them to the house. They gave me a receipt and it has your credit card number on it. You should be able to get a replacement card from the company. When I get back to Spartanville, I'll go over to the DMV and see what I can do about getting you a replacement Drivers License."

"Oh my goodness, I had completely forgotten about the car. Thank you for taking care of that and checking me out of the inn. You are a model of thoroughness, Mike Tolliver."

"Not a problem. I also contacted the people in town that have been coordinating the collection of personal effects from the accident site. They will be on the lookout for your purse and cell phone and if anything crops up, they'll call you."

"I totally forgot about all that stuff. I guess I have been out of it a little."

He smiled. "Just being of service, ma'am. It's a product of a trained legal mind. Well, I guess it's time to get you to your temporary home."

"It may not be so temporary if Nathan makes good on his threats about our marriage. I couldn't believe the look in his eyes. It's like nothing I'd ever seen."

"I'd be a liar if I didn't admit that I wouldn't be too unhappy if he did. You deserve a man who will support you in any circumstance, especially where motherhood is concerned. I know that it's not my place, but he seems to be totally insensitive to your emotional needs."

Miriam was taken aback by Mike's frankness. They had never discussed her relationship with her husband before; Nathan was always in the shadows in their relationship. Now here was Mike making a veiled suggestion that she should divorce her husband. *Could Emily be right? Does this man sitting by my side harbor romantic thoughts about me? I haven't really considered that, but now that I am, I couldn't choose a better man.*

"Anyway, the ball is in his court now. To be honest with you, having seen his true colors, I hope that he does go through with terminating our marriage and if he doesn't do it, I probably will."

It took every ounce of courage to make that admission, even more to look Mike in the eyes and say, "I don't want to go to the Peyton's house right now. Can we go back to where you are staying for a while?" Such a suggestion was risky. There was no doubt what it implied. Was Mike in a like mind? The answer came quickly. He dropped a twenty dollar on the table, grabbed her hand and led her back to the car.

They entered his room and in less than a minute they were both undressed and making love on the king-sized bed. They climaxed quickly in a burst of passion, both falling back on the pillows to catch their breath. They looked at each other, somewhat surprised at the intensity of their lovemaking.

Mike was first to speak, "That was beautiful; you're beautiful."

"I bet you say that to all your female clients."

"No, you can believe me or not, but in all the years that I've been in this business, I have never slept with a client." He added, with a big grin on his face, "either male or female."

She poked him in the ribs as she answered, "That's really comforting to know."

Mike sat back on his pillow and took her hand. "I don't know where all this is heading, Miriam. I just know where I would like it to go and that I want you to be an important part of my life from now on. I'm hoping that this time together means that you feel the same way."

"Of course I do. The only fly in the ointment is Thomas's recovery. It has to be my priority for now and I don't see how I can do this too."

"That's perfectly understandable. Whatever we build together from this point on has to be around Thomas's rehabilitation. I'm willing to wait, knowing that you feel the same way about me as I do for you."

She rolled over to kiss him, but he had something else in mind. This time they moved slowly, enjoying the other's body as only lovers can.

* * *

The ride to Emily and Walter's house was short. They spotted it easily by the red rental car parked by the curb. Emily and Louise greeted them at the front door and welcomed Miriam to her new home.

Speaking to Emily, Miriam said, "I want to thank you again for your hospitality. It's comforting to be close to the most important people in my son's life. Mike and I have had talks about how I should introduce myself to Thomas. I know that between you, Walter and Louise, we'll know the right time."

The three ladies did a group hug.

Mike said his goodbyes and left to return to Spartanville.

Looks as if the budding romance has been moved to the back burner for now.

CHAPTER 46
IN THE MEANTIME

The Town of Owensburg was slowly recovering from the devastating stage collapse. Business was still far from normal, but the majority of those injured sufficiently to require hospital care were back at home: some still requiring care on an outpatient basis. Only thirty-five concert goers remained under Owensburg General and neighboring hospital care.

Owensburg General proved that it deserved the high national ratings that it had earned over the years. Not only did they perform well handling the sudden large inflow of patients, many with life-threatening injuries, but also managing to overcome being blindsided by an E-Coli epidemic.

* * *

Owensburg High reopened, but not until all students were given the opportunity to meet with counselors from the school and several volunteers from companies in the vicinity. There were a lot of hugs and tears as the students met in the auditorium before the start of classes. Outside parents and well wishers gathered with flowers, well-wishing signs and even some care dogs to offer comfort. Asked by reporters why they had showed up for the school opening, most answered "We're just here to help our students rebuild their lives."

Temps filled in for the two teachers that were killed and for the one that remained in the hospital with a serious spine injury.

The Town of Owensburg didn't fare as well. Within a week they were beset with over two-hundred and twenty lawsuits, mostly for negligence and wrongful death. They hoped that the insurance policies that the town carried would cover most of these. Time would tell. Fortunately for the Town Council members none of them were named in the suits, allowing them to function without the proverbial "Sword of Damocles" hovering over their heads. They met almost daily with an ever-growing list of problems exclusively attributed to the disaster. Normal town issues were in abeyance indefinitely, except for the selection of a candidate to take over as Mayor of Owensburg.

The press was active in all venues, especially seeking out human interest stories, of which, given a disaster of this magnitude, there were many. Not a day went by when the residents of Owensburg weren't treated to at least a half dozen stories or columns about the accident and the recovery; some really heart wrenching. It was becoming very evident that this level of press activity would continue for some time to come.

The clean-up of the so called "Crime Scene" hadn't progressed much, either, due to the investigations going on at the Federal, State and Local levels. After a visit from the Governor, the town was declared a Disaster Area and became eligible for low cost loans to rebuild the Tiecher Park theater area.

A panel of experts attributed the cause of the collapse to the breaking of the guy wires behind the stage. The State Inspectors insisted in determining a secondary cause on the premise that the wires were intended as a back-up safety feature and not as a primary support for "The Beast". The Lead Inspector was overhead to say, "If you erect a super-structure you must ensure that it is designed to bear the load. If there were structural abnormalities in the base stage, they should have been addressed by more substantial offsets than just a few guy wires."

He was right of course but proving negligence in the original stage construction would be close to impossible now that the stage was demolished, but their insistence on puttering around in the debris was delaying the overall cleanup of the site and prolonging painful memories of the incident.

CHAPTER 47
TWO WEEKS LATER

Dr. Freenold scanned Thomas's chart. He was very pleased with the progress that Thomas had made in the past twelve days. When they brought him out of the induced coma, he responded immediately to the visual, auditory, touch and smell stimuli. Thomas knew his name and all the other questions usually asked a person returning to consciousness. The responses were both quick and certain, giving Freenold reason to be optimistic.

More tests were needed, of course, but it was clear to the Doctor that two significant events could be scheduled for the next few days. First would be the removal of the protective helmet, replacing it with headgear similar to the ones used by boxing sparring partners. The second, the more important one, was permitting visitors into the ICU for a brief visit. Visitors would be important stimuli at this early stage.

As the Family Spokesperson, the call about visits to Thomas's ICU came to Emily. When she received the call, Emily's knees went weak. Finally, limited contact with Thomas was approved. Dr. Jensen was allowing the four to visit with Thomas in his room for up to fifteen minutes depending on the strength of the patient. She spread the news as quickly as possible to Louise, Miriam and Walter.

When they arrived, Dr. Jensen greeted them with the rules regarding Early Stage ICU visits. The rules being that they would have to wear surgical masks and adhere to a prohibition regarding cell phones and cameras and they would have to stand behind a blue line painted on the floor about two feet from the bed. At all times they would be guided by and under the supervision of the nurses and attendants on duty. In cases of a negative reaction from the patient, they would be required to exit the room immediately. Dr. Jensen asked them to sign a form agreeing to these visiting stipulations.

That done, he led them into Room 333. Emily and Walter went to the left of the bed and Louise and Miriam to the right.

Thomas looked a lot better than he looked the first time they saw him. As Dr, Jensen had promised each succeeding visit showed more improvement to the point that they could at least recognize that it was a human being in the bed and not a mummy. Many of the wires and monitors were gone taking away much of the "emergency" appearance.

The occupant in the bed still didn't look like Thomas. The gruesome helmet that had obscured his face was gone and was replaced by red headgear. White dressings still covered the top of his head and gauze pads were taped over his eyes so that the only part of his face finally uncovered, was from his cheeks to his chin. In spite of some swelling and lacerations, which were healing, what they saw was the most they had seen of Thomas up until now. His arms lay on both sides with tubes and wires taped in place. He was propped up in a sitting position and appeared to be resting peacefully when they entered the room. In the background, the bank of monitors and pumps offered a cacophony of beeps and hums; sounds they would become accustomed to and suppress over the weeks and months ahead. A technician and a RN stood nearby, ever vigilant to the needs of their patient.

Dr. Jensen spoke, "Thomas, this is Dr. Jensen speaking. Do you remember that we spoke yesterday about you having visitors? Well, you have some here now. Do you want to speak with them?"

Thomas stirred. He answered softly, "Of course…who is here?"

Jensen nodded to Emily that it was okay to speak.

"It's mom, Thomas. I'm here with Walter, Louise and Miriam Walton, who was at the park when you were hurt." She looked at Miriam and she nodded back; having agreed earlier that it would be sometime down the rehabilitation process before it would be safe for Miriam to introduce herself to Thomas. Now was certainly not the right time for such a revelation.

Thomas took a few moments to reply. "Mom?" He took a deep breath before continuing. "I can't see you, but I'm happy to hear your voice."

"Louise?" They strained to hear him as his voice lowered almost to a whisper.

Louise answered, "I'm here sweetheart. We're all going to be here to help you past this."

"Louise, I'm sorry I didn't get a chance to show you my moves."

It was an inside joke, so only Emily and Louise smiled.

"That's alright, sweetheart, but you can show me next time."

Those words seemed to affect Thomas. The expression on what little they could see of his face changed and he seemed restless. It was several minutes before he answered. His voice trembled as he said, "I'm so sorry"

Walt interrupted, "Now, don't you talk like that, Son. You have nothing to be sorry about. You had no way of knowing that 'Beast' was going to collapse. You just happened to be in the wrong place at the wrong time. Dr. Jensen tells us that you're making excellent progress. Keep it up and before you know you'll be walking out of here as good as new."

They hardly heard him as he said, "That's hard to imagine, given the way I feel right now."

Then he added, "I sure hope you're right, Dad."

Louise burst in, "You and I have some plans to make. As soon as your system can tolerate us, we'll be here a lot to help you get better. I love you, my Tommy."

Those last words seem to enliven him, resulting in an involuntary rising of his bed sheet that brought smiles to the grown-ups faces and redness to Louise's. With his strongest voice of the last few minutes, he answered, "I love you too, sweetheart. I can't wait 'till I can see you again."

Dr. Jensen observed the changes in Thomas's voice, glanced at the monitors, saw that Thomas's blood pressure was rising slowly and decided that it was time to cut the visit short. "I'm afraid that I'm going to have to end today's visit, but don't be concerned. We'll have lots of time to visit in the weeks and months ahead. Right now, Thomas needs to rest."

They said goodbye to Thomas and followed the doctor out the door. As soon as they were out of range he turned to them and commented, "I think that went well for a first visit. It broke the ice and will make future visits easier. Thomas has made such extraordinary progress, but he admitted to Dr. Freenold that he felt guilty about being in the accident and although he's been assured that the accident was unavoidable, it appears that he continues to feel guilt about letting it happen to him. I can only surmise that it has to with feeling out of out of control temporarily and totally dependent on others for every aspect of his life. I'm hoping that as his rehabilitation goes on he'll be too busy to waste any time on remorse."

Walter agreed, "Thomas has always been very self-confident and self-reliant. I'm sure he feels that this incident pulled all the supports out from under him."

Dr. Jensen nodded his head. "Then we're all going to have to be on guard to avoid any conversations with Thomas that suggest that he has lost anything. Our focus will be on his *recollecting* rather than regaining lost senses and memories. The differentiation between the two approaches is striking and using the technique of recollecting means that we are assuring him that he knows the subject and that we are only trying to resurrect the memory, thus avoiding the negative of forgetting or losing them.

"I was very impressed with the results of cognitive testing that Dr. Freenold conducted. At this stage, the responses to stimuli should be only around two or a three out of ten, but Thomas is responding at level eight. I hope I'm not speaking out of place, but from what I've seen so far, I believe that Dr. Freenold will begin concentrating more on the physical, that is dealing with the surgeries, limb mending and movement, than on the recovery of cognitive, emotional or emotional issues. Those don't seem to have suffered from the accident."

Emily responded, "Thank you for being candid with us Doctor. We'll try to keep that in mind. Thank you for setting up this visit. We'll be waiting for the next one.

"I can't make any promises. It all depends on Thomas's progress. At least we've made it into his room. In cases of severe Traumatic Brain Injuries that's always a major step. I'll be in touch."

Dr. Jensen returned to Thomas's room. "I'm sorry that I had to cut their visit short, Thomas, but I noticed that your vitals were showing an increased level."

"That's okay, Doctor, it was getting hard for me anyway." His voice had regained the strength and clarity that he exhibited in their recent talks. "Not being able to see or feel their touch was frustrating. Laying in this bed twenty-four/seven has given me a lot of time to run over in my mind exactly what it will be like when that day finally comes. This will sound strange, but as much as I wanted them here, I was glad when you ended the visit."

"I understand, exactly. It won't be long, Thomas, I promise. You've made such extraordinary progress that Dr. Freenold needed to establish a totally new set of protocols for your rehabilitation agenda. If the tests planned for this afternoon pan out, we will start the next phase of your rehabilitation. In the meantime, get as much rest as possible. Your body is still doing a lot of healing."

"Can I ask you a question?"

"Certainly."

"How did they all look?"

"They all seemed well. Of course they looked worried, but that's to be expected. The woman, Miriam Walton was very pale, but she was released from the hospital recently. She was at the park that night and received a concussion, then while she was in the hospital she was infected by E-Coli and went through an agonizing time."

"The poor woman, but why did she come to see me?"

"That's a long story. It appears that she met your mother and father somehow and when she heard what happened to you, she volunteered to help them with your rehabilitation. She has a B. S. in Kinesiology which is an adjunct of sports medicine. I guess your folks thought that she might be able to help, especially since she was there at the park when the accident happened. Let's not look a gift horse in the mouth; it's one more person pulling for you."

"She must be a really nice person to want to help an absolute stranger."

"Yes, I'm sure she is. Now let's get you some rest."

"I'll probably say this a thousand more times before I walk out of this hospital. Thank you for everything, Doctor."

"You're welcome, Thomas."

Well, so far so good. Stay tuned as this drama unfolds.

CHAPTER 48

Mike Tolliver returned to Spartanville to work on another case, but he couldn't stop thinking of Miriam. Several times in the week since he came back, he spotted Miriam's husband; once on the street and another time in a supper club. He recognized Nathan from pictures he had in his file.

Now that the Parkinson case is finished there is nothing keeping me here in town. I think it's time to get on back to Owensburg and look in on Miriam. She must be lonely out there by herself.

* * *

"Hello Emily, this is Mike. Is Miriam there?"

"No. I'm sorry, Mike, she and Louise went to the mall. How have you been?

"I'm good, thanks. Say, I'm in Owensburg and I'd like to come over to see you all."

"That would be wonderful. Walter is due home in about two hours and I'm sure Miriam and Louise will return any time now. Why don't you come on over and wait for them? I just made a pitcher of sweet ice tea and I'm sure I can scare up some cookies."

"How could I say no to that? I should be there in about ten minutes."

"Great, I'll see you then."

When Miriam and Louise returned from shopping, Mike was standing at the door. They hugged a little longer and closer than "just friends" normally do, which didn't escape Emily or Louise, who gave each other a wink.

Miriam asked, "Will you be in town long?"

"I'm not sure. All I know is that I'm case free for a few weeks and deserving of a little R&R. I'm staying at the Owensburg Inn."

"I'm so glad you're here. I have so much to tell you." Miriam turned to Emily, "Would you mind terribly if Mike and I went out on the sun porch to do some catching up?"

"Of course not, Louise and I have some work to do out in the kitchen. You'll be staying for dinner, won't you, Mike?"

"I'd be happy to."

Miriam led him to the porch where they settled, next to each other, onto a bamboo love seat.

Mike spoke first. "I saw your husband around town a couple of times. Once he passed right by me on the street the other time I saw him in the bar of a supper club with a very young, curvaceous blonde hanging on his arm."

Miriam showed no emotion, "He always had an eye for blondes. As the saying goes, 'there's no fool, like an old fool'. He didn't waste any time, I see. I only got the divorce papers two days ago. He made me a very generous cash settlement offer, contingent on no alimony payments. That's not a problem for me. Since I have money of my own; I really don't need his. This way I can wash my hands of him and move on with my life."

Mike suppressed the feeling of joy he felt. Now he wouldn't feel guilty about pursuing another man's wife. "You sound relieved. Were you expecting him to follow through on his threat to end your marriage?"

"I'm not really sure. A part of me felt bad because it was my issue that caused the problems between us, but when Nathan showed his real colors by totally rejecting Thomas, I wanted nothing more to do with him. Either way, I am pretty sure that our differences could not have been reconciled short of me abandoning Thomas and there is no way in hell that that is ever going to happen; especially, now."

"What do you mean?"

"We were allowed to go into his room the other day. We had to stand behind a line again, but none of us minded. He was awake, and we could talk to him." Tears were flowing down her cheeks as she continued, "He didn't have that hideous helmet on and a lot of the wires and tubes you saw had been removed. He couldn't see us because of patches over his eyes, but when Emily, Walter and Louise spoke to him, he recognized them right away. He actually looked human even with the eye patches and the headgear he still has to wear. He knew I was with them, but he thinks that I'm just there to help with his rehabilitation. His voice was weak, but that is to be expected. Dr. Jensen says that he is progressing way ahead of what they expected, given the seriousness of his injury."

"That's such great news. When do you see him next?"

"That depends on the progress he makes with Dr. Freenold. He's the one that calling all the shots. I sure hope it's soon."

She leaned forward, and Mike guided her head onto his shoulder. "It looks as if things are moving along for you, what with your divorce and the good news about Thomas. You may not need my shoulder to cry on, after all."

Alarmed, she looked up, "That doesn't mean you're leaving?"

"Me? No way. I just meant that now we can have happy thoughts to talk about and not the gloomy stuff. Don't worry; you're not going to get rid of me that easily."

He leaned over and kissed her; she kissed back. After a lengthy kiss, he took her head in his hands and looked into her eyes. "I see the same feelings in your eyes that I have in my heart. I've loved you for some time now, Miriam, but I didn't feel it was proper to say anything while you were still married to Nathan. Now, I want you to know how I feel."

"I feel the same way, but I can't rush into anything. To be completely honest with you, my mind and heart are concentrating mostly on Thomas. I don't know if I can put much emotion into a relationship right now."

"I understand that entirely. I wouldn't want to get in the way of what you have to do. Look, we're on this quest together. I'll be here to shore you up when you need it. As long as we're on the same track *we* can wait"

"You are such a lovely man. I feel so fortunate to know you."

"I'm the fortunate one. Who could have known that the day you came into my office looking for help to find your son that we would land up together now? It's got to be Kismet."

Miriam moved her head back to the crook of Mike's shoulder; a comforting smile on her face.

Well, so far things seem to be working out for Miriam and Mike.

Time will tell.

CHAPTER 49

Dr. Arnold R. Freenold was shaking his head as he read Thomas Mortinson's chart. "I'm still astounded by the progress Thomas is making. I've done dozens of Craniectomies and no patient has ever made this kind of progress six weeks after being brought out of an induced coma. I've never seen such a rapid healing; his was one of the worst cases I've ever had to treat. He must have a good relationship with the man upstairs; that's all I can say. He has progressed to the point where we can implant the prosthetic bone and stitch up his scalp."

"I would be honored to assist you when you do the procedure. This will be my first observance of a Craniectomy."

"Of course, Frederick, I would be honored to have you at my side. Clear your schedule for 8am, Wednesday morning. We might as well ride the crest of this phenomenon."

"I'll reserve the operating room and arrange for the synthetic skull replacement to be moved over there. Do you want to inspect it before the procedure?"

"I'll take a look at it, but I've ordered these prosthetics dozens of times. As long as my specifications were followed to the letter, everything should be just fine. I've always had a perfect fit from them. What's nice about the prosthetics from Chesterton, is that they make them with an eight-inch flexible edge, so that if the patient's skull has expanded or contracted even the slightest, it will still be a perfect fit.

"You will have to inform his family about the operation and that the visiting rules will revert back to red line for five days and then blue line for another five days. Explain to them that we must take the same precautions as we did for the first procedure. I'm sure they'll understand."

* * *

Everyone was home when Emily received the news from Dr. Jensen that the following morning, Dr. Freenold would complete the Craniectomy by sealing Thomas's skull with a prosthetic bone.

Louise was the first to respond to the news, "I know that it had to happen someday, but it seems like a set-back."

Emily was quick to respond, "It does seem that way, doesn't it, but closing up Thomas skull has to be done. Dr. Jensen said that the procedure should have no impact on the progress that Thomas has made so far. I signed the authorization papers last week. Now we'll just have to pray that all goes well and remember that Thomas is in the hands of one of the top neurosurgeons in the country."

Walter added, "You're right and after whatever recovery is necessary, we can look forward to continued progress with his rehabilitation. Let's not forget that we still have a long road ahead of us; this is just a rest stop along the road to recovery."

Miriam laughed, "That's right, Walter. You have a real flair for this. You should be writing pamphlets for the Hospital."

"Oh, go on…you know exactly what I'm talking about."

"Of course I do. I'm just kidding you."

Emily asked, "Then are we all satisfied that this operation is a good thing and that the sooner it's behind us, the better it will be for Thomas and all of us?"

They nodded their agreements.

"Well now that we've agree on that, I have to share some bad news."

She waited until the vocal reaction to her words subsided before finishing. "There is a downside to this operation. It's nothing serious, but visitations will revert to the rules we started with."

Louise, answered with anger in her voice, "You mean the damn hall and red line again?"

"Unfortunately, yes, but it will only be for five days. Then we'll be allowed to be in his room behind the blue line for another five days. "She ignored the moans. "Wait a minute, think of what that means. If we are restricted to only five days behind the blue line, the implication is that we should be able to approach his bed right after that…maybe even be able to hold his hand. At least that's what I read into it."

Walter agreed, "I would think so. That sure would be great."

Emily went on. "Dr. Jensen also told me that after the ten days, the patches covering Thomas's eyes will be removed, too, so he will be able to see us."

"Oh, that will be so great," Louise said. I can't wait to look into his eyes again."

"The Doctor plans within the next two weeks to hold a Rehabilitation Review meeting with us to lay out a preliminary schedule for the coming months. Miriam, if Mike is still in town he is certainly welcome to attend the meetings with us."

"Thanks for thinking about him. I'm sure he would be happy to attend with us and I could use all the emotional support I can get."

"Well, that's all I have. We'll just have to wait to hear from Dr. Jensen about the post-operation schedule for visits."

CHAPTER 50

"Thanks for assisting me, Frederick." He smiled as he said, "That scalp stitching was superb. You are a couturier extraordinaire of TBI."

Smiling back, Jensen remarked, "It was rather good, wasn't it? Of course that perfect fit of the prosthetic bone that you made, did make it a lot easier to close up the scalp."

They high-fived and continued to remove their medical gowns.

"How about joining me in my office for a well-deserved libation? I know it's not noon yet, but I think we earned it. I've got some fine Johnny Blue or Crown Royal."

"I'm very tempted, Frederick, but I have a lot of reports to fill out and I've got to be sharp while I do them."

"Well, then, how about at my club for dinner. The last I checked, even top-ranking Neurosurgeons have to eat."

"You're right, of course; I'd love to join you."

"How about seven-thirty then?"

"I'll see you there."

* * *

Dr. Freenold was watching Thomas move about. "Can you hear me, Thomas?"

His jaw moved and his fingers started to twitch. "Doctor Freenold?", he responded, his voice quivering slightly.

"Your operation is now complete. You've got your head back together again."

His voice took on a newfound strength. "Thank God. Did everything go the way you expected?"

"It couldn't have gone any better. I closed up your skull and Dr. Jensen stitched your scalp back into place. It was a veritable tour de force, if I must say so. Pardon the braggadocio, but everything about your case has been superlative. I'm not taking all the credit; you, of course, are the major player in this drama.

"You may suffer from minor headaches for about a week. If this happens be sure to tell the attending nurse. They know how to deal with these and will give you something to relieve the pain.

"How are you feeling now? Do you feel strong enough to go over the agenda for the next week?"

"You know I'm anxious to get this behind me. I'm for anything that will get me out of this place…no disrespect intended."

"None taken, Thomas." He smiled and added, "Actually, that attitude is exactly what I'm looking for. I seem to thrive on patients happy to see the end of me. Who knew?"

Dr. Freenold pulled up a chair and opened a folder. "Well then, let's get started. Let me go over the whole schedule first and then we'll talk about it. Okay?"

"Fire away."

"First of all, we will need to repeat the cognitive tests we did previously to assure that your responses haven't suffered from the final surgery. When we remove the patches from your eyes, there will be an additional battery of tests to check your ability to recognize shapes and colors, to test your vision range and to be sure that you are able to read. I have every confidence that these tests will go quickly although it's not uncommon for a TBI patient to experience blurred vision at the start.

"Once those tests are out of the way, we'll move to next phase involving motor skills. That's when we will be bringing in a number of specialists that will concentrate on your physical functions. Normally a patient with the severity of your TBI will experience fatigue, sleep disturbances, sensitivity to light and/or sound, leg or hand tremors, ringing in the ears, loss of taste and/or smell and a gait imbalance. That said, there hasn't been anything *normal* about your recovery, so we will have to wait and see how things progress.

"That being said, until we get the positive signs that I'm expecting, we must restrict visits for the next two weeks. Your family will not be allowed in your room for a few days and then they will have to stand two feet from your bed for an additional few days. The good thing is that during the second period your eye patches should be off, and you will be able to see your family again."

"I don't care too much for the first part, but I can't wait to see them again."

"I'm not promising anything, mind you, but if all goes well with your healing, we should be able to allow limited physical contact soon."

"You mean I can hold hands and touch faces."

"Something like that. It will be limited of course. We still must err on the side of being super cautious. I'm sure you understand."

"Of course…" he said, stopping in mid-sentence."

"What's the matter?"

"Oh, nothing."

"Come on, now. Thomas. I know you better than that. What's bothering you?"

His head moved from side to side. "I just started to think about what they will see. Whether or not they will be disappointed?"

"About what?" the doctor asked.

"Just about everything. This was a serious accident. I have no idea what impact it may have on me short and long range. What if I'm different? You know, what if they don't see the same Thomas Mortinson that they were used to? I've been looking forward to the day that I can see them and hold them, but that's me. What will they be expecting? Hell, I don't even know what I'm going to look like. Will I have physical scars as well as emotional ones? I know that the tests show that key areas of my brain were unaffected by my accident, but there is so much more that could be damaged; some of it unseen. Stuff we haven't touched on yet."

Thomas caught Freenold by surprise with this sudden negativity. "You are absolutely right, of course. They have expectations just as you do. There are some mysteries yet to unfold along the roads to recovery, but there is no reason to suspect that they will unveil negative elements. That's why we have a team of specialists in every discipline to detect and deal with anything out of the ordinary."

"How do you know what's ordinary for me? You know very little about me."

"That's true, but that's where you and your loved ones come in. This is a true team effort, Thomas. Don't you think that they have been influenced by your accident in much the same way that you have? They will be at your side helping you to recall everything about your life that defines you. Don't you realize that all they care about is that you are alive and are getting better?"

"You think?"

"I most certainly do. For years I've been helping TBI patients recover their personas. Of course there will be changes in you as well as in them; that's to be expected. My god, Thomas, we all changes every day and our friends and families are constantly adjusting. That's part of life. No one will be judging you, if anything, given the situation; they will be cutting you some slack. You would do the same if the positions were reversed. True?"

"I guess you're right. I didn't think about it that way, but I see your point."

"Okay, then, let's not talk about that anymore. I'll schedule your testing for noon today."

* * *

Dr. Freenold arrived on time at the Owensburg Country Club.

"I'm over here, Arnold."

Dr. Jensen had reserved a booth away from the bar so that they could hear each other better.

The bar at the club tended to be a raucous mix of golfers either bragging or complaining about their day on the course.

Frederick had a Johnny Walker Blue label on the rocks in front of him. "What'll you be having, Sir?"

"I'll have a vodka martini."

Frederick caught the attention of the waiter. "Get my friend here a vodka martini. Make it top shelf."

Minutes later they raised their glasses for a toast. Frederick offered, "Here's to the continued remarkable progress of our favorite patient, Thomas Mortinson."

Arnold added, "And to the continued successes of the team dedicated to his full recovery."

"So how did Thomas respond to the operation?"

"Very well, for the most part. My initial post-operative cognitive testing showed only a slight diminution from the original testing. From what I can tell, the operation was a success."

"That's good news. I can't think of a nicer reason for us to celebrate. Check out the menu. I recommend the steak and lobster combination; the chef is top rated."

"I think I will do just that. Those are two of my favorites."

When the waiter brought drink refills, he took their food orders and left them to continue their conversation.

"There is one small thing that came up while Thomas and I were reviewing his schedule. Out of nowhere he expressed a concern that his family might be disappointed in the *Thomas* that emerges from this incident. He's worried that the accident and operation may have lasting effects on him physically and mentally. Of course, he's right. There is no way that he and his loved ones could go through the severity of a GCS 5 and all that it entails and not suffer some noticeable changes. The point that Thomas fails to see is that changes are to be expected. That doesn't mean that the changes that do occur are so significant that they won't be compensated for. If I recall correctly, your report of the first blue-line visit said that Thomas apologized for being in the accident."

"Yes, he did, and his father quickly assured him that he in no way was responsible for what happened…that he was just in the wrong place at the wrong time. He seemed to be satisfied with that assurance."

"Yes, but it's something that we must be on the lookout for. When a TBI patient opens up avenues for negative thinking, it can quickly turn to depression and hamper any continued progress toward a full recovery. I think we talked it through, but it's something we need to keep an eye on, in case it returns. I hope he will work his way through it. I'd rather not administer antidepressants, with the healing from the Crainiectomy still going on.

"I'll make a note of that and make sure that everyone on my team is aware of that possibility. We'll do everything possible to keep things upbeat."

The food arrived, and they did their best to keep the conversation light for the rest of the meal; if you consider the presidential race to be light conversation.

CHAPTER 51

Peter Westlake was ushered into Walter's office by a female police officer. It was one of the more attractive town offices, having been decorated at cost by an interior decorator friend of the Peyton family.

"Peter, it's good to see you. How are things down at City Hall?"

"As good as can be expected given the circumstances and certainly a lot better than a month ago. That's part of the reason for my visit, but before I start how are things coming along with Thomas?"

"A lot better than the doctors originally thought. He's finished with the surgical procedures and we'll be concentrating on his physical rehabilitation."

"I'm so glad to hear that."

"Well, have a seat and tell me what's on your mind."

"I'm chairing a sub-committee vetting candidates Mayor and your name is at the top of the list."

"Are you serious?"

"Very. Please hold any questions until you hear me out. To begin with, you have an outstanding record as Sheriff, but the thing that impressed us the most was the way you handled your department during the crisis. We had a lot of complaints about other public servants over the past six weeks, but not one about you or your department. That says something about your leadership skills. The town needs that kind of leadership now. My fellow committee members and the Council as a whole are unanimous in your endorsement for the next Mayor of Owensburg.

"Now before you say anything, let me tell you about changes we made in the position. The Council made several changes that make the Mayor's job more attractive. For one, it is no longer an elective office. The Mayor will report directly to the Council. We realized also that the position will have many demands placed on it due to the accident out at Tiecher Park. To ease the burden, a new position, that of Vice-Mayor has been approved. The Mayor will choose his Vice-Mayor.

"I know that you have strong ties to the Sheriff's office, but as Mayor, you will have oversight, so it will still under your purview. Now as for administrative issues, your salary will be bumped thirty thousand dollars a year to start. All accrued benefits and employment records will be transferred to the new job.”

"Walt, I'm not going to sugar coat this offer; it is what it is. It will be hard work, but we are confident that you are the man for the job.”

Peter stopped talking and sat back in his chair to await Walter's response.

"Peter, first let me first say that I am honored to be offered the job as Mayor and I am flattered by your assessment of my qualifications. These are difficult times for Owensburg and all of its residents have an obligation to support the town leadership as they go about restoring order. I will consider your offer very seriously, but I need time to discuss this with Emily. I will give you my answer tomorrow morning.”

"That's all I can ask for. In the interim, if you have any questions, here is my private cell phone number. Don't hesitate to call about anything that concerns you." He handed Walter his business card, shook hands and left the office.

* * *

"What do you think? I told him I would give him an answer by tomorrow morning.”

Walter had just gone over the details of Peter Westlake's offer. He couldn't tell from her expression, whether or not Emily liked it.

"It looks like a wonderful opportunity. After all you didn't plan on being Sheriff forever. This is like a gift from heaven, but of course it's your decision."

"So, you think I should accept the offer?"

"Absolutely. You're a good leader and administrator. The town needs you right now."

'But, what about Thomas?"

"What about Thomas? A different job isn't going to affect your participation in his recovery. He has a team supporting him, remember?"

"You're right and the extra salary will help with those expenses not covered by insurance. Okay, then give the new Mayor a hug."

They hugged for several minutes and then Emily suggested that he call Peter right away to get things moving. He grabbed the phone and dialed the private number Peter gave him.

After two rings, Peter answered. "This is Peter Westlake, how can I help you?"

"Peter, Walter here. I've decided to accept your offer."

"That's great. You won't regret making that decision. You are just what the town needs right now. Is tomorrow at noon too soon to swear you in? I'm sure that I can round up the Council and the Press by then. Bring the family and weather permitting we'll conduct the ceremony on the City Hall steps.

"I'll appoint Deputy Sheriff Wes Kaufman immediately to take over for me on an interim basis until I can make it official. He's well qualified to take over my duties. Tomorrow at noon will be perfect. I'll see you then."

It looks as if events are working out well for Walter and Emily Peyton, but will that be the case for the rest of our characters? Let's take a look and see.

CHAPTER 52

Visits for the first five days, back behind the red line in the hall, were frustrating for the foursome, but all was forgotten when, on the sixth day, they were ushered into Room 333 and greeted by Thomas, sans the eye patches. Although they still had to stand behind the blue line, being able to look into his eyes and see the love they projected, made any inconvenience they had to go through well worth bearing.

Thomas's eyes darted from one to another as he experienced the emotions of a man finally returning to a world of sensibility. He wasn't the only one in the room whose eyes began welling with tears. As some drops began the journey down his cheeks, a RN stepped forward with a cotton pad and sponged them up.

"I can't tell you all how it feels to be able to see you. The last time you were here I could only hear your voices, and my heart was crying out to be able to lay eyes on you. Hi, Mom, Louise, Dad. Looking straight at Miriam he said, I guess you must be Miriam Walton. I'm very pleased to meet you."

This was the first time that her son had spoken directly to her and the experience was disconcerting. She had played the scenario over and over in her head very often and had worked up dozens of rejoinders…all of which totally escaped her at the moment. All she could come up with was, "I'm pleased to meet you too, Thomas."

Walter asked, "Are the eye patches off for good"

"According to Dr. Freenold, they are. It took me almost twelve hours to get my eyes back in focus, but according to the tests they've been conducting my eyesight and figure/color recognition is now normal."

Louise responded, "I'm so glad, dear. This is all so wonderful. Dr. Jensen says that next week we'll be able to hold your hand. I'll be so glad to get rid of this darn blue line. It's exasperating to be so close and not be able to reach out to you."

"I feel the same way. It's like being confined behind a glass wall…look but don't touch.

When did you say that would be?"

"It's supposed to be when we visit next Monday."

"It can't come fast enough." He looked toward Walter. "Dad, you look like the cat that swallowed the canary. What's up?"

"Show some respect there, young man, you're talking to the new Mayor of Owensburg."

"You're kidding."

Emily jumped in, "No he isn't. He was sworn-in on the steps of City Hall yesterday."

"That's so awesome, congratulations"

"Thanks, son."

Next, he turned to Louise. "I really miss you. I'm glad you're staying with my folks."

"I miss you too, but I'll be here every day they allow us to and hopefully we'll get you out of here soon."

"Dr. Freenold says I'm making great progress: the fastest recovery he's ever seen. I'm going to do everything I can to stay on that track." He switched his attention to Miriam.

"I understand you have experience in Sports Medicine. Have you ever seen anyone as messed up as this?"

Miriam smiled, "Are you kidding. How about a quarterback that got jackknifed by two three hundred-pound tackles? If ever there was a candidate for a full skeletal transplant, he would be it. He had to mend over twelve individual bones and relearn how to stand, walk and lift. He even needed to learn a new way to breath. It took him over twenty-four months to complete his therapy and then he was only operating at about seventy-five percent of his previous capability. From what I have heard about your case, so far, you will not be dealing anywhere near that level of rehabilitation."

"Well, that's good news. I really want to thank you for taking an interest in my recovery. Have you recovered fully from your own concussion?

"Yes, I have, and thanks for asking. Personally, and professionally I know what you are going through. I'm just thankful that your family is allowing me to make whatever small contribution I can towards your rehabilitation."

He smiled, "It's not small and it is greatly appreciated. You're a very special person. Miriam Walton."

After several seconds, Miriam replied, "I'm happy I can be of help." *I can't believe this. My son thinks I'm a special person. I hope he still feels that way after he finds out the truth about me.*

Yes, but we've got a lot more story to tell before that happens

CHAPTER 53

He was surprised by a knock on the door of his room. 11:30pm is a little late for visitors.

"Whose there?"

"It's me, Miriam."

Mike rushed to the door and threw it open. In the hall stood Miriam soaking wet from the brief storm that had blown over about five minutes ago.

"My god, get in here. Get out of those wet clothes." He couldn't tell whether the drops rolling down her cheeks were tears or from the rain; most likely rain.

She shed the raincoat and fell into his arms. They kissed, feeding on the hunger that they both had felt since the moment they professed their love for one another. Mike swept her up and carried her to the bed. "It's been a while…too long.

"I just couldn't stay away. There's no sense in depriving myself of your love."

"I'm glad you realized that," he said, as he gently removed her clothes and then his bathrobe. As they did the first time, they made love passionately at first and then tenderly as they lost themselves in the joy of the moment.

Once their emotional and physical needs were sated, they laid back on the pillows their heads towards one another.

"I'm sure glad you decided not to wait."

"I am too. I've been going to sleep every night with an image of you on my mind. All day my thoughts drift to you… and us. I don't know why I was so fearful that I couldn't be with you and still be there for Thomas."

"Speaking of Thomas, how is he coming along?"

"Just wonderfully. They finished the operation on his skull and took of the patches from his eyes. I got to look into his beautiful blue eyes. They were just like his fathers, but the really great news is that he talked to me about my being there to help him. He actually said, 'You're a very special person, Miriam Walton.' God, I hope he feels that way when he finds out the truth. What if he hates me?"

"Now don't talk like that. You are in an envious position of being able to work with your son during his rehabilitation. He will get the opportunity to know you over that time. Besides, you have the full support of Emily, Louise and Walter. I honestly don't think you have anything to worry about."

"You've had other clients with this problem. How did it go with them?"

"You're right, I have had at least half a dozen cases like yours and only once did the child refuse to have anything to do with his birth-mother. The child was seventeen and on drugs and he made it clear that if she ever came anywhere near him he would kill her. Social workers involved in the case reported that he blamed her for his condition and that nothing they tried would convince him otherwise. She was very depressed and overdosed with sleeping pills the next day."

"Oh, my god, how awful."

"Yes, it was. That was the last case of this kind I undertook, before you showed up in my office one day. I almost turned you down, but there was something special about you that prompted me to listen to your situation. I'm sure glad I did."

Miriam leaned over and kissed him. "I'm glad you did too. Speaking about your practice, have you done anything about getting a license to practice here in Ohio?"

"I spoke with someone the other day. There is no reciprocity between Pennsylvania and Ohio, so I would have to apply to take the Ohio bar exam. That's not a problem. The person I spoke to has a practice here in Owensburg and he seemed interested in taking on a partner."

"That's wonderful. Is that really what you want to do?"

"Well that depends a lot on you and your long-range plans"

"I think you know what they are. Even after Thomas recovers completely, I will still probably make Owensburg my home again. There's nothing for me back in Spartanville."

"I know this is going to seem very sudden, but I want to be where you are. I've worked with you for so long now that I probably know you better that anyone else. What I'm saying is that I want to marry you and settle down."

"Oh, Mike. You don't know how much that means to me. I want the same thing. My life has been in such shambles, with Nathan walking out on me and Thomas being hurt."

They kissed again.

"How do you think we should go about this, what with all that is going on?"

"That's a good question. It's not just us we have to be concerned about."

They both got quiet, neither wanting to suggest anything that would delay their desired union. Finally, Mike offered, "What if we make plans to get married in about six months? That way Thomas will be well along with his rehabilitation, and I should be set up with a practice here in town."

"It sounds like such a long time to have to wait."

"Yes, it does, but I can't see how we can do anything sooner."

"I'd opt for getting married right away, but for one thing, how it would look."

"I'm not worried about what some narrow-minded busy-bodies will think. I've long since given up letting other people run my life. Is public opinion the only reason?

"No, actually, I was thinking more about how much work I'm going to have when the physical rehabilitation kicks in for Thomas. I've worked with enough injured athletes to know that your time is not your own. I wouldn't be much of a wife for you while that is going on."

"I see your point. Now that I think about it taking the bar exam and setting up a practice would tie me up a lot. When it comes to the heart, I hate doing anything *practical,* but it does seem to work out best if we postpone our nuptials until the dust settles in our lives. Let's announce our engagement, though; ring and everything and pick a date six-months from now. What do you say, Miriam Walton…will you be my wife?"

"Yes, of course I will."

"I guess you wouldn't consider moving in here with me until we can find suitable lodging."

"Shame on you, Mike Tolliver. Are you trying to besmirch my reputation in this town?"

"You can't blame a guy for trying."

"There will be no more talk like that."

"Yes, Ma'am."

They rolled over and made love again, this time complete with a vision of their future together.

CHAPTER 54

It is not unusual for family members of TBI patients to have many questions about the recovery and rehabilitation of their love ones. How long before they will be back to normal?

What will be the long-term effects of the brain injury? How well will they function in the future? What if they never are the same again?

Unfortunately, there are no easy answers. TBI research is a relatively new area and how a patient will function months and years out continues to be beyond the pale of predictability. A multitude of physical and behavioral issues can complicate the process making it near impossible to predict the outcome of a TBI procedure. For instance, age and pre-injury condition can have a major influence on the outcome as does the timing of the initial corrective surgery and the temperament of the patient.

The types of injury to the brain and secondary damage also have a bearing on the eventual outcome. Depending on the area of the brain affected, brain functions can be impaired requiring addressing memory, speech, decision making, balance, physical coordination. If extensive testing indicates that a brain function cannot be restored, then the patient must learn how to compensate for that function.

It is the aim of the staff at the George Bennett Baxter Trauma Center to address these issues utilizing the most up-to-date technology and Neurosurgery experience available. It was towards that end that they invited Dr. Arnold R. Freenold one of the top Neurosurgeons in the country to head up the team that would be responsible for the care of Thomas Mortinson who entered the Center with a Glasgow Coma Score of 5. Dr. Freenold had a world-wide reputation for the successful rehabilitation of dozens of patients with GSC scores less than 7.

* * *

Thomas completed the drill for the third time. Two Physical Therapists worked with him for the past three hours concentrating on simple movements of the arms, hands, legs and feet; all done while he laid flat on the bed. He found the exercises tiring at first, but the encouragement of the therapists and progress he was making using his limbs kept him going.

Dr. Freenold joined the team as they completed the last set. He watched and made notes as Thomas made the movements required of him.

"Bravo," he said as clapped at the final exercise. "That's excellent. You're doing great, Thomas. Why don't you rest a few minutes while we'll give these fine people a chance to pack up their gear and then we will do some special movements?"

Minutes later they were alone except for an RN watching the monitors.

"What we're going to do now is work on your neck muscles. Your head has been restrained from the first minutes that you were discovered. It's time now for us to restore normal movement to your neck and shoulders. I'll need a few minutes to remove the Head and Neck Support System; you won't need that any longer. When it's gone, just lay your head back on the pillow and then we'll begin a series of movements that will reeducate all your neck and shoulder muscles and nerves.

It took Freenold and the RN over ten minutes to disconnect the equipment from the bed without jostling their patient too much in the process. When they were finished, Thomas was able to lie back on the pillow for the first time since he arrived at the hospital.

Finally, Dr. Freenold said, "There you go…free at last."

Thomas smiled, "That's one way of putting it."

"Now before you make any sudden moves, keep your head still for a few more minutes.

We'll be doing a series of movements in a special order. They will sound easy at first, but you will probably experience some difficulty simply because most of those muscles have been immobile for a long time."

During the next hour Dr. Freenold ran Thomas through a battery of tests that required Thomas to exert specific muscle groups in a specific order; the intent being to stretch his neck and shoulder muscles. Thomas responded well to the exercises until they came to his shoulders. There he experienced pain in his left shoulder. This wasn't entirely unexpected in as much as he had broken his left collarbone in the accident. To offset this, the Doctor started a new set of exercises aimed at stimulating the area around the break. He continued these for over fifteen minutes until Thomas felt a relaxing of the shoulder muscles. That done, the original set was resumed, this time without any pain.

"We're almost done here. We'll repeat these tests tomorrow morning after your visitors leave. You will be free to hold hands with them, but I must caution you that you must not attempt to raise your body to hug anyone, because the muscles you would need to use haven't been resuscitated yet and to use them prematurely can cause a setback to the progress we've made so far. I know it will be hard not to hug them, but we can't risk using certain muscle groups until the proper time. Do you understand what I'm saying?"

"Yes, of course. I won't do anything that could impede my progress. Remember I'm the one whose looking forward to the day I can shake your hand and thank you for making me well."

The doctor smiled. "Okay then, but just to be sure, I'll remind Dr. Jensen to instruct your visitors about the rules. I know that they will understand that we must err on the side of being overly cautious."

"I'm sure they will cooperate."

"One other thing, after we have our session tomorrow, you will be scheduled to repeat the hand and leg exercises you did today. That way we can improve on the overall movements you were tested for.

"I guess we can end this session, now. As usual, you have outperformed my expectations. Just take it easy. Don't over exert yourself. Enjoy your new-found freedom. We have a lot of work ahead of us, still and we don't want to waste time going back to correct mistakes. You have a good night Thomas, and I'll see you in the morning.

"You too, Doctor."

CHAPTER 55

Emily, with the help of Louise finished setting up the family's dinner on the sun porch. Louise left to round up Miriam and Walter.

"Please sit down everyone. Let's say grace…Heavenly Father, bless this food and this gathering with your love. Continue to bless our Thomas as he recovers. Bring him back to our fold soon. Amen"

"Amen," by all.

"Okay, let's do justice to this roast. Walter, would you do the honors with the slicing?"

"Consider it done."

They spent the next half hour eating and engaging in small talk. As soon as the dishes were cleared away and the coffee and desert in front of them, Emily turned over the cover of a writing tablet. "While you're enjoying the cheesecake, why don't I bring you up-to-date on Thomas?

"I received a phone call from the Trauma Center earlier today. I think you're going to like what I have to tell you. First off, according to Dr. Freenold, Thomas continues to make extraordinary progress with his rehabilitation. They removed the neck and shoulder restraints and began a series of physical exercises to strengthen his neck, shoulders, arms and legs. The next phase of the recovery plan will involve restoring as many physical functions as possible.

The Center is initiating a new protocol that includes family and/or loved ones in the rehab sessions. Apparently, they have studies that show that when the families are involved in the exercises, the response from the patient improves upwards of thirty-five percent."

No one was eating cheesecake. They were hanging on every word Emily spoke.

Emily checked her notes before she continued, "For the next few weeks, the physical therapists will be concentrating on motor functions, coordination, basic movement, balance and simple skills involving getting in and out of the bed, using the bathroom, bathing, dressing and eating. These are skills that we take so much for granted, but to a TBI patient they can present major hurdles."

She turned to Miriam. "Dr. Jensen requested that you take part in the sessions they have set for next Monday, Tuesday and Wednesday mornings at 9am. He mentioned your experience with Sports Medicine and he felt that it would be especially beneficial if you participated in these initial sessions. Any future participation on your part will depend on the progress Thomas makes at these sessions,

Miriam replied, "Oh, that's great." She looked at Emily, Louise and Walter. "You don't mind if I go first, do you?"

In unison, all three responded, "Of course not."

"Thank you. That will be a lot less awkward than me going alone to visit him in his room."

Emily closed the tablet. "There is another issue that we need to discuss. After tomorrow's visitation, Dr. Jensen suggested that instead of a group visit, we limit the number of persons to one or two. His reasoning makes sense to me, but I want to get your take on it. When we are all there, Thomas appears to be overwhelmed. Tension builds as he has to direct his attention to more than one person at a time. Dr. Jensen feels that tomorrow is an exception, because it will be the first time that we can ignore the blue line and be at Thomas's bedside. We will be allowed hold Thomas's hand, but we have been cautioned not to attempt to hug him or kiss him since that could cause involuntary movement in his neck that could cause damage before they have a chance to restore normal functioning. We'll have to keep that in mind, but even so, just to be able to hold his hand will be a blessing after all these weeks."

"You can say that again," Louise said.

"While we're on the subject, we should probably discuss what the doctor said about limiting visitors."

Miriam volunteered, "I will be working with Thomas next week for three days, so I won't need to be involved with daily visitations."

"Thank you, Miriam, that makes sense. What I'm thinking is that Louise should be the first to visit him alone. After all, she was the last one to be with him before the accident. Walter and I can go together the next time."

Walter nodded his agreement.

"Thank you. Are you sure?"

"Yes, of course, Louise. You're the logical one."

"There is so much I want to say to him. The kind of stuff that's hard to say standing behind a blue line with other people party to the conversation." She thought a moment about what she had just said, "Oh, I'm sorry. I didn't mean that the way it sounded. I just meant that it's hard to express yourself when others are in the room. You know what I mean."

Walter answered, "Yes, Louise, we know what you meant, and I think you are the best choice to be the first."

"Well, now that that's settled, let's do justice to this cheesecake."

Miriam raised her hand, "Just a small piece for me. I have a date with Mike tonight and he always likes to stop at a small café for a light snack. I don't know how he does it. He has the appetite of a lumberjack, but he never seems to put on weight. I guess he has one of those overactive metabolisms takes care of those extra calories."

Walter rubbed his mid-section. "I sure wish I had me one of those metabolisms."

* * *

Thomas was anticipating today's visit in spite of Dr. Jensen reminder about the no-hug rule.

His eyes lit up as Emily, Louise and Walter entered his room. Emily and Walter went to the right side of the bed and Louise to the left. He immediately reached for Louise's hand as he felt Emily grasp his right hand.

"It's so great to touch you all again. It's funny how you miss something as simple as a touch; how often we take things like that for granted."

Emily let go of his hand so that Walter could hold it. Thomas immediately tightened his grip. "How is it going Mr. Mayor?"

"Just perfect, son. I see you still have a nice firm handshake."

"That will have to do for now. It'll be a while before we can arm wrestle again."

"All good things in time."

Louise was rubbing his hand against her face. "It's so nice to feel your touch again. I don't know if you heard yet, but Miriam will be working with the Physical Therapists for three of your sessions next week. And Monday afternoon I'll be visiting you alone for about a half-hour. I can't wait."

"Neither can I. That's really good news."

The rest of the visit was spent on bringing Thomas up-to-date on what was going on in Owensburg. When the half-hour was up, Thomas's dinner arrived so they said their goodbyes and left.

CHAPTER 56

"I can't believe that I will be working with the Physical Therapists three days next week."

Mike looked surprised. "You mean you will actually be working at the Center on Thomas's exercises? That's incredible."

"Yes, it is. They have a new protocol that includes family members and loved ones as part of the schedule. Apparently, they discovered over the years that patients respond better to the rigors of therapy if they go through it with someone they know. I thank god for getting such a chance. I was at my wits end trying to figure out how to get closer to my son and then along came this opportunity.

"I'm happy for you Miriam. You deserve a break. When will you be doing this?"

"Next Monday, Tuesday and Wednesday mornings at the Center's Physical Therapy suite. I'll have to go through some training myself, before I work with Thomas, but that shouldn't be a problem. I've done a lot of work with injured athletes at my job. I can't imagine that they do things too differently."

"I'll bet you never imagined that your job would be instrumental in helping you know Thomas."

"Not in a million years. It's funny how things work out. One of the reasons that I chose that particular vocation was because I wanted to help young men reclaim their lives after they were injured either playing sports or from driving accidents. It was my way at the time of giving something back. Does that sound strange to you?"

"Not at all, it makes perfect sense. That's why I chose Family Law."

Mike pulled her close. "You're a very giving person, Miriam."

The hug led to a kiss and subsequently to the two of them spending the next two hours in bed.

CHAPTER 57

Dr. Jensen did the introductions. "Miriam Walton this is Wendy Marshall. She's the lead Physical Therapist assigned to Thomas."

Miriam shook her hand, "I'm pleased to meet you."

"Same here."

"I updated Wendy on your experience in Sports Medicine."

"Yes. We're glad to have an extra hand, especially someone with your unique skills. I'd like to take a few minutes to outline what we will be doing for the next three days…"

Dr. Jensen interrupted Wendy," I don't think you will need me for the next couple of hours. I'll be back at eleven to wrap things up." With that he left them to their work.

The ladies sat down, and Wendy showed Miriam the plan for the morning. "Dr. Freenold chose the Turnwell Convention for our sessions. Are you familiar with that discipline?"

"Yes, we used it quite often."

"That's great. It will save me a lot of explaining. Well then, we might as well get things set up. They will be bringing Thomas down in a few minutes.

* * *

Dr. Jensen arrived just as they were getting ready to return Thomas to his room. "Well, Thomas, how did your first day of PT go?"

"If you're asking, 'am I exhausted', the answer is yes. If you are asking if I made much progress, you'll have to ask these lovely ladies here," he said motioning his head towards Wendy and Miriam.

"What do you say, ladies. Did our patient cooperate with the program?"

Wendy looked at her clip board. "It looks like he scored a seventy-two which is very good for a first day. We had a few rough spots and I even think I heard him utter an expletive under his breath, but that too is par for the course given the amount of exertion we demanded from him."

Thomas looked embarrassed. "I apologize if I said anything off-color. I must have been caught up in the moment."

"Oh, don't be silly. If I had a nickel for every swear word uttered in this room, I could take an extended all expenses paid vacation to Hawaii."

Dr. Jensen turned to Miriam. How does our work here compare to the Sports Medicine venue you work in?

"Actually, it is quite similar. Many of our sports injuries involved concussions so we use the Turnwell Convention quite often. It was by far the best option in those cases."

"Thomas, how was it working with someone from outside the center?'

"It was good, Doctor. She was just as tough with me as Wendy was and I was glad of that; maybe not at the time, but now that it's over I am glad she didn't cut me any slack. I know I'm not going to get out of here until I can do all this stuff right. So, Miriam, thank you."

"You're more than welcome, Thomas. You're no different than the jocks I've had to work with. They want to get well so they can get back on the field. The motivation for you is the same and I admire you for it."

"Thank you, that means a lot to me. I promise both you ladies that I will try extra hard tomorrow. You'll be very pleased with the results."

Wendy replied, "That's the spirit. I'm going to hold you to that."

Miriam nodded her agreement.

* * *

Once again, Dr. Jensen showed up at the end of the second day's session.

"So, how did it go for day two?"

They all looked down.

Wendy offered, "It didn't go as well as we expected. Score wise, only forty-eight percent."

Jensen looked surprised. "What happened?"

Thomas answered, "It wasn't them, it was me. I just couldn't do some of the exercises. I either didn't understand what I was supposed to do, or I just couldn't get my body to do what was required. Either way I just couldn't do any more."

"Well, don't let that bother you. It's not unusual to have setbacks, especially when you've been on a fast track. You go on back to your room and I'll have a look at what you did accomplish today. We'll resume our sessions tomorrow morning."

As soon as they wheeled Thomas out of the room, Wendy addressed Dr. Jensen, "Thomas gave an accurate assessment of what happened today. The demands of the exercises seemed to require more strength than he could muster. I could see that he was really trying to keep up, trying to do what we required, but he just didn't have the strength to do it. I know that he will eventually meet the requirements, but we're going to have to go a little slower. I hope I'm not speaking out of turn, but is

Dr. Freenold certain that Turnwell is the best discipline for Thomas's condition?"

"I'll certainly discuss that with him. Thank you for your honest assessment."

* * *

Dr. Arnold Freenold slammed his fist on the table. "So now my decisions are being second-guessed by Therapists. How many TBI cases have they managed? What's wrong with this world today? Everybody with a little experience thinks they're a damn expert."

"I'm sorry, Doctor. Perhaps I shouldn't have said anything. It's just that this has been the first significant setback for Thomas and it took everyone by surprise."

Freenold was silent for a few minutes. "I'm sorry for the outburst. I guess that was my ego talking. Of course, we must look at our choice of conventions. After all, this is supposed to be a team…all input should be invited and respected. Now let me see, Turnwell came the closest to meeting the needs of Thomas Mortinson. If that is failing us it appears that we need to be innovative in our approach. I'm going to join you tomorrow for his next session. Call a meeting a half hour before for you, me, Mrs. Walton and Wendy to go over alternative protocols."

He sighed and put his hand on Dr, Jensen's shoulder. "Frederick, sometimes this work makes me feel old"

"I know what you mean, Arnold. Why don't you join me at my club, tonight? We can discuss this some more."

"I think that would be a capital idea."

"I'll see you at seven, then."

CHAPTER 58

Louise hurried to Room 333 unaware that Thomas's morning rehab session had not gone too well.

"Louise, I've been waiting for you to get here."

Tears formed in her eyes as she rushed over to the bedside and sat down next to him. She grasped his hand and squeezed it and he did the same. "Oh, Thomas it's so wonderful to be this close to you and to hold your hand. I've missed you so much. I wish I had gone with you when you went to get the wine. Maybe things would have turned out differently."

"Yes, you'd be lying in a bed like this in another room with your head cut open and your body trying desperately to return to normal functioning."

"You don't know that. Maybe we would have returned to our table sooner and avoided the stage entirely when it fell."

"Yes, that's possible…but that's not what happened. Anyway, what's important is that you're safe and I'm mending."

She lifted his hand and kissed it softly. "You're right, I should concentrate on the now. You're getting the best care here at the Center and we should be thankful for that. How did your session go today?"

He got quiet and looked away. "Not well at all. I couldn't seem to muster the strength to do a lot of the exercises. I don't understand it. I did so well the first day. I got a good night's sleep and had a full breakfast, but my strength just seemed to drain out of me. I just couldn't do what they asked me to. I've never experienced that condition before. I used to do a lot of training when I played ball. We started slowly and worked our way up to the harder exercises, just as we are doing here. I was always exhausted by the time we finished, but it came on slowly. This thing today just overwhelmed me."

"What did the Therapist and Miriam say about that?"

"They were as surprised as I was. My scores were really low. They were talking about slowing down the pace a bit until I was ready. I feel like I let everyone down."

"Don't talk like that, Thomas. Isn't it possible that Dr. Freenold overestimated the level of your recovery and assigned an improper program?

What do they call it, a convention or something like that?"

"The Turnwell Convention."

"That's it. It is possible that they were misled by the rapid progress you've shown. He did say that each TBI case is different. Isn't it possible that they should be taking a different approach to your rehabilitation?

"Of course, anything is possible."

"Well then I'll discuss that with Miriam at dinner tonight."

"I don't see how that can do any harm. I just want to get back on track. I miss being with you. I hate being apart from you and not to be able to hold you and make love to you."

Louise's face reddened. "You sure have a silver tongue, Thomas Mortinson. You know I feel the same way. When I saw that 'Beast" fall on you I thought I had lost you forever. It was the worst moment of my life." Tears were cascading down her cheek.

Thomas reached out and tried to rub them away, but they were dropping faster than his thumb could erase them. "Please don't cry. Everything is going to work out for us. You'll see."

"I know, but just the thought of being without you tears at me. I can't help it."

"There is nothing that can keep us apart. In fact, I have a confession to make. I was planning to propose to you when the show was over. I had a ring and everything."

Louise reached into her pocketbook and brought out the ring box. "This ring?"

"That's it. Where did you get it?"

"It was with your personal things when you were brought here. Walter thought you would want me to hold it for you." She took the ring from the box and handed it to Thomas.

He took the ring and in the most somber of voices asked her, "Louise O'Neill, will you marry me?"

"Yes, of course I will. He brought her hand up to his lips and kissed it. "This will have to do for now."

She put the ring on her finger and held it out to admire it. "It's a beautiful ring and it's a perfect fit. How did you know my size?"

"Oh, I borrowed a ring from your jewelry box."

"The ring with the three pearls?"

"Yes, how did you know?"

"I was missing it one day. I looked all over and couldn't find it. Days later it suddenly appeared again in my jewelry box. I thought that I had just missed it while I was searching."

"I never saw you wearing it. I thought it would be safe to borrow it. Just my luck that you would suddenly miss it."

Thomas's voice became serious, "I wish that the circumstances were better. When I planned to propose, things were very different than they are now. I don't even know what I will be like when they finish the rehab. There are a lot of unanswered questions that usually don't come with a proposal of marriage. Are you sure you want to go through with this?"

"Now you stop that kind of talk. We're in this together. If the shoe were on the other foot, you wouldn't back out on me, would you?"

"Of course not."

"Well then I don't want to hear any more about it. We need to concentrate on getting you up to par. I'll talk to Miriam when I get home and see what this convention stuff is all about. In the interim I want you to get as much rest as you can and to keep upbeat."

"I will. I'm going to try harder tomorrow because I know that you and everyone else are counting on me. I don't want to let any of you down."

"Don't you worry about what others are expecting, Thomas, do your best because it's what you want."

He looked embarrassed, "You're right, of course."

They just held hands and looked into the other's eyes until the RN motioned to her that the visiting time was up. Louise kissed his hand and said, "I have to go now. I love you."

Thomas kissed her hand and said, "I love you too."

CHAPTER 59

"I called this meeting, because it seems that what we've been doing for Thomas Mortinson, may not be the best protocol for his rehabilitation. I recognize that those of you on the front lines, as it were, have a golden opportunity to see first-hand how our therapies are impacting a patient. I value that. Keep in mind that where Craniectomies are involved, the ability of the patient to react to a specific convention may vary significantly from the norm. That seems to be what we are dealing with in Thomas's case.

"There are several approaches we can take. One would be to try the Patel Convention or the Davis Convention, but they don't offer a significantly high enough response level. Another approach, one which I am recommending is to continue to use the Turnwell Convention, but to alter the exercises in a unique way. What I'm suggesting is that we use input from Thomas to guide us with the steps we take. In other words, Thomas will tell us how he wants to perform a required exercise rather than us telling him what we want him to do. The benefit from this will be that he will be suggesting steps that he feels he can perform. This alone should provide a psychological boost that is always desired in these cases."

"Wendy asked, "Wouldn't that drastically slow down the program? I would think that if the going got tough, Thomas would opt for the easiest exercises rather that the toughest."

"That is certainly possible, but we're dealing with a patient who has a strong desire to put this all behind him and get on with his life. I would think that Thomas's motivation would be strong enough to overcome the desire to take the easy way out. Dr. Jensen and I discussed this last night and he feels, that at this juncture, we have very little to lose and much to gain. We will still be following Turnwell, but we will be modifying our approach to the patient by involving him in the choice of individual steps."

He looked at Miriam, "What do you think about this approach?"

"I think that it is certainly worth a try." She turned to Wendy. "You know, yesterday when Thomas was struggling with the vertical lift and he let out an expletive, what if we had asked him right then how he would do it? Maybe he would have suggested another way and he might have been able to complete the drill."

Wendy thought for a minute. "You may be right. At this point I'm for giving it a try."

Dr. Freenold smiled, "I'm glad we are all on-board. Let's go in there and make it work."

* * *

Thomas liked the idea. "Quite a few times I was sure that doing a set differently would have worked better, but I decided that you were the professionals and knew what was best for me, so I kept quiet about it. I'm ready to give this a try if you are."

They worked with the new discipline for a half hour longer than planned, but by the time they finished they made up the lost time from the previous day and recorded scores in the high eighties.

Dr. Freenold was very pleased with the results and didn't waste a minute letting everyone know. "That's what I love about working in science, there is so much to learn; so many things to try. I'm very proud of you Thomas."

"Thank you, Doctor. I'm very tired, but it's a good tired. That change was obviously the right choice to make. Thank you all for coming up with it."

Miriam and Wendy helped him back into the wheelchair. Wendy remarked, "If you keep up this kind of progress it won't be long before we can trade in this chair for a walker."

"I look forward to that day and then to the day I can walk out of here under my own power. Again, thank you all for your patience with me. I know it can't be easy standing by and watching a person struggle to do basic moves that everyone takes for granted. I'm blessed to have you all working with me."

As the nurse started to wheel him back to his room he added, "I'm really looking forward to tomorrow's session."

Dr. Jensen said, "As are we, Thomas. See you then"

* * *

The doctors met in Dr. Jensen's office.

"Who knew? If you had suggested to me that before Thomas's rehabilitation was complete, we would be making a major change in the Convention, I would have told you that you were out of your mind. We continue to demonstrate how little we really know about the human brain."

"How true. I'm as surprised as you are about how successful the new approach was. Not because of the results per se, but because the scores took a quantum leap. Arnold, I think you are on to something major, here."

Freenold laughed, "Hold the presses at the New England Journal of Medicine…we have a major breakthrough."

"You may laugh, but this variation of the Turnwell Convention is significant, and we have the figures to prove it."

"You think? Maybe we should start calling it the Freenold Convention."

"All kidding aside," Jensen suggested, "I think you should keep that in mind as you document Thomas's progress. This is the very thing that advances in our field are built on.

You saw the difference with your own eyes. Many of the exercises that Thomas aced today were impossible for him yesterday. His participation in the decision making was key to his success. I've never heard of taking that approach before and I've been in this field for over thirty years. I'm current on my journal reading and I attend several major mental health conventions every year. This is new and it's genius. I'm proud to be working next to you while you are fine tuning it. This is a real boon for the Center."

"You flatter me, Frederick. Remember it was me who got his nose out-of-joint when I heard that the therapists were questioning whether my choice of Turnwell was the right convention for Thomas. It just goes to prove that inspiration can come from any venue.

"I think you may be right. If this wasn't a GCS 5 I wouldn't consider such a thing, but by documenting a new convention, we have the opportunity to offer to our fellow Neurosurgeons a discipline that can possibly make the difference between their patients living a trouble-free life or one where their future is full of limitations.

"Think about it for a minute, the way things work today, if a convention is followed to the letter, we settle for whatever condition the patient ends up in and send them off to live life to the best of their ability. What a travesty this is and to think that you and I have been proponents of this approach for much of our professional lives."

He high-fived Frederick. "By George, let's do it. I want you to co-author this new convention with me."

Surprised, Jensen immediately accepted, "Thank you, Arnold, it would be an honor."

"Great then. N.E.J.M. here we come. I think that this calls for a celebration. It's my turn to treat. Do you know a good steakhouse; someplace where one can get a nice juicy steak and a couple of Vodka Martinis? You choose the spot and make the reservations."

"I know just the spot. It's new, but they have the best steaks in town. I know the chef, so there won't be any difficulty getting in. How does seven sound?"

"Great, that will give me time to go over my notes so that everything is in line with our new enterprise."

CHAPTER 60

"What's the good of being the Mayor if you can't pull a few strings now and then? Your new office furniture will be delivered tomorrow. Try to use that old stuff until then."

This remark was in response to his Vice-Mayor, Cal Bronson's request to make changes to the office space that the Town Council had him assigned in the Owensburg Town Hall building. It wasn't the size or location of the office, not even the lack of a window that bothered Cal, it was the outdated furnishings that were thrown together to constitute office furniture.

"I sure appreciate it, Walt. That desk must have come with the building when it was established in 1923. It's got grooves all over the top where people wrote messages without a blotter or pad underneath. You can even make out some of the words. It's like a history lesson, but definitely unsuitable for use as an office desk."

"That is certainly not the way for us to welcome our new Vice-Mayor. It's apparent that somebody dropped the ball on this. I apologize."

"Oh, I know it's not your fault. I'll make do until the new furniture gets here. It's not like I'm going to get a lot of visitors today. Heck, nobody even knows I'm here."

"Well that's going to change quickly. I just heard that the State Safety Commission has concluded its investigation of the accident and is expected to make a ruling tomorrow morning at nine at a press conference up in Columbus. I'm going to ask you, as your first official act, to take over the coordination of town affairs related to the clean-up and restoration of the Tiecher Park Theater Area. Once we're given the okay, I want to waste no time getting things back to normal. Owensburg has suffered enough. We can't have this thing dragging out any longer than is absolutely necessary. Just stay clear of any law suits; Payne Easton and a law firm the town hired are taking care of all litigation matters."

"Sounds like a plateful. I'll get right on it."

"You're going to have to walk on eggshells, Cal. There are a lot of people out there that have issues and they are going to be looking for someone to be a punching bag for them."

"Don't worry about that. I've lived in Owensburg for over thirty years and I know most of the people in town."

"That may be so, but this is an extraordinary situation and when people feel they have been disenfranchised, they often forget who their friends are. Just be careful, is all I'm saying."

"I will. Thanks for the advice,"

Walter smiled as Cal turned to leave the office, "If you have any more issues that require me to wave my magic wand, just give me a holler."

"Will do."

CHAPTER 61

Dinner time at the Peyton household was quickly becoming meeting time for updates on Thomas's recovery. Tonight was to be no exception. The "team" was there in addition to Mike Tolliver, who was becoming a regular since his engagement to Miriam.

Emily announced dinner and they came from all over the house. "I hope you all are hungry. I couldn't get a smaller roast than this and I don't have a lot of room in the refrigerator for left-overs."

"Mike volunteered, "Seconds for your meals have never been a problem for me. I think we'll do justice to it."

Walter said, "Amen."

Halfway through the meal, Emily asked, "How did today's session go?"

Miriam answered, "Dr. Freenold joined us today. He tried out a new convention where we look to Thomas for his ideas of how we should conduct specific exercises. It's kind of a radical approach, but it worked better than anyone expected. Thomas's scores rose to the eighties. It was so heartwarming to see the smile on his face as he was able to perform some of the difficult drills we put him through. It looks as if the new approach could speed up Thomas's recovery."

"That's really good news. I was so concerned after he had a problem the other day. Louise said he was really down about it."

"Yes, he was very frustrated by not having the strength to do everything. He especially was upset because he thought he was letting us down. We had a long talk and he promised me to stay positive. It looks as if this new concept didn't come along too soon."

"I'm reminded about the time he had a bad softball game," Walter interjected. "He was routed with ten consecutive hits on thirteen pitches. They hit everything he served up. He was ready to give up pitching. All I heard was, 'I'm no good' and 'I stink.' It took a lot of persuading to get him to calm down and to accept the fact that he would have an occasional day on the mound when he would not have 'his stuff'."

"I remember that night. Your talk with him took him from the dumps to an hour of practice with you in the back yard. I'm sure glad that Dr. Freenold is flexible enough to try new things. I guess that's why he is one of the best Neurosurgeons in the country."

"So, what else is going on. How about you, Mike?"

"I got some good news today. It looks as if I can take the Ohio Bar Exam next month. When they have a back-log of candidates, they give the exams in-between normal qualifying dates. In the interim, I can practice as long as I'm connected with a practicing lawyer; which of course, I am."

Miriam turned to him with a big smile on her face, "I'm so happy for you. Would that mean that you can practice in Ohio and Pennsylvania both?"

"That's right. That could prove to be an advantage with my new partnership. There aren't too many attorneys that practice in two jurisdictions."

Louise, Walter and Emily added their congratulations.

"Your Mayor hired a Vice-Mayor today. His name is Cal Bronson and I assigned him the job of coordinating the rebuilding of the Tiecher Park Theater Area. The State finally concluded their investigation and we can start removing the debris and rebuilding. It can't happen soon enough for me. The town is still in turmoil and I guess that it will go on for some time yet. I think Cal is going to be a great help to me with my new responsibilities."

Turning to Miriam, Emily said, "Well, that catches us up, so maybe this would be a good time for us to discuss when and how you are going to tell Thomas who you really are. It must be tearing at you, working with him on his rehab and not being able to tell him you are his mother."

Miriam looked uncomfortable; not expecting to discuss the subject so soon. "To be honest with you, Emily, I haven't thought about. I'm just so happy with the time I'm getting to spend with him…getting to know him. It even occurred to me that maybe he never needs to know."

Louise wasn't alone in being taken aback by that remark, but she was the first to speak up, "What on earth are you talking about. Of course he needs to know. You can't come this far and then back out."

"It's not a case of backing out, I'm just been wondering lately, with all that has happened to him, whether it is his best interests to dump this on him. I'd never forgive myself if I caused a setback in his condition. Right now, I have a vicarious connection with him that will allow me to be a small part of his life for some time to come. He can know me as a friend of the family, without any further involvement. He doesn't ever have to know the truth, not if it might cause irreparable harm. I could live with that."

Louise countered, "That's ridiculous, Miriam. You know that he has been harboring a deep seated need to know about you. Surely you must realize that it wouldn't be right to let him go the rest of his life without ever knowing that you brought him into this world."

Emily backed up Louise, "I agree. I was his foster mother for over twenty-one years, so that's got to count for something and I'm telling you that if you don't make yourself known to Thomas now that you have this golden opportunity, it will be the biggest mistake of your life. It will be even worse for Thomas if you withhold from him the one chance he has to know the wonderful woman who brought him into this world. It would be a far worse tragedy than the mistake you made when you were a scared young woman. Now let's not hear any more of that kind of talk. We'll get through this together."

Mike put his arm around Miriam. "You should listen to these ladies. They know Thomas a lot better than you do. We have time yet. Thomas is getting stronger every day. You are an important part of that. Of course, I can't know for sure, but I'd be very surprised if Thomas didn't welcome you with open arms. You have the opportunity to be an essential part of his life from now on. It wouldn't be fair to him and it certainly wouldn't be fair to you."

Miriam was bewildered by the outpouring of support. "Maybe, you're right. I just thought that something as mindboggling as this might have the opposite effect and set him back."

Emily took exception, "I don't believe that at all. I think that if we handle this properly, it could be the very thing Thomas needs to complete his recovery. I said *if we handle this properly* because I think we have to do some careful planning about how and when you tell Thomas. We should probably involve both doctors in this before we do anything."

"I hadn't thought much about that, but you're right, of course. So you all think I should go ahead and let Thomas know about me?"

Walter looked around the room and said, "I think it's unanimous. The trick will be to determine the best time. I don't have any doubt at all that Thomas will be happy to have you in his life. I remember when he was about eight, when we asked him if he would want us to formally adopt him. His answer was no. He was very happy living with us but felt that if he was legally adopted, it would make it hard for him to learn his true identity. What that tells me is that he has a deep need to know about his birth mother. Nothing that I have seen since that time would lead me to believe that that need has gone away. Also, you heard Louise say that they had discussed the subject on the day of the accident and he agreed to their hunting for you together. Now if that doesn't prove that you have to tell him, I don't know what does."

"Okay, I agree that Thomas needs to know. I'll listen to what you and the doctors have to say, but when I finally tell him, it will have to feel right. I'll know when the time is right."

They all assured her that it would be her call and offered to help in whatever way they could. To that end Emily suggested, "I suggest that we ladies schedule a meeting with Doctor Jensen to get his take on it. He can do the checking with Doctor Freenold. After we get their input, I think that the five of us should meet at least twice a week to develop plans for getting this done. Maybe there are things that can be done to make everything easier."

She turned to Miriam, "Thank you for letting us be a part of this. I realize that it won't be easy telling Thomas about yourself, but I firmly believe that it is not only the right thing to do, but will ultimately bring us all together as one big happy family."

CHAPTER 62

"Well, Thomas, looks like another successful session this morning. If you keep this up, we're going to have to rewrite the medical journals for the 'Thomas Mortinson Protocols'."

Dr. Freenold was referring to the results he had just received on Thomas's morning session with the Physical Therapists working on his motor skills.

"That's okay with me, Doctor. I'll be happy to set new records from here on out. I was surprised, though, when they insisted on sticking to their prescribed exercises. I made a few suggestions like you said, but they told me that they had to stick with the procedures laid out for them."

"Oh, I'm sorry about that. The new discipline that we introduced yesterday only applies to the work done following the Turnwell Convention. The morning exercises are a totally separate part of the rehabilitation process. I should have been specific about that."

"That's okay, it's not a biggie. I was just surprised."

"Okay then. Let me take a few minutes to explain what we will be doing this afternoon. First of all, I will be participating on the floor for the duration of your Convention treatment. What we will be doing from now on could impact the recoveries of hundreds of future TBI patients and I want to observe every minute of it. Your participation in the decision-making process is now an important part of your rehabilitation. Try not to over exert yourself as we go through the steps. It is normal to want to want to please the Therapists, but I want you to exercise restraint if you are asked to do something that is beyond reason. Your participation is a two-way street. You not only will be expected to make recommendations, but in cases where you can't improve on the way a step is done, you must also point out why we shouldn't ask you to do anything that you feel is wrong. Does that make any sense to you?"

"It does. I think I understand what you are saying. The second day when I couldn't do some of the exercises it was because I was afraid that I would hurt myself if I tried. I didn't know how to express it at the time except to break down…and that's what I did."

"That's good, but for the future, when you get that feeling, you need to tell us. That will provide an opportunity for us to evaluate that step and either modify it or eliminate it."

Freenold put Thomas's file on the table. "Let's talk about you for a few minutes."

"Sure, what do you want to know?"

"Well, for one, I've been working with you for a couple of months, now and I never asked you what name you prefer to be called by. Is it Thomas, Tommie, Tom or something else?"

Tomas cringed, "Definitely not Tommie: I hate that name, it sounds so juvenile. For some reason most people just naturally call me Thomas, so I'm good with that."

"Okay, another thing I'd like to know has to do with your casual time activities. For instance, do you play golf, bowl, jog or ride a bicycle?"

"Basically, I'm a couch potato. I was very active when I was in high school. I played softball, I bowled and played some soccer. I was pretty good at most of them, but since high school I haven't done much of anything when it comes to athletics. I lift some weights at least twice a week to keep toned." He got quiet for a few seconds and added, "I guess I won't be doing any of that stuff when I get out of here."

"That's not the case at all. As long as you avoid activity that could possibly result in a head injury, there is no reason why you can't be physically and sexually active. Golf, bowling, walking all would be in the safe category. Anything that would involve physical contact or the potential of being struck with an object or falling would be out including soccer, football, baseball, softball, cycling and ice skating,"

"Well, then it doesn't look as if I'll be making any sacrifices in that department." He couldn't hold back a grin as he asked, "Does that mean that rough sex is out? "

The Doctor broke out laughing. "That's the first time a TBI patient asked me that. Well, I would go easy on that for a while."

"I'm just pulling your leg; that's not my style. What else do you want to know?"

"The next question is rather personal. You don't have to answer if you don't wish to, but it would be helpful to me in planning the rest of your rehabilitation.

"Fire away, Doctor."

"It's not unusual for adult TBI patients to become very dependent on their family. It comes from the feeling of being out of control that is normal after an accident. The feeling is exacerbated by dependence on the family during the therapy. That being said, have you given any thought to what you will do when you leave here? You will have your fiancé, your foster parents and the volunteer Mrs. Walton, all wanting to play an active role in your post-rehab life. Sometimes this support is overwhelming for patients who have finally broken free of dependent care."

"No, I haven't given it any thought, but I see what you're getting at. I just thought that I'd rest up a month and then get back to work. You know…business as usual. Actually, I would expect that everyone would be glad when that happens. I know this whole thing has been very trying for each of them. It's sort of taken up their whole lives."

"Yes, that's true. Well, if no one has said anything about your post-hospital plans, we'll just have to wait until it happens. Of course, you will have to have a six month and twelve-month checkup, but I know several very competent Neurologists out your way that can complete the Post-Therapy examinations."

Dr. Freenold took a few minutes to reflect on the discussions so far and followed up with, "So you are certain with regard to your family and friends expectations?"

"No one has said anything so far. They all just want me to be back to normal and put this whole experience behind me."

"I'm happy to hear that, but promise me that if you see a situation building and don't know how to deal with it, that you will speak to me immediately. Sometimes a dispassionate view from an outsider is helpful. That goes even after we're through here and I'm back home.

Agreed?"

"Yes, of course. Thank you."

"It's my pleasure, Thomas. Well, I think that will do it for now. I'll see you at the next session this afternoon. We will be concentrating on getting you back on your feet unaided by crutches or a walker. It may not be as easy as it sounds. For some TBI patients the lower extremities pose a special set of difficulties; a loss of muscle strength in the thighs and legs. It has something to do with certain neurons being disrupted and it sometimes takes a period of time to get them back on track. Often, we need to use mild electrolysis to stimulate them back in line. It's nothing to worry about though because if that is true in your case we'll know it right away and we'll take immediate action to correct it. So, I'll see you in a few hours. In the interim, get some rest."

"Thanks for the heads-up, Doctor."

"That's what I'm here for."

* * *

Dr. Jensen's office looked cluttered with the extra chairs that an orderly brought in from the lounge. They were brought there for a meeting that Emily had requested.

"Do you know what this meeting is about, Frederick?"

"I haven't a clue, Arnold. I just know that my secretary got a call from Mrs. Peyton asking for a meeting with us. She said that she, Mrs. Walton and Ms. O'Neil would attend."

Exactly at noon, the ladies strode into the office.

"Please have a seat, ladies. What can we do for you today?"

Emily began, "We're here because we have a specific problem that we don't think we should handle alone. She nodded to Miriam.

Miriam said, "I'll get right to the point. I am Thomas's birth mother. I came to Owensburg on a search for my son and discovered, for sure, that it is Thomas. We all believe that he should know about his birth mother, but we realize that with the seriousness of his injury, it is a delicate situation that must be well thought out."

Dr. Freenold answered, "I sensed that there was more to your involvement than that of just being a volunteer, but I didn't want to pry. You were right to speak to us. This is a situation that needs to be handled carefully."

Dr. Jensen asked, "You say that you're all agreed about telling Thomas about his birth mother. Does that include your husband, Emily?"

"Oh, yes, definitely. He has agreed to let the three of us work with you to find the best way to do it."

Dr. Freenold took a sip of water before he commented. "I can't say that interjecting a personal issue into a TBI rehab program is new to me. I had a case a year ago where the patient's wife decided to divorce him while he was still in rehabilitation. The patient went into a depressive state and we had to suspend our sessions while he worked with a psychiatric team. It set us back four months. I'm not saying that that will happen with Thomas.

"As luck would have it, he and I had a discussion about personal matters this morning and I find him to be pretty level minded when it comes to his expectations about post-therapy life. At the moment I can't give you any advice as to how you should approach telling him about Miriam. Obviously, it is an emotionally charged issue that must be handled carefully. I think it would be best if you didn't do anything at least for a few days. Let me discuss this with Dr. Jensen and have some exploratory conversations with Thomas."

He saw concern on their faces and added, "Don't worry, I'll be very discreet, but I want to get a feel for how he would handle a surprise of this nature."

Emily assured him, "Louise and Thomas discussed the subject of his birth mother on the day of the accident. He seemed willing to do some exploratory checks with her on the web. When he was a young child, when we asked him if he would want us to adopt him, he said no so that he would be open to someday finding out who his birth mother was. So, I don't think it would be a total shock to him. He'll be surprised of course, that's to be expected, but we believe that he will welcome her with open arms. The fact that it turns out to be Miriam should make it easier for him to accept."

Freenold looked at Miriam and then back at Emily. "I hope you're right. In any event, give us a few days to think it over. Let's meet again at the same time on Friday."

The ladies looked at each other and nodded in agreement.

* * *

The two doctors sat in Dr. Jensen's office reflecting on the Miriam Walton news.

"Boy that sure came out of left field. It's almost like one of those hospital soap operas."

"Yes, except we don't have a script to work with. We're going to have to ad lib the whole process." Freenold sat back in his chair and took a sip of water. "What's your take on this?"

"I know that this type of thing is happening a lot these days, what with the States opening up their files, but I don't have any personal experience with anyone it's happened to. I realize that once the cat is out of the bag, we're going have to deal with any repercussions, good or bad. That's the problem with issues like this. They are deeply emotional and there is no way of knowing on which side of the Emometer they will fall."

Emometer? What the hell is that?"

"That's my word for an emotional gauge that I operate in my mind. The needle sits on zero. Depending on a person's reaction, the needle will move left if it's negative and right if it's positive. The grade either way is from one to one hundred."

"It sounds like one of those Scientology meters."

"No, it's not that complicated. In fact, I've used it for nearly thirty years and in the absence of any other scientific tools; my patient files are replete with Emometer notes."

"That's the damnedest thing I've ever heard; and yet it's so creative. So, what does your Emometer tell you about how Thomas will react to news of his birth mother?"

"That's a good question. Of course, this is new to us, but my first thought is that Thomas will react with a positive thirty or forty when he first hears of it and move higher to a seventy or eighty as he assimilates what it will mean in his life."

"On what do you base your readings?"

"First of all, Thomas's current mental state is good. Even in the face of defeat with his therapy, he maintained an optimistic attitude. He has accepted our protocols without any resistance, demonstrating his willingness to accept life as it comes along. Apparently, he has exhibited an interest in finding out about his birth mother. Of course, that doesn't necessarily mean that he wants to be in contact with her, but it's a start. He has developed a friendship, probably even a liking for Miriam Walton, but again that may be only because she is giving of herself to help him get better. How will he react when he finds out? As I said before, I think it will be mildly positive."

"Interesting. I must say that I concur with most of your analysis. One thing is for sure, those women are going to have their way. Thomas is going to find out about his birth mother and it's going to happen on our watch. So, we must assure that it is an event that happens under our auspices; no surprises"

"They seem to be amenable to that, or else they wouldn't have come to us in the first place."

"That's a good point."

"Okay then, do you have any ideas as to how we can go about this? I would like to have a plan that we can present to the family so that we can weave it into our therapy schedule."

"You know, Arnold, this is a bit alien to our backgrounds. I'm thinking that we should set them up with the resident Psychiatrist. He or she should have a lot more input than you or I would have."

"You make a good point. Who do we contact?"

"I can handle that part. Let's you and I determine what we expect them to do and then set up a meeting with the family."

It took twenty minutes for them to outline their request and another five to set up the meeting.

* * *

The meeting with the Staff Psychiatrist, Dr. Philip Dalton took over two hours. By the time the family left, they felt comfortable with the plan laid out for Miriam to break the news to Thomas. Basically, it called on waiting until Thomas regains control of his motor skills and passes a psychiatric exam. Once the go-ahead is given, the family would be free to approach the subject with Thomas in whatever way they deemed best.

They met in the Family Room to make plans.

Emily spoke first, "Miriam, I think you should take the next visiting time and have a one-on-one with Thomas. Your therapy involvement ended yesterday so it would be natural for you to visit him in his room."

"I think you're right. It would give us a chance to get to know each other. I need him to like me as a person before I drop the bombshell on him."

Louise and Walter nodded in agreement.

"Then it's settled. The next visitor's slot is yours."

It looks as if we're getting closer to moment of truth.

CHAPTER 63

The town council meeting was open to the public for the first time since the Tiecher Park accident. Every seat was taken, and the council members knew that it was going to be a long and a trying meeting.

After Marge Nelson took attendance, Peter Westlake introduced their new Council member, David Cooke who was the owner of the town's most fashionable restaurant. David joined the Council to fill the vacancy caused by the death of Wendell Philips at Tiecher Park. Before getting down to business, Peter addressed the crowd of onlookers.

"Before we get down to our official meeting, I would like to apologize to you for the series of closed meetings. As you can imagine, much of the content of our meetings had to do with private and sometimes confidential information that the Council decided was best kept within the confines of these four walls. I would also like to remind you that the rules of conduct for these meetings require that any members of the public attending these meetings abide by the Council rule that only allows public participation during the question and answer period at the end of the meeting. Any disruption during the meeting will result in ejection from the hall. I assure you that there will be sufficient time for your questions."

The new and old business sections of the meeting took forty-five minutes to complete.

Peter banged his gavel to close the formal part of the proceedings and open the meeting for questions from the audience.

A tall, burly man was the first to approach the microphone that was attached to a lectern located directly in front of the Council table. He taped the microphone and appeared satisfied with the thump emanating from the four speakers mounted on the walls. "Good evening, my name is Ralph Nyquist and I live on Miller Lane. I want to know whether the town is going to suffer financially from lawsuits filed against them by victims of the stage collapse or their families."

Payne Easton fielded the question. "I understand how you might be concerned about lawsuits being targeted at the town. As you no doubt know, the State has fixed responsibility for the stage collapse solely with Mystic Times, the owner of the stage show called "The Beast". Early on Owensburg was named in a number of suits filed immediately after the accident. All of these have since been withdrawn. In addition, we have engaged the services of a law firm that specializes in suits of this nature and Owensburg will be filing a number of civil actions against the owner as well."

"Thank you, that's all I wanted to know."

Next came a woman who lowered the microphone before she spoke. "I just want to compliment the town for the way they handled the children returning to classes after the accident. My Gwen got to talk with a counselor that helped her get past the loss of two of her best friends. I can't thank you enough for the caring."

John Clark addressed her comment. "Comforting our returning students was as monumental undertaking that required that teachers, parents and trained specialist deal with a number of emotions and concerns. Credit for accomplishing the task goes to them and to the employees of the Schnieder Corporation who donated their time to help out.

A couple stepped up to the microphone next. "We're Mike and Betty Carson. We live on Oakdale, a block away from Tiecher Park. Needless to say, our street has been a mess during this situation. They finally took away the last of the debris last week, but they left behind a torn-up road, damaged trees and lots of sand and mud. We want to know what is being done to restore the park and our neighborhood."

Peter stood up to answer, "I can understand your concern about your neighborhood and I can assure you that restoration of the park and vicinity is a high priority. Engineers have already chosen a site for the new bandstand. Construction should be completed within three weeks and a full cleanup and restoration of the environment in the park and surrounding residential areas will be mounted at that time. We appreciate your patience while we get this job done."

The Carsons were followed by an elderly man. "My name is Ed Dashel. I've lived out on Dixon Road for over forty years. I just wanted to congratulate the Council for choosing Sheriff Peyton as the town's Mayor. Walter Peyton is a dedicated public servant who was the best Sheriff we ever had."

Peter responded immediately, "I couldn't agree with you more. We were fortunate that he agreed to take over the leadership of Owensburg during this critical period of our history and I thank you for your vote of confidence."

Ten more townsfolk made their way to lectern expressing their concerns or offering appreciation for the way the Council was handling the crises. Each appeared to be satisfied with the response from the Council members and on the dot of 10pm, Peter gaveled the meeting to an end.

On the way out of the hall, Peter turned to Payne, "This sure is far from the position we expected Owensburg to be in when we started planning for our 200th anniversary celebration. It's amazing how just a few minutes can change the course of history."

CHAPTER 64
GETTING TO KNOW YOU…

"May I come in?"

"Come in, Miriam. When I heard that you were on the visitor list, I was very happy. I thought that since your work with the sessions was over, that I might not see you again."

Miriam crossed the room and went to Thomas's bedside. She leaned over and gave him a soft kiss on the cheek. "Just because I don't have any assignments any more, doesn't mean that I won't be participating in your rehab. Hell, I won't be at rest until I see you walking out of this building under your own steam."

"Please sit down" he said as he gestured to the chair next to his bedside.

"You know, Marian, I still can't figure out why you have helped me. I was an absolute stranger to you and still you stayed in town, so you could be a part of my therapy."

"You're forgetting that I was in the park that night too. I saw that stage fall on you. How could I not volunteer to help, especially when I am trained in Sports Medicine? I couldn't turn my back on you, Thomas Mortinson."

"You are an exceptional human being, Marian. Anybody else having gone through what you yourself suffered that night would have been happy to put this town behind them as fast as possible, but here you are, just like a Fairy Godmother, worried about my recovery"

"Well, we Ohioans aren't made that way." Marian choked back tears as she almost blurted out, *"Thomas, I'm not your Fairy Godmother, I'm your mother"*. Recovering, she added, "And besides, we have something special in common. I went to Owensburg High, too. Go Panthers!!"

"What year did you attend?"

"Shame on you, Thomas. A gentleman doesn't ask a lady a question like that. Suffice it to say, it was quite a few years before you. I was a jock too. I played on the ladies tennis squad and basketball team. I wasn't a star like you, but our basketball team won the All County trophy for three years straight.

"How cool. I don't know what it is about you, Miriam, but I feel, I don't know…safe when I'm around you. Weird, huh?"

"Not so weird. It's very common for a bond to develop between a therapist and patient."

"No, it's more than that. I feel especially close to you and I don't feel that away about any of the others. It's like there is some kind of an invisible link between us. Don't you feel it?"

She wanted to say, "*Of course I feel it, I'm your mother"*, but instead said, "I do feel a special attachment. It's nothing I can put my finger on, but I felt it the first time I saw you."

"What do you mean?"

Miriam realized that she was going too far. It was time to tone down the rhetoric before she slipped and told him the truth. "I just meant that sometimes in my line of work you come across someone who you sense has special qualities and you just want to do your best to help them get better. That happened when I saw you for the first time. You are a fine young man, Thomas Mortinson, I knew that from the start. I'm proud that I am participating in your rehab."

"Let's move away from this *woo woo* stuff and get back to learning more about each other"

"Okay, I notice that you are wearing an engagement ring. My mom told me that you are engaged to an attorney. Where did you meet him?"

"We both were living in Spartanville, Pennsylvania when we met. He came out here when he heard I was in the hospital with a concussion. He took an instant liking to Owensburg and last week he went into a partnership with another attorney here in town, so it looks like we'll be house hunting here soon."

"Wow, that's great. This accident has caused me to do some reflecting as well. I'm thinking about moving back here when Louise and I get married; she likes the idea too. It's only a short commute to where we're working."

"That's terrific. It doesn't look as if we will be separated from each other after all." After the words left her mouth, a feeling of dread came over Miriam, *"What if he can't accept me as his mother? That would be very awkward for everyone."*

Thomas noticed the sudden change in her demeanor. "Why so glum, chum?"

It only took his smile to bring her back. She reached out and squeezed his hand. "It was really a happy thought…the two of us coming back to our roots. It's serendipitous."

"Yes, it certainly is."

"I graduated from Miami University in Oxford, Ohio with a BS in Kinesiology & Health.

I got a job in Sports Medicine right away and that's what I've been doing ever since. I'm happy to be working in a field where I can help people recover their lives.

"There is one other thing. I was recently divorced from Nathan Walton. Irreconcilable differences they called it. Everything worked out well and I've put it all behind me."

"Did you have any children?"

Miriam hesitated for a moment, "Nathan and I were childless." She looked him in the eye and commented, "Now, enough about me. It's time for you to unveil your past."

"Well, you already know a lot about me. I went to Ohio State after I left High School. I graduated from there last year with BS in Finance and took a job with Matson Steel in Akron. It's a good job and they are great people to work for. They even told me to take all the time I needed to get better. They are holding my job until I'm well enough to go back to work."

"That's wonderful. I wish more companies were like that."

"I met Louise at a frat party at school. Her sorority and my fraternity sponsored a charity event for the homeless. We landed up on the same committee and took an instant liking to each other. We've been together ever since. She's got a BS in finance too. She was working for a different company in Akron, but when I got hurt she quit because they wouldn't give her an extended leave of absence."

"That's quite a story. You two must be very much in love."

"We are. We are very compatible. Louise spent a short time in a foster home when her parents were killed in an auto accident. As soon as she could, she went off on her own. She got a full scholarship to Ohio State and earned a BS degree in Finance just as I did. After graduation we moved in together in a small one-bedroom apartment near Akron. She got a job with a Non-Profit Charitable group. She really liked the work, but unfortunately that's over for her now."

"You know of course that I spent my childhood as a foster child. Emily and Walter couldn't have been better parents. They reared me as if I was their own child. The gods really smiled on me when I was placed in their care.

"Have you ever thought about searching for your birth parents?"

"Of course, quite often. It's been twenty-three years now. The only thing that I was ever told was that my father died in the war. His name was Thomas Wendell Mortinson. I know nothing about my birth mother, but I guess she must have had a good reason for giving me up."

"Have you thought about trying to locate her?"

"Not really, but Louise and I were talking about that recently. I'll probably give it a try sometime. This accident has quickened my thinking about mortality. I can't see where I'd have anything to lose by finding her. Who knows, she may even be looking for me. Wouldn't that be a kick?"

"It certainly would be." Treading deeper into the dangerous waters, Miriam asked, "How do you feel about her? She must have had a sound reason for giving you up?"

"Of course, I'm sure that she did. Look, I lucked out by growing up in a happy home with the Peytons. Of course she wouldn't have had any way of knowing that I would end up in a good home, but nevertheless, I'm willing to keep an open mind about what happened."

"You are a very compassionate young man. Louise is very fortunate to have found you."

"I'm the lucky one and to think that I might have been handicapped by my accident."

"What does that have to do with anything?"

"You know what I mean. What if I wasn't able to be a man for her? She deserves more than that."

Miriam reflected back to the files she read about the tests given to Thomas to test his responsiveness to various stimuli. When shown pictures of naked women in various positions, he had an instantaneous response in that department. "It's natural to think about that, but I'm pretty certain that you will not have problems in that area. Now, do you have any other concerns?"

"None that I can think of right now. You know, I really enjoyed this time together, Miriam."

"So did I. It's a shame that it took a tragedy like a stage collapse to bring us together. Well, it's getting near your dinner time, so I better be getting along. Have a good night, Thomas. I'll visit again."

"I look forward to it. Goodnight, Miriam.

* * *

"He seemed to want to know all about his birth mother."

"You didn't say anything did you?"

"Of course not, Mike. I agreed to wait until everyone thinks it's the best time, but after today I don't think it's going to be much longer."

Mike sat back with Miriam's head resting on his shoulder. "We've come a long way, haven't we? I couldn't have imagined just a short time ago, that not only would we be this close to Thomas knowing about you, but that I would be planning on marrying you and settling down here in Owensburg. Life moves in mysterious ways."

"Yes, it does and I couldn't be more elated about our visit."

"Finish your wine and let's move to the bedroom."

Hang on, we're almost there.

CHAPTER 65
THREE WEEKS LATER

"Frederick, Dr. Dalton believes that any time now it would be safe for Mrs. Walton to have her private talk with Thomas."

"I'm glad to hear that, Arnold. I was wondering when they were going to get around to that. What's your feeling about it?"

"The present would certainly be an ideal time. Will you pass that information along to Emily? This afternoon is open. He has no therapy sessions scheduled."

"I will be happy to set that up. Do you think that either of us should be in attendance when she does tell him?"

"Definitely not. That has to be a very private meeting; the fewer people around, the better."

Dr. Dalton offered to be on standby in case he is needed, but he said that he was sure that Thomas will be receptive to what she has to tell him. I agree with the doctor that Thomas will be receptive to the news. It shouldn't have any impact on his progress; in fact, it might even have a positive effect on his post-rehab outlook. You go ahead and set it up, the sooner we get it out of the way, the better."

"I'll be glad to get that out of the way. I'll get right on it."

* * *

Emily, Miriam and Louise were excited as they waited for Walter to return home.

"Louise spoke first, "I would be happy to be there with you when you tell him."

Emily added, "I would be also."

"No, I appreciate the support, but I have to do this alone. Thomas and I have had several lengthy visits together. We've gotten to know each other very well. We've touched on his heritage a few times and he seems to want to know about his birth mother."

Louise reached out and grasped Miriam's shoulder. "I think so too. With his rehab ready to end in about thirty days, his spirits are very high. I've never seen him so enthusiastic about anything. If there is ever a time, this has to be it."

Walter, arrived home, and went over to kiss Emily on the cheek. "I just about got to the office, when I got your call. So, today's the day."

Emily replied, "Yes, it's finally here. We were just talking about it. Louise and I offered to be there with Miriam when she tells him, but she's decided to go it alone"

"I can understand that. This time should be just between Mother and son. How are you setting up the visit, Miriam?"

"I haven't been there for a visit for two days, so it won't be unusual for me to just show up. I have to admit, that I'm a bit nervous. I've played the visit over and over in my mind at least a dozen times and you would think I would have it down pat, but I keep coming back to the uncertainty of his response. Will he welcome me as his mother? Will he be disappointed that it's me?"

"That's silly talk, Miriam and you know it," Emily said. "You've told me yourself that when you and Thomas talked about his birth mother that he was curious enough to want to engage in a search when he's released from the hospital."

"Yes, I did say that, and I know he talked to Louise about doing that." She hesitated for a moment. "But I'm still worried that he might have changed his mind."

Emily, hugged Miriam. "You have no reason to expect anything other than Thomas embracing you as his mother. Now stop all the negative talk and let's work on finding the right dress for you to wear for your visit."

Walter, gave Emily a peck on the cheek and said, "It doesn't look as if I'm needed around here, so I'm going to go back to the office. Don't worry about a thing, Miriam, Thomas is a practical young man and he'll realize right away how fortunate he is to have someone as wonderful as you for a mother. You've got my word on it."

"Thanks, Walter. I sure hope you're right."

"I know I am."

Getting closer.

CHAPTER 66
THREE WEEKS AND COUNTING

"Arnold, how much longer do you think Thomas's rehabilitation will last?"

"As best I an tell, if he continues on the path he's been going, he should be ready for release by the end of the month."

"I still can't get over it. When he came here with a GCS 5, there was no indication that he would be able to leave here in less than a year and a half and now here we are ten months later talking about his release. Arnold, I salute you."

"Frederick, I don't want any salute. You know as well as I do that this was a team effort and that a good measure of the credit goes to Thomas, himself. I have never seen a patient with a more positive attitude, especially a patient that required a Crainiectomy. This is definitely one for the books."

"Speaking of books, how are you coming with the documenting of our Freenold Convention? I was thinking the other day that there could be a problem since the first part Thomas's rehabilitation was done under the Turnwell Convention?"

"That's not the case at all. While it is true that the sessions leading up to the Thoriatic Balance exercises will be virtually the same as those for the Turnwell, Thorndike and Faraday Conventions, it is at that critical point that the Freenold Convention begins to involve the patient in the determination of how and when to complete the steps of a prescribed session. Since the exercises up to that point are basically the same for all current conventions, they've become a matter of public domain. As a whole, the Freenold Convention is fundamentally so different than any of the current Conventions that it justifies its own classification. There is no question in my mind that the review boards will give their complete support to naming it a new convention. Frederick, we have something here that is monumental. This will revolutionize TBI rehabilitation and we, my good Doctor, are in on the ground floor. I firmly believe that by this time next year, at least half the country will be choosing the Freenold Convention for the treatment of severely head-injured patients. The reduction in total recovery time, alone, will assure its selection."

"I wish I had your conviction."

"O ye of little faith. When you've worked with the hierarchy of the Institute of Neurological Disorders and Neuroscience Centers as long and as often as I have, you get to know how the major medical institutions function. Trust me when I say that they will welcome the new convention. It's been six years since Turnwell was introduced. A new convention is overdue for a science that is so often referred to as the last scientific frontier. The powers to be cannot ignore the significant reduction in healing time and the improvement in the patient's mental outlook that we are offering with our new convention."

"I'll take your word for it."

"By the way, what's happening with Thomas's mother? Is that all set up?"

"They will be meeting at one today. I sure hope that it goes well. We've been operating too long with a 'sword of Damocles' over our heads waiting for this to happen. I'll let you know how it works out as soon as I hear anything. I've got a good vibe about it though. I think that it's just what Thomas needs at this point in his recovery."

"I agree with you on that. Thanks, Frederick. I wait to hear from you.

* * *

Wendy Marshall sat down with Thomas to go over the morning's session. "As usual you aced those exercises. How does it feel to walk without support from the bars or the walker?"

"I don't think I'm ready for any treadmill yet, but it sure did feel good being able to walk from one wall to the other without any support."

"There were three muscle groups we needed to work on today, the gluteus, quadriceps and Sartorius. All three, for some reason are impacted by TBI more than the others and when you add months of inactivity they required our special attention. That's why I had you doing those squats and lunges earlier. How do your legs feel right now?"

"They feel a little tight, but I'm certain I could walk more if I had to."

"Excellent. That's the exact response I was hoping to hear."

"Happy to oblige."

"I wouldn't plan on doing any marathons any time soon. Even though you have a purposeful gait right now, there is still a lot more to be done on the remaining muscles. Unfortunately, they work contrary to each other, so the exercises must be done over a period of time and with countless repetitions. When you leave here, you'll have a list of exercises to do for at least the next six months. Many of those will have to do with maintaining strength in your leg muscles."

"I will do them gladly. You'll remember that it wasn't too long ago that I had fears of never being able to walk again."

"I remember that, and I remember that Marian told you that you would be up on your feet if she had to drag you across the floor, herself."

Thomas smiled. "Yeah, I remember that. I think she was serious too."

"You're damned right she was. She's some tough cookie when it comes to motivating patients. She told me some stories of a few young football players who feared the loss of their potential professional career. They got so depressed that a few of them tried to take their own lives. It took successes in their rehab sessions to turn them around and she got them by riding herd until they could think of nothing but to complete the exercises to get her off their backs."

Thomas laughed. "That sounds like her. She got tough with me a few times. I'm sure glad she did. She's quite some lady."

"She sure is. We were lucky that she came along when she did. I don't think we would be so far along without her input." Wendy thought a minute and added, "I'm not trying to take anything away from your efforts. Hell, I've been in this business for five years and I've never seen a TBI with such a good attitude. You were not without your down times, of course, but in general you are enthusiastic and up-beat. It's funny when you think about it, but this is one occupation where someone in my position is happy when they are not needed anymore."

"That's true. I said something like that to Dr. Freenold one day and he cracked up."

"That's another thing that you can be thankful for. You had one of the best neurosurgeons in the country, perhaps even the world. For him to be assigned to your case was a gift from God."

"Don't I know it. Even being treated here at the George Bennett Baxter Trauma Center was a stroke of luck. My dad told me it's one of the highest rated trauma centers in the world. I have a lot to be thankful for. Things couldn't get any better for me."

Don't be too sure of that, Thomas.

CHAPTER 67
AT LAST

Miriam knocked on the door before she entered Room 333. Thomas was sitting in a chair next to the bed wearing a navy-blue bathrobe.

"Come in Miriam. I saw your name on the visitor's list. It's good to see you again. I miss you at our sessions."

"Not as much as I miss being there." She leaned down and kissed Thomas on the cheek before sitting down on the chair next to his.

"How are you doing today?"

"Really great. I walked several hundred feet on my own this morning. Wendy says I'm ahead of schedule, but I still have a bunch of leg muscles to tone up. I can't tell you how great it felt to push that wheelchair aside and say goodbye to those parallel bars."

"I'll bet. I'm so happy for you." She reached over and patted his arm. "I have a special reason to visit with you today. I'm a little nervous about it, so if I'm acting a little strange, I hope you will understand."

Thomas looked concerned. He had never seen Miriam so serious. "What's wrong? What's troubling you?"

"I don't know any other way to do this, so I'll just come right out with it. Thomas, I'm your mother." She said no more; simply looked at him and waited to see how he would react.

"What did you say?"

"I'm said that you are the son I had to give up when you were first born. I came here to find you, and this is where I landed up."

His mind raced as he attempted to make sense out of what he had just heard. He closed his eyes and choked back words that he wanted to say. His balance gave in to the shock and he had to reach down to the chair seat to keep from toppling over. Finally, he looked up at her and reached out to hug her; holding her as close as their positions would allow. He continued to hold her as he said, "I always wondered what you would be like."

Tears were pouring down her cheeks. She pulled back and looked him in the eyes. "Thomas, I never set out to give you up, but it was the best thing I could do for you; providing you with a chance to grow up with a nice family. I'm not excusing myself, but when your father died overseas, before we could get married, and then you came along, I had to make decisions about what would be best for you. Things were different twenty-three years ago for unwed mothers. Keeping you would have meant not being able to give you a decent life with two parents and all the things that a growing boy needs. So, I gave you up without ever getting to hold you in my arms or feel your face against mine. I only saw you for a minute or two. You were so beautiful." Her lips fell silent as she searched his eyes for some sign as to how he was receiving this life-changing disclosure.

"Somehow, I knew that someday we would meet. I wondered if you find me or if I would have to do my own search. I'm totally at a loss for words…*Mom.* This is so overwhelming. Why didn't you say something before now?"

"I wanted to, but I was concerned that if I did, it might set you back. I couldn't risk that happening. Everyone thought that it would be better if you had a chance to get to know me first. I just lucked out that I had the Sports Medicine skills to be a part of your rehab. I had to promise them that I would wait until the doctors felt that you were of the right frame of mind to be receptive to the news.

"So, everyone knew but me. Wow. I thought my folks and Louise acted strangely at times, but I never would have guessed that this was the reason. This sure isn't what I expected today's visit to be like." He hesitated a moment and said, "To think that you came along at the time in my life when I needed you the most. That's so serendipitous.

Looking into her eyes, he said, "I love you, Mom. I have from the first time that Emily and Walter told me about how I came to live with them. There's been a special part in my heart since then reserved for you, which will be there until the day I die."

"I'm so relieved that you can forgive me."

"Forgive you? What are you talking about? I have nothing to forgive you for. I know that you would never intentionally hurt me. I can't imagine what it's been like for you."

"My son, I love you. I want to be a part of your life from now on if you'll allow it."

"Of course I want you in my life. Now that I've found you, I don't ever want to lose you again"

Holding each other, the mother and son reunion continued for the balance of the visiting time.

Finally, Thomas said, "I hate for you to leave, but the strictest rule they have around here is that visiting hours are non-negotiable."

"I'll be back as soon as I can, Thomas. Wild horses couldn't keep me away from you now that we're reunited." They kissed and hugged again as the nurse came in to escort Miriam from the room.

"Goodnight, Thomas."

"Goodnight, Mom."

Now wasn't that worth waiting for?

Let's see how the rest of the story goes.

CHAPTER 68

Miriam sat in her car for an hour, going over in her mind what had just transpired. Her journey had finally come to an end. Her son had told her "Of course I want you in my life. Now that I've found you, I don't ever want to lose you again."

When she began her journey to reunite with the child she gave up for adoption some twenty-four years ago, she was well aware of the emotional rollercoaster she had gotten onto.

Months earlier while sitting at home thinking about meeting Thomas for the first time, she fantasized dozens of scenarios, with only a handful of them having a happy ending. Not only were the odds of finding him stacked against her, but the odds of him accepting her into his life were even more unfavorable.

Mike made her aware of all this when she first met with him, but to her way of thinking, if she didn't try to find him, she would continue to have that nagging feeling that was causing her much discomfiture. Mike's record at locating lost persons, which in essence was what her son Thomas was, was outstanding, and as it turned out he lived up to his reputation by not only locating Thomas, but also guiding her as she finally made contact with Thomas.

Marian knew that she was probably luckier than most mothers searching for a lost child. She was fortunate to have a support system that came out of nowhere; aside from Mike, she had Thomas's foster parents, Emily and Walter and his fiancé, Louise solidly on her side.

She mused about what the journey had cost her. Of course, there was her marriage to Nathan. While she had harbored fears about how he would react when he found out about Thomas, she never anticipated that it would cost her her marriage of eleven years. The biggest surprise came from Nathan's stubborn refusal to understand her feelings about Thomas. *I still feel justified in not to tell him before we got married. I couldn't have known at the time that my buried need for closure would turn out as it did. I guess in a way I am fortunate that I got an opportunity to experience the cruelty that Nathan was capable of. Who knows when that could have cropped up and it might even have turned into violence.*

As it turned out, I was lucky enough to find a good man who loves me for who I am; a man who would travel to the end of the world to be with me. Thank you, God, for this blessing and for all your help in reuniting me with Thomas.

It's so great that Mike will be working here in Owensburg. We'll get ourselves a nice house and settle down with our new family and friends.

CHAPTER 69
ALL'S WELL THAT…

The dinner table had an extra setting this evening; it was Thomas's first night home. They were all gathered around the table as Walter raised his glass to make a toast. He wanted to say something that would celebrate Thomas's victory over infirmity, Miriam's triumphant quest to be reunited with her child, Thomas's and Louise's forthcoming nuptials, and Mike's and Miriam's recent marriage. He chose, "Here's to Thomas; here's to never giving up; here's to clinging to hopes and dreams until they become manifest and lastly, here's to never ending love."

They raised their glasses, each reflecting on the part of his toast that impacted their lives.

For Miriam it was double barreled. Not only did she gain a part in her son's life, but she also found and married a wonderful man. They planned to settle down in Owensburg where she would be close to Thomas and her new friends. Life was certainly good for her. *I'm the luckiest woman alive.*

For Louise the toast signified her fiancé's successful recovery from a potential fatal TBI and their plans to be married within a month. *I'm so happy everything worked out.*

For Mike it meant the beginning of as new life in Owensburg with a law firm partnership and his recent marriage to Miriam the love of his life. *I've got a great fresh start.*

For Emily there was nothing but jubilation over how well everything turned out. Thomas not only recovered fully from a potentially life-threatening brain injury, but was planning to marry a lovely girl. Most of all he was reunited with his birth mother and enthusiastically welcomed her into his life. Her newly formed BFF turned out to be Thomas's birth mother. Walter was now the Mayor and was being hailed by the press as being the town's savior. *I have so much to be thankful for.*

Thomas thought about everything that had happened to him since that fateful day almost a year ago. He realized that he never would have made it if it wasn't for all of the people who were standing in front of him raising their glasses in a toast. He was getting a second chance at life that would include his birth mother. *I've been truly blessed.*

After Walter made his toast he reflected on the meaning of his words. How great it is that all these people found the inner strength to rise above the impact of multiple tragedies. *God bless them all and God bless the town of Owensburg and all its residents. Give me the strength to serve them to the best of my ability.*

They sipped from their glasses and sat down to dinner.

"That was a lovely toast, dear," Emily said.

The others nodded.

"It said what was in my heart. We've just lived through a memorable time of our lives. None of us could have imagined the events of the past months, but together we got through everything and came out stronger for it."

Thomas looked around the table. "I could never have made it without each and every one of you. Thank you all again for being there for me when I needed you most. Oh, by the way, I'm really looking forward to Louise and my wedding reception. I'll finally get a chance to show you all my *moves*."

Miriam, Emily and Louise fought back tears. Even the slightest recollection of what Thomas had gone through did that. The guys just chuckled.

Emily picked up a plate with thin sliced roast beef and started passing it. "Let's get to this meal before it gets cold."

The meal proceeded with light conversation more in keeping with a family get-together. After dessert and coffee, Mike, Thomas and Walter went out on the porch to enjoy a cool afternoon breeze.

Walter commented, "It's so delightful out here most summer days. When the sun moves around to the front of the house in the afternoon it drops about ten degrees back here. That's something both of you should remember when you choose where you're going to live. It doesn't have to be a deal breaker, but if you have a choice between two houses that you like equally, if one has a backyard and bedrooms that face east, pick that one. When Emily and I moved into our first house, we had the sun in the back yard and coming into our bedroom during the late afternoon and evening. It was a constant battle to keep the bedroom cool for sleeping. Most people don't think about those things until it's too late."

"Miriam and I found a house we liked the other day. I never gave the direction of the sun a thought. I'll have to check it out."

Thomas added, "I will put that on my list. I now have about twenty things we need to check on. We plan to live in our new place for a lot of years, even raise children there if we are blessed. We don't want to have any regrets about not planning ahead."

The ladies made their entry after cleaning up the dinner dishes.

Emily asked, "What are you men discussing?"

Walter replied, "Believe it or not, we were talking about the sun."

Louise asked, "Is that the male variety or the astronomical sun?"

"The latter."

Miriam asked, "What's so interesting about the sun?"

Mike answered, "We were talking about how important it is to choose a house that is positioned properly, with respect to the sun."

Walter turned to Emily, "I told them about our first house and how hot our bedroom always was."

"Oh, god, I remember those days. Walter's right, especially if the house is two stories."

Thomas turned to Louise, "I added it to the list."

Mike said to Miriam, "That's something we'll have to check on at the Sanderson's house. I never would have thought of it if Walter hadn't mentioned it, but it makes a lot of sense. It doesn't look as if builders give much consideration to a houses position on a plot when they design the room layout."

"I would have never thought about that either. Now I understand why some people insist on living in a house for a few days before agreeing to buy it. Even if it means sleeping on the floor in a sleeping bag, it at least gives you a feel for what it will be like living there. That's so important if you're planning on living there for a long time. Do you think the Sanderson's would let us stay there for a night?"

"They might if the house hasn't sold before they move out. I could write up an agreement with them that the sale of the house is contingent on our staying in the house for two days to decide on its habitability for us. It's different, but I'm sure that it's been done. We have nothing to lose by trying?"

Miriam hugged him. "That's what I love about being married to an attorney."

* * *

The Town Council Meeting ended with a rap of the gavel; but not before Peter Westlake reported that, after a year, the town was finally returning to its old charm. The new bandstand and parking lot were built, and the first show was attended by a record number of Dixieland Jazz enthusiasts. An arboretum and a sculptor commemorating the lives of those who died in the accident, sat in place of the old bandstand.

* * *

"How is everything at the Center these days?"

"Couldn't be better, Arnold. The last of the Tiecher Park patients was released last week."

"That's good to hear, Frederick. I've got some good news. After months of review and testing, the Institute of Neurological Disorders authorized use of the Freenold Convention." He hesitated a moment and added, "We did it."

"That's great news."

"You should be getting some papers this week for us to apply for a Copyright for the sessions. I signed my part already, so just use the return envelope to get it back to the attorney. We did very well, my friend."

"Have you spoken to Thomas recently?"

"He called last week with some questions about workouts at the gym. He is doing very well. He has a slight problem with sleep; something about an over active mind. I gave him some advice about specific pre-sleep activity and offered to prescribe a mild sedative, but he said he was already taking more pills that he cared to. I think he'll be okay. He has an outstanding support team backing him up."

"I'm glad to hear that. I'll be interested in seeing the results of his six-month checkup. Okay, then, give me a call if you have any questions about the Copyright papers."

"I'll do that Arnold. Have a good day."

"You do too."

AUTHOR'S NOTES

I would be remiss if I did not take advantage of this opportunity to mention the Foster Care System that played such a prominent role in the plot of *Tenderly Beats the Lonely Heart.*

The information that follows was obtained from the Adoption and Foster Care Analysis and Reporting System (AFCARS) and represents data for FY 2014 made available by the Child Welfare Information Gateway (https://www.childwelfare.gov)

What is the Foster Care System?
Foster Care is the arrangement by which 24-hour care is provided outside their own homes for children whose birthparents are not able to care for them. I may be arranged through the Court System or result from placement by a social agency and can be for a period of time measured in days up to the age of 18 or the completion of high school. (Some States have extended the age limit to 20 or 21.)

Children in foster care live in a variety of placement settings. These foster care settings include, but are not limited to, non-relative Foster Family homes (46%), Relative Foster Homes (29%), Institutions (8%), Group Homes (6%), Pre-adoptive Homes (4%) and Others (7%).

What kind of numbers are we talking about?

On September 30th, 2014, there were an estimated 415,129 children in foster care. During FY2014, 264,746 children entered the system and 238,230 children exited foster care.

How did Foster Care work out?

Of the estimated 238,230 children who exited the Foster Care System in 2014, 51% were reunited with their parents or primary caretaker, 21% were adopted, 9% were emancipated, and 19% had other outcomes.

How long did they stay in Foster Care?

Of the estimated 238,230 children who exited the Foster Care System in 2014, 11% were there for less that 1 month, 35% for 1-11 months, 28% for 12-23 months, 13% for 24-35 months, 8% for 3-4 years and 5% for more than 5 years.

What are the ages of the children in Foster Care?

Children can enter Foster Care from infancy to 18 years of age (in some States 20 and 21).

For the statistical year shown, the median age of the children in foster care was 8.0 years, the median age for those entering the system was 6.4

years and the median age for those exiting the system is 8.0 years.

How does race and ethnicity factor in?

Of the estimated 415,129 in the Foster Care System in 2014, some 42% were white, 24% were black or African-American, 22 % were Hispanic and 12% were either other races, multiracial or were unable to be determined. The general population of the United States for the same period is 62% White, 12% black, 17% Hispanic and 9% others.

What happens after Foster Care?

With a system that culminates at age 8 (some States, 20 or 21) we should not expect to learn much about what happens to a child after they "age out". Most of the information we have gotten came from via private agencies or journalists looking for an attention getting story or column. What I found was a mix of mostly bad news and some optimistic news. By their mid–twenties, 80% of foster care children who have aged-out graduated from high school or earned a GED diploma, 5% obtained a college degree, almost 60% of the young men have been convicted of a crime, 80% have been arrested, 75% of the young women have become pregnant since they aged out and 25% of the total population have been homeless.

These dire statistics haven't gone unnoticed. Many States have developed Transition Programs to help these children move from Foster care to independence. The programs aim at providing safe and stable housing, temporary Medicaid coverage, job training and educational vouchers. Most of the programs begin two years before the foster care ends to ease the child's transition to adulthood.

* * *

In the novel, *Tenderly Beats the Lonely Heart,* Thomas Mortinson entered the Foster Care System at birth and only a fortunate series of circumstances allowed his case to fly under the bureaucratic radar until he left for college at 17 1/2. It is rare for this to occur, but certainly not impossible. His foster parents provided a very stable home (after all his foster father was the town sheriff), which did not require excessive visits by an overly worked Civil Service Agency; out of sight, out of mind. This was a success story, there are many like it, but the bad news greatly outweighs the successes.

The Foster Care and Adoption Systems need to be revamped. States must provide the funds to gut and rebuild the structure of the Civil Service agencies that administer the programs. The future of our country depends on making good citizens of all our youth including those unfortunate enough to get the short-end-of-the-stick when it comes to parents or guardians. **Make your voice heard.**

ABOUT THE AUTHOR

Ken is a multi-genre novelist living in Ohio with his wife and miniature Schnauzer. He was born in St. Louis, Missouri, but moved to Long Island, N.Y. when he was 8 years old.

Reading and writing fiction have always been a big part of Ken's life. As a child he wrote about outer-space and in high school he was the editor of the school's literary newspaper. During that period, he wrote mostly short stories and novellas.

Ken earned a BS in Logistics from NYU. His career in NYC was spent in management positions at several large companies, including Exxon, Metropolitan Life and J.C. Penney. During those years he had little time for writing as his career required extensive travel and he was busy raising a family.

In the early eighties, as an empty-nester, Ken moved to Centerville, OH with his wife, Jeannette. There he retired early from the bicycle manufacturer Huffy when they went into bankruptcy.

Now, as a full-time writer. Ken writes because he feels that there are stories that need to be told. He enjoys the process of writing and firmly believe that you do your best writing when you are well read. To that end, he reads at least one novel a week.

Blood Money, Ken's debut novel centers on a private investigator, Mark Matthews, turned FBI agent. In the novel Mark topples an association funneling money to terrorists. It was published as an eBook in November 2011.

Fatal Dose, the second Mark Matthews Mystery exposes a drug mafia distributing counterfeit prescription drugs and revisits some of the villains from *Blood Money*. It was published as an eBook in March 2013.

Siblings, is a captivating family saga and an introspective of the hierarchy in sibling families. This tale of the Symington family runs rampant with romance, gambling, psychedelic trips and infidelity. It was released as a paperback and eBook in August 2015.

The Journey, Eight Postulates to Live By is a about a modern-day Everyman, It introduces a way to enter the Kingdom of Heaven on earth. It is scheduled to be published as a paperback and eBook on April 3, 2017.

In His Fathers Shadow is a multi-genre work about three generations of the Westbrook family. The protagonist, Adam Westbrook III, provokes each of the main characters with a series of ruthless actions until one is driven to hire an assassin to kill both Adam and his father and burn

Westbrook Manor to the ground. It is currently unpublished

Before starting a novel, Ken does extensive research. For example, while writing *Blood Money* and *Fatal Dose,* that feature an FBI agent as the protagonist, he met with local FBI agents to verify details used in his stories. For *Siblings* he needed to learn about psychedelic drugs and abortion procedures.

With three published thrillers and one Family Drama/Romance novel under his belt, Ken is turning to romance novels and those addressing social issues and topics with spiritual/inspirational themes.

Member of ITW, WFMA and INTA